PERFECTION

Perfection © 2003 by Anita Mason
All rights reserved

First edition published May 2003
10-9-8-7-6-5-4-3-2-1

Spinsters Ink Books
P. O. Box 22005
Denver, CO 80222
USA

Cover Design:
Jodi Wright

Interior Design:
Attention Media Group

Library of Congress Cataloging-in-Publication Data

Mason, Anita

Perfection / Anita Mason. -- 1st ed.

p. cm. --

ISBN 1-883523-54-0

Printed in Canada

PERFECTION

by Anita Mason

Spinsters Ink Books
Denver, Colorado
USA

Other Books by Anita Mason

The Yellow Cathedral
Angel
The Racket
The War Against Chaos
The Illusionist
Bethany

1 The Playwright

There was a man in a ditch by the side of the road not far from the Three Weavers. Surprisingly, he still had his hat. He did not look as if he had much else. His pockets had been turned inside out and his purse taken. He lacked a jacket. His face was bruised as if he had been fighting, and under that he was very pale. Before falling into the ditch, he had been sick on the roadside. Dogs had cleaned up most of it.

There was a trickle of water at the bottom of the ditch, and although it was not enough to put him in danger of drowning, he was certainly in danger of catching a serious chill. Nevertheless, of the dozen or so people who had passed by since dawn and seen him there, none had attempted to pull him out. He did not look like a man it would be worth rescuing. Several of them, in any case, knew who he was.

It was a dog licking his face that brought him round. He was conscious first of something rough and warm probing the bruise on his cheek. He turned his head aside, wincing. The warmth of whatever it was made him aware that he was cold, and as soon as he became aware how cold he was he realised how very ill he felt. A part of his mind which had not succumbed to the general wreck told him his situation was bad, but that the worst could be averted if he could overcome the raging pain behind his eyes for long enough to get out of the place he was lying in.

As soon as he moved, the dog got in the way, almost sitting on his chest in its excitement. He threw it off, and managed to get his feet under him before it came back again, thrusting its muzzle into his ear. He cursed and hit out at it, missing and striking himself on the temple. Thunder lit in his head.

He got out of the ditch by pulling on an ash sapling that was growing a short distance away. His legs, arms and face were covered in mud. His boots were soaked through. He noticed that his jacket was gone, but that he still had his hat. It was now lying at the bottom of the ditch. He picked it up, shook the water off it and put it on his head. As an afterthought, he wiped the mud from his face with the back of his wrist.

He began to walk down the road. The dog trotted beside him. His head drummed, and the morning light cut his eyes cruelly. His stomach heaved and wanted to relieve itself, but there was nothing in it.

The events which had brought him to the ditch began to present themselves to him in sharp and random fragments. The play. The jeering fellow at the front of the crowd. Melchior, sulking because he had to play two parts and getting his revenge by giving the angel a drubbing, which was not supposed to happen and had not been popular. Not surprisingly, the angel had subsequently limped and forgotten his lines. And the castle had fallen down. In the midst of all this, what use had been his own fine characterisation of Herod? Probably no-one had even heard the great last speech. He recollected going to the tavern afterwards, telling the rest of the company that as far as he was concerned they could go on to the next place without him. After that he remembered very little.

The dog raced off after a cat, and, having chased it up a tree, returned to his side. He tried to kick it but didn't have the strength. He didn't like dogs much. They ate food that humans could have eaten, and had a habit of telling people where you were when you would prefer no-one to know. A dog had nearly got him hanged once.

He walked on, and turned the corner. A man with a brazier of hot coals was selling chestnuts. Gratefully, the playwright warmed himself at the fire. The chestnut-seller asked him if he was going to buy some chestnuts.

"I've no money," he said.

The chestnut-seller told him to clear off, in that case.

"A bit of human kindness wouldn't hurt," he protested, spreading his hands to the coals."

"I don't give to beggars," said the chestnut-seller.

"I'm not a beggar." He brushed some dirt from his elbow. "I'm a man of letters." He walked away.

It occurred to him that he could sell his hat and buy something to eat. He took it off and inspected it. It was inconceivable that anyone would want it in its present condition.

He realised that he must wash. His hair and beard stank, his clothes were clogged with mud and worse things. He was quite likely to be locked up simply on the strength of his appearance. The solution was at hand: the street he was on bordered a canal. There was plenty of water in Holland. It wasn't always cleaner than what you washed in it, however.

This canal was black and scummy. Nevertheless he could not bear the feeling of himself, so he took off his hat, filled it with water and tipped it over his head. Involuntarily he swallowed some: it tasted vile and shocked him with its coldness. The dog, excited, pawed his back. He snarled at it, and took off his boots and rinsed the muck off them. He hoped the leather wouldn't shrink, because he had no money to buy another pair. They were expensive boots, soft calf with fashionably high heels. Then he saw, with despair, that one of the heels was coming loose.

He would have wept if his teeth had not been chattering.

The idiot dog laid its head on his knee as if to comfort him, and he thought with bottomless self-pity that this was the point to which his life had been leading, all the high hopes, his talent, his looks, all the chances grasped, missed or squandered, they had brought him to a canal bank with his pockets picked and a cur for company.

He wrapped his arms around himself and rubbed his skin through the wet shirt in an attempt to get warm. And that was what he was doing, sitting shivering on the canal bank, when the Spanish soldiery came down the road with their prisoners.

At first he saw only the marching troop, and he rose to his feet and put himself at a healthy distance. The soldiers halted a few yards from the water's edge and broke rank. Then he could see the three men and two women who stood together, barefoot and with their hands tied, in the midst of them. Curious citizens from further up the street began to drift down and take up position under the trees, watching. More soldiers arrived with rough wooden chairs, and set them down at the canal's edge.

The prisoners were made to sit on the chairs. It was like a play. They sat in a row with the canal at their backs, mutely facing the growing audience of townsfolk. Then they were tied, at wrist, leg and ankle, to the chairs. Finally a rope was passed around their chests, binding them to the chair's back. It took a long time for the work to be done to the satisfaction of the sergeant, who walked up and down inspecting the knots. The audience ate chestnuts, gossipped and commented on the proceedings.

Sure of Heaven, and resigned to the dreadful price they would have to pay to enter it, the prisoners looked straight at the crowd, appearing not to see it. The playwright, still shivering, studied them. He wondered where they found the strength for this. He could not imagine why they did not recant.

The roping was finished. A plump Franciscan stepped forward holding up a cross. He held it out to the heretics. Their eyes moved to the nailed figure, and moved away again with what seemed to be indifference.

"D'you see that?" said a woman among the onlookers.

The man with her said, "Matthys's people. Hard as stone."

"Why haven't they caught him yet?"

"They're trying, aren't they? Raised the price on his head."

An order was barked. Four soldiers at once seized the chair on which the first prisoner was sitting, lifted, swung and hurled it over the water. For a long moment, the man on his chair seemed to be rushing backwards in some extraordinary, newly-invented contraption for human flight. Then the chair reached the highest point of its trajectory, seemed to hang motionless for an instant, and plummeted with its burden like a stone. There was a very loud splash.

The onlookers, quiet now, inched forward. The soldiers stood around the second stool. A woman was tied to it, worn-looking, with straggling grey locks which, blowing about her face, made her look deranged. Her eyes stared. As the soldiers lifted her from the ground she seemed about to speak, but nothing came from her throat. After that, the only sound was the swish of air as she travelled through it, and then the splash.

And so with the five of them. By the time all had been thrown in and the soldiers were marching away, the sun was higher in the sky and a little warmth was making itself felt on the playwright's skin. The crowd pressed forward to the bank and peered down with an avid curiosity. It was impossible to see anything, owing to the inkiness of the water and its disturbance. Ripples were spreading to either bank, each concentric set confused and interrupted by the neighbouring ones, while from the black depths rose glistening chains of bubbles which expired in tiny, useless breaths on the surface.

The playwright stood at the water's edge and looked down into it. Its depths were inscrutable. Raising his head, he pulled the damp city air deep into his lungs. It was tainted with smoke and rotten fish and something from the dyeworks. There was a metallic edge to it, too: someone was smithing iron nearby. He found it wonderful, this tainted air; he gulped it.

He began to walk towards the centre of town. The dog was trotting beside him again. He placed the flat of his foot against its flank and pushed it, scrabbling, into the water.

He went to the square where the players would be if they had waited for him. They had not waited. They had left before dawn.

That same day, Rothmann preached against property in Münster.

He preached from an upturned wine-tub outside St Lambert's. The Town Council had banned him from preaching inside. It was stupid of them, because when he preached outside more people came to hear him.

There was by any reckoning a large congregation. It was composed of extremely diverse elements. Respectably dressed citizens stood next to rank-smelling skeletons in rags, apparently without noticing the fact. A bunch of out-of-work weavers had planted itself in the middle of the gathering. Also present was an assortment of beggars, tradesmen, disbanded soldiers, apprentices, country people who had come to market, shopkeepers, thieves and mystics who received personal messages from God.

Rothmann was telling them things they were not used to hearing from a cleric.

"How does it come about that some of you possess nothing, not even the clothes that would keep you warm through a winter night, when there are other people who have so many possessions they don't know what to do with them? And why is it that so many of you are out of work? Do you think it's by some decree of Almighty God, who has decided that from now on there shall be less work in the world?"

No, they didn't think so.

"It's by decree of the men who sit in counting-houses and want to increase their profit. Guild labour is too dear, they won't pay for it."

A shout of agreement went up.

"You who come from Holland know this, too. Two Dutch clothworkers unemployed for every one in work. Isn't that so?"

There were a number of Dutchmen in the crowd. They were practically destitute. They stood together, listening intently and nodding fiercely when something struck them. They nodded now, and clapped their fists into their palms.

"And all the time rents and taxes go up, and the cost of food rises, and the only thing there's more of is the number of beggars. Is it true?"

Loudly the audience told him that it was.

"And, brothers, what is behind it all? One thing, one single thing. Property!"

"Down with property!" cried a woman with her bonnet on askew at the edge of the crowd. She was known as Crazy Kate, and she always went to Rothmann's sermons. He smiled at her tolerantly.

"Property is the dividing up of the earth by man," said Rothmann. "In the beginning, there was no ownership: the earth was given to all of us to share. But ever since Old Testament times, people have been squabbling over 'yours' and 'mine' and trying to get more for themselves. They devote their whole lives to doing it. They make laws to protect what they have and to prevent anyone else from stealing it, although they stole it in the first place. They don't care that to increase their profit they are taking bread from a child's mouth. That's business, they say. But, brothers, it is not business, it is murder!"

A great roar of assent rose from the crowd. It was not rhetoric to talk about bread in Münster. The price of rye had trebled in a year.

Now Rothmann's voice rang out and tears stood in his eyes, as he cried, "But a new time is coming!" The joy of that longed-for time transfigured his face. It was as if he saw it before them, dawning in the smoky afternoon over the fish market. And many in the crowd saw it, too, because they began to cheer and weep and take off their hats and kneel down in the place where they'd been standing, and some of them gave voice to the Spirit.

"A new time is coming!"

"Praise God, the Lord is coming!"

"He shall wipe away the tears from our eyes!"

"The proud and the oppressor shall be cast down! Praise God!"

A group of ex-nuns who had abandoned their convent began all at once to talk in tongues, to the great interest of the people standing near them. After a while, a cobbler who had the gift of interpretation started to interpret to the crowd what was being said. The excitement grew.

"Amen!" cried Rothmann, his arms raised above the growing tumult as if to draw down to himself the divine lightning. "Come, Lord Jesus!"

The playwright's earliest memory was of dampness and the dangerous proximity of a pair of wooden-shod feet. The feet clumped to and fro, narrowly missing him. Under his buttocks, the floor was cool and hard. All around him were mountains of cloth from which steaming vapour rose. There was a great din in his ears of things clashed together, water sloshed and raised voices, the voices of women.

It was always women. He felt his childhood had been passed among women. Probably it wasn't so; men must often have come swearing and roistering into that female world he remembered, but when he cast his gaze back, all he could see was the women. Women in the laundry where his mother was a washerwoman, women bustling in the kitchen of some fine house, women in the market where once his mother had sold ribbons and he had wandered among the stalls, young and pretty enough to get a bit of pie from the pie-seller and a cup of milk from the country girls, and with luck too young and pretty to be suspected of thieving.

His father was a great man, his mother told him, a dignitary in some neighbouring town. The boy met him once. Already tall at twelve years of age, he looked down on a little, spare, bald, officious man who had a shrill way of talking and never stopped fussing with the rings on his hand. This man gave him a leather purse with some coins in it, and a piece of advice. The money went on a set of clothes, and the advice could not be forgotten since it had not been listened to in the first place.

He was the constant star in his mother's life. She moved from place to place, occupation to occupation, trailing him after her, through tribes of other women and other children. She always encouraged him to think of himself as better than the people they were among. She had no need to. He believed it already, had received it from some other source in his earliest infancy. He knew he was marked out for greatness.

He loved the world, when the time came for him to elbow his way in it: he loved its clamour. And it liked him. As a result, he made his way tolerably well. He had scraps of schooling and picked things up quickly: it was enough for him to spend an evening in an educated man's company to come away with a gloss of education himself. But his most important asset was that he had a way of getting people to do things for him. Women, particularly. Men either took to him or distrusted him. He developed ways of dealing with the distrust, and one of them was to acquire practical knowledge: other men respected you if you knew how to do things. Learning a bit about everything in any case suited his temperament, which did not take to steady work. In the course of a few years he was a journeyman tailor, a millwright's labourer, a fish-salter, a horse-breaker, a peddler of herbal remedies and a clerk in a warehouse, where he learnt among other things how to falsify accounts. He did a bit of soldiering and enjoyed it, but when he was offered a commission he refused. He thought fighting other men's wars was a stupid way to spend your life.

At twenty-two he still did not know what his destiny was. His mother had died while he was on the road selling remedies. The loss disturbed him: he dimly realised that her faith in him had been part of his faith in himself. He took jobs here and there; work was getting hard to find, people said, but he never had any trouble finding work, he had trouble keeping it. He became bored almost at once with whatever he was required to do.

He made an effort to settle down. In Leyden he took over the running of an inn, and acquired a wife without really meaning to. One afternoon, bored witless, he went to a play in the marketplace. It was a lamentable play. The jokes limped, the characters had no life in them and the dialogue was old-fashioned. He went home and wrote his own play, sitting up all night over it, and took it to the players in the morning. When they left Leyden a few days later, he was with them. He had not seen the inn, or his wife, since.

And now he had come to the end of that road, too. This time, he had not the faintest idea what to do next.

The events of the past year in Münster had left the city with only one monastery, out of the four monasteries and eleven convents it had formerly boasted. This monastery was in St Egidius Street, and was supposedly protected by the treaty the Bishop had made with the citizens.

Not long after Rothmann had finished his sermon, knots of people began drifting towards it and congregating around its entrance. They were clearly waiting for something. After a while, cheerful shouts were heard and the apprentices came swinging down the street. They held aloft poles from which the Bishop dangled in obscene effigy. The crowd laughed and let them through to the gate. It was a stout oak gate, but the apprentices' boots made short work of it. They broke down the inner door and raced through the halls and corridors, scattering monks in panic.

Behind them came the townsfolk, who knew what this fight was about and that it had been coming for a long time, but were not averse to putting the boot into a few monks on their own account. The apprentices threw over tables and broke several windows on their way through the building, but did not allow themselves to be distracted from their real goal, which was the workshops.

Six monks were at the looms. They had continued with their work when they heard the noise, but now they paused and looked up. The apprentices bunched their fists and grinned. There were thirty of them, more or less, with the crowd at their back. The monks stood up.

The boys came vaulting over the looms. At first it looked as if they didn't mean to damage them, and it was all a game. But the monks defended their looms, and the apprentices drove hard young fists into their faces and stomachs and kicked with hard young feet, and it was not long before an apprentice had drawn a knife and cut the strings of a loom, and then all were being cut, the work slashed to ribbons, the wooden frames attacked with an iron pole, amd the monks themselves fleeing from the room and from the building, and locking themselves in the safety of the church.

Then someone with less sense than the others set fire to some weavings, which put an abrupt stop to the activities because the fire service had to be called at once before the flames spread.

The apprentices and the crowd, having made a few ineffectual attempts to extinguish the blaze, retired to a distance to watch it. Fortunately it was soon brought under control by means of a chain of buckets filled from the river, but not before a tiler who was noted for seeing signs and visions had discerned in the burning roof-timbers the shape of the horseman of the Apocalypse who for the past two weeks had been seen in the western evening sky.

"Have you heard of a man called Matthys?" the playwright asked a bargee. The wind was chill. It was late in the afternoon.

The bargee looked at him sharply, and then went on stowing his gear on the boat. "You're a fool if you go asking for him," he said.

"But is he here in Haarlem?"

"They say so." And that was all he would say.

He tried next with a serving-girl who pretended she didn't know what he was talking about, although from the fright in her eyes he knew that she did, and then with a rabbit-catcher in the market. The rabbit-catcher smiled slyly at him and shook his head.

"What does that mean?" asked the playwright. There were people loitering by and looking at the rabbits. It was a stupid place to ask.

"Whatever you want it to. Going to buy a rabbit?"

"My money's been stolen."

"You want to be more careful," said the rabbit-catcher.

After that he tried asking in the tavern, where he beguiled the girl into giving him a drink in return for a kiss planted in the palm of her hand when the mistress wasn't looking. But there he was told, by someone who overheard him, to keep his mouth shut. The girl found him a hunk of cheese and somewhere to sleep in the stables. He might then have given up—after all, it was a wild idea and dangerous—but something pushed him to keep trying. It wasn't as if he was working completely in the dark: he knew the leader of the heretics was in Haarlem. He always made it his business to find out what was going on in whatever place the company stopped (it was a good idea to slip local references into the play), and the first thing he had found out was that Matthys was in town. The Baker they called him, because that was what he'd been.

The following day he went on asking. He chose the poor parts of town, around the market, and in the weavers' district. Mostly he was ignored or laughed at; some people cursed him. One woman threatened to call the soldiers. In the course of the day he became aware that a boy of about fifteen, a sandy-haired boy with a hare-lip, was following him.

The playwright let this go on for another day, and then walked slowly back to the canal bank where the Anabaptists had been thrown in. He sat down, and waited for the hare-lipped boy.

After a short interval the boy appeared. He came and sat on the bank.

They watched the water for a while. A barge went by. Then the boy said, "Why are you looking for Matthys?"

"Do you know him?" the playwright countered.

"Why are you looking for him?"

The playwright had an answer ready, but he took the one that tumbled out of the sky.

"I want to change my life," he said.

That night the boy took him on a journey through the dark streets of Haarlem. It was a long and baffling journey. The playwright did not know the part of the city he had been taken to, but he was aware that they many times changed direction, doubled back on themselves and went in circles. Every now and then an armed patrol went by, and they had to hide in the shadows. His plan was hopeless, he concluded. He would never be able to guide the soldiers to the place. The only person who could find Matthys in this warren was one of his own.

At last, in a narrow, mean street like all the others, as dark and evil-smelling as all the others, they came to a house like all the others and knocked. A man whose face was obscured by a large-brimmed hat opened the door, stood back and directed them up a steep, winding staircase. The playwright had no candle, and had to feel his way. The boy was behind him, or he thought he was, but when he reached the upper floor, which was a single long room with a slit of a window, he turned and found himself alone. Alone, that is, except for the man who sat with his back to that narrow window, and with his hands on a table on which a stub of candle burned.

"Matthys?" he asked.

"You will have wasted your time otherwise." The voice was low and harsh. "Come nearer and sit down."

A wooden bench stood against the table. The playwright sat on it. The room was very cold. There was no fire. The only tiny warmth came from the candle flame.

"What is your name?" Matthys asked.

"Jan Bockelson."

"And how old are you?"

"Twenty-four."

"What's your trade?"

"I've practised many. Until a few days ago I was an actor and playwright."

Matthys said nothing more for a while, and the playwright began to feel uncomfortable with a discomfort that was more urgent than the chill of the room. He had the frightening sensation that the man sitting opposite him could see every detail of his face and clothing, could see the Italian dagger he wore and his fashionable (the heel was still holding) boots, and his now-stained, ruffled shirt from a tailor he had not paid in Groningen, and more, although he could not possibly see all this in the light of the candle, and he certainly could not see Jan's boots, which were under the table.

"Why have you come to see me?" asked Matthys.

"I told the boy…"

"He is called William."

"I told William that I wanted to change my life."

"Yes, but did you mean it?" Matthys did not pause for a reply before going on, in that harsh voice, "I will tell you two things about yourself. One you know, and one you don't. The first is that, when you set out to come here, you intended to betray me, but you gave up the idea because you realised you would never be able to find the place again. The second thing is that, although you thought you came here of your own accord, you were sent."

Jan was so alarmed by the first statement that for a moment or two it was the only part of Matthys's speech he registered.

Then the second statement made its way through to him. He was bewildered. "Sent?"

"Yes."

"By whom?"

Matthys made an impatient movement. "Who do you imagine is in charge of the affairs of this world?"

"Some people believe it's Satan."

"Only the stupid make that mistake."

"If God is in charge of the world, I've seen few signs of it," said the playwright with an attempt at bravado. He did not in fact believe that the God described in the Bible existed. Who or what had created him, and why, was a question he did not trouble his brains with.

"Who do you think you are, to judge God? God can blow you out like a candle."

The candle flame at that moment flickered and almost died in some tiny current of air. This coincidence increased the playwright's unease.

"Once I was walking down a street, cocky with youth and with all my sins on me, just like you," said Matthys. "The Lord struck me down. I fell down in the street. I was carried to my lodging and I lay there paralysed for three days and nights. On the third night, the Lord spoke to me. He told me to find a certain man called Hoffmann and become his disciple. When dawn came, I got up from my bed."

"Did you find him?"

"Of course. We aren't told to do things which are impossible."

Jan longed to be out of the room which contained this madman. However, he did not know how to take his leave without giving offence, which might have who knew what consequences, and in any case he did not know how to find his way out of the warren of streets. He had walked into a trap which he had set himself. It might even be a fatal trap. If Matthys and his friends decided to murder him, no-one would ever be the wiser. He was inwardly furious with himself for such stupidity.

"You are quite safe," Matthys told him. As the playwright stared at him with a thumping heart, he continued, "It frightens you that I can see your thoughts, doesn't it? It's very easy. I can see through you as if you were a drop of water."

The small molten pool below the flame of the candle brimmed over in a river of tallow.

"A moment ago you were angry with yourself because you thought you had been stupid to come here. You don't like to think you've been stupid: you're used to considering yourself rather clever. Better than other people. You probably think you deserve a great future. However, your prospects aren't good: I can tell that by looking at you. You have no money, although you like to dress well. Because nothing is good enough for you, you won't soil your hands with honest work. Look at your hands" — they were clasped on the table in front of him. "You keep them like a woman's. You're beginning to lose hope of this great future. You're running out of time. You have to change your life: you have no choice. What you said to William was the simple truth."

Astonished, and also fascinated, the playwright listened.

"You have been searching for your master, as I searched for Hoffmann, but without knowing it. Well, you have found me." A pause. Sharp eyes interrogated him. "So, what will you do?"

"Do?"

"Must I spell it out for you? You were meant to come here. But you do not have to accept the cup which is held out to you."

The playwright laughed. "Usually I can see what's in a cup that's held out to me."

"I will tell you what is in this one. You will have to give up everything. Your possessions, if you have any, your friends, if you have any. Your fashionable clothes. Your good name, if you have one, though that I doubt."

"And?"

"Become one of us. We live communally, we share everything we have, and we share our danger. Every one of us is under sentence of death."

"Then I would be mad to become one of you, wouldn't I?"

"On the face of it, yes. We are all mad, in the world's eyes. But the world is afraid of us, and that is why it kills us." He paused for a long time. Then, sombrely, he said, "Five days ago, five of our people were martyred. They were Peter, Marius, Mary, Hannah and Bjorn."

The uttering of the names had an extraordinary effect in the chill, dark room: it was as if the dead had come into it.

In a sudden, startling movement Matthys half-rose and pulled a sword from his belt. Jan, who had not suspected that Matthys was armed, recoiled and his hand went to his dagger. Matthys smiled grimly and laid the naked weapon on the table.

"Soon," he said, "I shall unsheath this sword and not sheath it again until Peter and Marius and Mary and Hannah and Bjorn are avenged, and the world is clean."

"Clean?"

"In the days to come, Good will battle against Evil until Satan is chained," Matthys said. "Then we, the Chosen, will reign with Christ for a thousand years in the New Jerusalem." He fixed Jan with a stare which caused the playwright's hairs to rise on his neck. "The Last Days are very near: we know it, we have been given many proofs. It will be next year. And it is we, the despised, who will bring it about when we rise against our oppressors. Brother, ahead of us lies the greatest adventure in the history of the world! Don't you want a part in it?"

2   The City

All the printers and apprentices were gathered by the press reading something over each other's shoulders when Martin got to the printing shop. He took off his scarf and went to look.

It was the text for a pamphlet. He'd never seen anything that went quite so far. The hand was scholarly but had a certain plainness to it. Rothmann's, of course.

Tenckel, who was holding the paper, went off with a little smile and started setting up the type.

"Are we really going to print that?" someone asked.

"We always do Rothmann's printing."

Tenckel was half way through the typesetting when the master printer, Peter Eck, came down. He ran his eye along the field of lead in its wooden frame and pointed out a word with a missing letter. He asked when the job would be ready.

"Three o'clock," said Tenckel.

Master Eck went back to his cubbyhole at the top of the staircase which was the only place in the building that was warm.

When Tenckel finished the printing, he laid the sheets on the pine table in the centre of the workroom floor so the ink could dry. They gathered round again, abandoning their own work for a few minutes to admire Tenckel's composition of the type and refresh their memories about the things the pamphlet said. As the sheets were being put into piles, Master Eck came down again to look them over. A little after that, two boys came in and took the finished pamphlets away.

There was still about an hour of daylight left. Martin went on with his work. He was typesetting a book on the use of herbs in treating melancholia. Just as the light was fading, four militiamen walked in. Two of them clattered up the frail wooden staircase to the master printer's office, and the remaining two began to walk around the printing floor. They stared at the iron presses, peered at the type set up in the forms, which of course they couldn't read, not having the printer's skill of reading backwards, and looked over the shoulders of the apprentices as if expecting to find them committing a felony.

The two who had gone up the stairs came down with Master Eck between them. The master printer opened a drawer of the big table and drew out Rothmann's text. The chief militiaman seized it and thrust it into his pocket. He said, "And where is the type?"

It would have been possible, Martin thought, to show them almost anything and they would have believed they were looking at the type for the pamphlet. But the master printer led them straight to the press where Tenckel had left the type standing, and without even a glance at the letters they started ripping lead out of the frame and stamping it underfoot.

When they had done that, the chief pointed at the bits of lead on the floor and ordered, "Melt it down."

A ripple of amusement ran round the journeymen and apprentices. Dimly aware that they had made fools of themselves, the militiamen strode out of the printing shop.

"Sort it out, lads," said the Master Eck with a nod at the scattered type, and went back to his office. The apprentices picked up the letters and began to sort them. Sorted, they would be put back in their boxes, and then not even the Pope would be able to tell which letters had been used for printing Rothmann's pamphlet against infant baptism and which had been used for printing a civic ordinance about rubbish in the streets.

Martin told the story when he got home that evening. His wife, Susannah, was salting pork. She laid two trotters side by side on the bed of crystals in the stone jar, and wiped her fingers on her apron.

"They left it too late, if they didn't want anyone to read that pamphlet," she said. "It was put up on half the doors in town. There was one on ours. 'Tis over there with the apples."

He laughed. He loved his wife. He kissed her on the neck, and she turned round and kissed him on the lips. He pulled her closer. "Not now," she said, wriggling. "I'm in the middle of salting, look." But then when he went on holding her by the waist she put her tongue in his mouth. It was warm and wet and tasted salty. He was on fire at once. He pulled at her clothes, she expertly unpicked his, and there they were rolling giggling on the rushes and doing it again. A little later, when the room was smelling deliciously of heated man and woman and salted pork, Jakob, who had lived with them for a month, came in. Martin covered himself hastily and got up.

The Dutchman grinned, took an apple from the bowl and bit into it with his grey teeth. "Don't let me stop you," he said. Susannah, pink in the face, smoothed down her apron and went back to the salting.

"I hear there was some trouble at the print shop," remarked Jakob. Martin told him about it. He had the feeling that Jakob already knew as much as he did. The Dutch were always well informed about what was happening, and they were clannish.

Jakob nodded sagely. Then he said, "After you're rebaptised, you'll have to go through another marriage ceremony, you know. If you married under the old law, you're living in mortal sin."

Susannah turned quickly. "We're doing no such thing. We're man and wife in the sight of God."

"He's teasing you," said Martin.

"Teasing you, am I?" said the Dutchman. "We'll see." He munched the apple. "There's a great change coming, that's certain, and we must all be ready for it. And another thing that's certain is that many of those who think they're ready for it will find when it comes that it's not what they thought."

Jakob was given to making pronouncements like this. It irritated Martin, but he told himself that the Dutch had suffered a great deal and that was probably why they behaved as if they were the only ones who knew anything. He didn't really mind, and he was glad they had offered Jakob shelter in their little room under the roof.

The mob broke into the church of St Egidius late in the afternoon. They found the padlock on the gate broken already, and flooded into the churchyard. An advantage of the place was that it was some way from the centre of the town.

Among them were men from the slaughterhouse. They'd come rushing out to join the crowd as it passed, and were still wearing their bloodstained leather aprons.

Some of them were still climbing over the railings, impatient of the crush in the gateway, when there came a sound of splintering wood. A bull of a man with a square black beard was attacking the church door with an iron pole. His clothes proclaimed him to be one of the Dutchmen. He laboured at the door with savage intentness. After a while, when he stopped to wipe his face, another man, almost as wide in the shoulders, pushed his way through to help him. This got a cheer. The second man was the local gravedigger.

Soon afterwards the door gave, with a soft crunch of tortured wood. The next moment the mob was flowing irresistibly into the dark, incense-smelling, cold interior.

There they stopped. It was the darkness, or something else, that stopped them. It was like a hand. They stood there, rubbing their shins where they'd barked them on the pews through not being able to see, feeling all that weight of darkness above their heads. Through that darkness, the angels on the ceiling bosses looked down at them. Through the darkness they sensed how the pillars rose to the roof and Christ laboured with his cross along the nave, and the gold gleamed on the altar.

They moved uneasily, and a few of them backed towards the door. Then someone spoke angrily, and a light was struck. It illuminated the bearded face of the man who had broken the lock. He lit a candle and held it over his head.

The light loosened their limbs. They scrambled to find more candles and light them from the first. The big Dutchman walked up to the altar with his iron pole. They watched as he held it out at the full stretch of his arm, then swung himself sideways so that the candlesticks, the Cross and all the other things that were on the altar sailed into the air and flew into the choir stalls, where they bounced off the wood and landed on the tiled floor of the sanctuary.

A shiver went through the crowd as the golden candlesticks hit the floor. Some people looked up, as if they expected the roof to fall and bury them. But moments passed and nothing happened. Stone remained stone. The carved angels were fixed and sightless. The sacred air was empty.

Someone laughed. It broke the enchantment that held them. At once, men began breaking up the choir stalls with their boots. A youth set about knocking the glass methodically out of the Nativity window with a brick. In the midst of the activity, the gravedigger could be seen holding the lectern in his arms as if it were a dead child, before throwing it across the chancel.

At the back of the church was the font.

It was old. It had been carved out of a hard grey stone, and its plainness was relieved by a frieze of ivy leaves cut into the outside surface just below the rim. It had an austere beauty, and some of them who knew the church were reluctant to harm it. But it was the font and of all the bad things in that sacrilegious building it was the worst.

They rained blows on it with picks and hammers, until they had reduced it to ugly chunks of stone. Then they threw the chunks outside in the churchyard. They stood there, breathing heavily, with their feet covered in powder and chippings. Someone said, "Well, that's that, then."

It wasn't, at all.

Sister Agnes, who was sometimes known as Crazy Kate, was looking at a small white cloud in the palm of her hand. At first it seemed to be all fleecy softness, but then she saw that right in the centre of it, like a seed in a pod, was a tiny crystal of sapphire.

As she gazed at it, the sapphire began to grow. It became as big as her hand, and then it filled the whole kitchen, and then it was everything there was and she was inside it. She was standing on a white seashore.

She could hear singing. Apart from the singing, everything was still. The sea had been turned into something like glass, and she could see the fish frozen in its depths, with their mouths in an O and their pretty scales glimmering like flakes of gold. On top of the motionless waves were perched motionless fishing boats, with motionless people in them.

Then a dark and ugly shadow passed over the sea. Sister Agnes looked up to see a very large bird, unlike any bird she had ever seen, flying overhead. It was half bird and half bat. It had a fierce curved beak and in its talons was hooked a piece of bloody flesh.

Then, thwick! An arrow pierced the bat-bird's breast and it fell. It tumbled on to the seashore, not far from where she stood. There it lay.

She turned to see who had shot it. The Lamb stood behind her, holding a bow and arrow. He told her that the bird had been Antichrist.

And now the seashore vanished, and she was still looking at the Lamb, but he was seated in a golden chair. The chair had two wings like an eagle's wings, and they were slowly beating the air. She was able to look around a little, and saw that she was in the sky, standing in a kind of rush basket. Beside her was an angel, who leaned over the side of the basket and pointed downwards. Sister Agnes leaned over and looked down, and was just in time to see the blue sea below shrink together like the skim on milk and vanish.

The air filled with the singing she had heard before. Looking up again, she saw the sky start to crack and unpeel like the bark of a dead tree.

The Lamb was growing brighter and brighter. It was impossible to look at him. The basket in which Sister Agnes and the angel were standing began to burn.

Just in time, before the flames reached her, she was lying on the kitchen floor with Ruth bending over her asking if she was all right. Sister Agnes smiled as best she could, and said she would be as right as rain shortly.

Tylbeck knotted his hands over his chain of office. The other Burgomaster, Sachs, had taken to his bed as the troubles increased.

"Gentlemen," said Tylbeck, "What are we to do about these constant disturbances?"

He cast his eyes the length of the polished table. Men of weight, all of them, in several ways. Their sober cloth with its trimming of fur, the heavy rings on their fingers. Their seamed faces. They were men of business, they were used to risks and they knew about human nature. They could deal with those things, but they did not know how to deal with what was happening in Münster.

Tylbeck's eyes came to rest on a councillor called Vogel. In a roomful of men accustomed to be blunt, he was the bluntest.

"Call in the Bishop," said Vogel.

The room instantly divided itself into two opposed camps.

"I won't see Catholic rule brought back here," said Krechting, the timber importer, and thumped the table to prove he meant it. He had been moving towards the Anabaptists for some time.

"None of us wants that," protested Vogel.

"So, with his soldiers in the streets again, what's to stop him?"

"The treaty."

Krechting sneered. Most of the room was with him. When a vote was taken, on Vogel's motion, there were three in favour, fifteen against and the rest were abstentions.

Tylbeck repeated his question: "What are we to do?"

"Expel the men responsible for these disturbances," said Gebler, who owned the paper mill.

A councillor called Bernard Dolling, who featured prominently in Tylbeck's sleepless nights, eased himself forward on his chair.

"Are you going to name names?" asked Tylbeck.

Gebler said that everybody knew who the main instigator was.

Vogel said, "Why beat about the bush? It's Rothmann who started all this, and is still stirring things up."

"There isn't a man in this room who doesn't owe his seat on the Council to Rothmann," said Dolling loudly.

"By the time he's finished there'll be no Council, no Council chamber, there won't be one stone standing on another," growled Vogel.

"If a building's rotten it deserves to fall down," remarked Dolling, which had the desired effect of making several councillors very angry.

Tylbeck banged his little wooden hammer on the table.

"He stirs up rebellion," said Gebler. "We all know it. Inflammatory rubbish against authority, against property, against religion... And who's his audience? The mob!"

"He preaches to the poor and homeless," said Dolling.

"He preaches to all the riffraff that's drifted into the city. Dutchmen, beggars, the nothing-to-lose brigade..."

"Driven out of their homes by Catholic persecution," noted Krechting. "If you were a Christian you'd share your house with them."

"I don't notice that you do."

"Everything Rothmann preaches and writes is taken from Scripture," said Dolling. "Not one of you can fault it." He looked round the table. "Or if you can, then do so now."

"This Council is not competent to debate theology," said Gebler.

"Then it is not competent to decide whether Rothmann should be expelled from Münster."

"Hear, hear," said Krechting.

The room erupted. Tylbeck banged the table again. "I shall take a vote on whether to issue an expulsion order against Rothmann."

"I petition that the vote be delayed until other methods of quelling the disturbances have been discussed," said Dolling.

According to procedure, Tylbeck could not refuse this. He granted it with visible reluctance. Dolling smiled, having returned the meeting to chaos.

Tylbeck asked, once again, for suggestions. This time the militia was mentioned. So far it had proved unreliable: too many of its members were in sympathy with the rioters. But the militia took them back, irresistibly, to the Bishop's troops, and this time the proposal was made that the Council should ask the Bishop for the loan of a few hundred of his soldiers on conditions that would be negotiated.

"We can't hold him to conditions," said Krechting. "Once his troops are in control, he will say that the terms of the treaty have been breached."

"How can he say that?"

"Because we have allowed this wretched Anabaptist superstition to infect the city," said Vogel.

"Then we must get rid of Rothmann!"

"Do we really have to go through this rigmarole?" put in a councillor called Mollenbecke, a stiff fellow who was a master armourer. "It's ridiculous to hazard our freedom of religion for the sake of a few hotheads whom we could deal with between us with a few feet of steel."

Dolling had been waiting for precisely this. He threw in his pinch of gunpowder.

"What freedom of religion? There is no freedom of religion in Münster! The Catholics are allowed to worship as they please, the Lutherans are allowed to worship as they please, but we, who only ask to be allowed to worship God as the disciples did, are denied it. Our preachers are threatened with expulsion… "

Every man in the Council chamber was on his feet, shouting.

Tylbeck, getting no response with his wooden hammer, picked up a heavy brass candlestick and banged that on the table.

"Gentlemen!" he bellowed. "We are here to govern a city, not to brawl."

"This city has gone past governing," said Vogel.

It was true.

Jan had been re-baptised. He lived in an Anabaptist household, and earned his living selling plates and bowls for a wood-turner.

His life had slowed down (or perhaps, he sometimes thought, stopped). He had got used to rising early, going to bed at a time which previously he would have found incredible, and weeding the curses out of his speech. He ceased to think about nothing but how to get hold of money and how to improve his standing in the world, and thought instead about how to win the esteem of Matthys.

Matthys governed his flock with an iron hand. However, if he was harsh to them, he was ten times harsher to himself. He ate like a sparrow. He rose long before dawn and was awake long after the brethren had gone to their beds: Jan wondered if he slept at all. He owned nothing except his clothes, a Bible and that sword.

Jan was surprised to find he was married, because his life seemed untouched by any kind of softness. Yet Jan found him one afternoon in the company of a young woman with fine features and clear brown eyes, whom he introduced as his wife, Devera. She had been a nun, one of those incarcerated by their families as children, who came flooding out of the convents like freed galley slaves as the Reform spread. She was beautiful, Jan saw with astonishment, because how could a woman like this have accepted a man like that as a husband: and did Matthys know she was beautiful? He stared at her, and then hastily lowered his gaze. Dangerous. Much too dangerous. He must try to forget that he'd seen her. It was too late already.

"You should have a wife, Jan," said Matthys.

"I do," he said. He regretted it at once. Normally he would have had his wits about him enough to dissimulate, but he had been thrown completely off his guard.

"Where is she?"

"In Leyden."

"You should send for her."

"Yes, I will."

They were very strict about marriage and relations between the sexes. Marriage was godly, and was for the procreation of children. Everything else was fornication, and you were cast out for it.

Casting out of the community was their punishment for all serious offences. Jan was surprised by its mildness (for Matthys was not a mild man) until he realised what it meant. For its members, the community was all there was. Rejected by it, they were deprived of everything that went to make up life.

Nothing in Jan's previous history suggested that he would be able to endure all this, or indeed any of it. The first week was the worst: twenty times a day he was on the point of throwing it in, walking out of the house, the workshop or the prayer-meeting in disgust and leaving them to suffocate in their piety and martyrdoms. But he knew that this period would not last long, that Matthys did not expect it to last long, and this helped him to keep his patience. He nourished his patience, too, on the bait Matthys had offered him. It was an intoxicating bait: merely the whiff of it had turned his head. It was the more potent for being mysterious. At times, indeed, it appeared delusion—both Matthys's delusion and his own—and then he fell into a deep dejection. What pulled him out of it was the unfailing belief of those around him in that very dream. He realised that, contrary to what he had expected, he had in a way become one of these people. They shared the same hope. It was just that he did not think of it as Heaven.

His main preoccupation was that Matthys would not trust him enough. He was still unclear what Matthys intended to do. He would drop a hint, say something cryptic about a time or a place, and then retire for days into an impenetrable silence. Jan did not dare to ask him a direct question. He had not got over his fear that Matthys still thought of him as the man who, if only for an hour, had intended to betray him.

Jan tried hard to please him. Flattery of course was not only useless but downright dangerous: he would see through it at once and wonder what you were after. But it was possible, Jan decided, to flatter him more subtly by listening with care to what he said and returning later to discuss it with him on a level he had not anticipated. When he had done this several times, he felt that he was growing in Matthys's estimation: Matthys even called him a thinker. This gratified Jan greatly until, suddenly suspicious, he turned one day and found Matthys laughing at him. He should have known: Matthys had no time for thinkers or theologians, he had nothing but contempt for learning. But he did like it that Jan was apparently applying himself to the brotherhood's teachings. In his cold and awkward way he seemed to grow quite fond of his new disciple.

Jan was determined that, whatever Matthys proposed, he was going to have a major part in it. And that, indeed, was what Matthys seemed to intend. But if he was to have a major part in it he needed to know what it was, lest it turn out to be so outlandish as to be completely impossible.

He had a sense that Matthys, who oversaw the domestic business of his little flock very efficiently, would not prove able to direct a great and dangerous operation, a military operation, without disaster. And if what Matthys had been talking about at their first meeting was not a military operation, Jan did not know what it could be.

Matthys said eventually that he had received a vision, as a result of which everything was now clear. The time when the New Jerusalem would be established was very close, and he knew the place. That was all he would say, despite increasingly anxious promptings. It seemed he was going to keep it all locked up in his own head until the very last moment. Then, thought Jan, he would announce that the day of the final battle was upon them, issue a set of orders which could be carried out by no human agency, and wait for the arrival of the heavenly host.

Bernard Dolling sat in his study with a glass of wine at his elbow and a ledger in front of him. His eye moved down the column of figures. Then it moved up again, more slowly, checking the addition. His hand reached for the pen, and he dipped it in the inkwell. At the foot of the page he appended a note about a shipment of cloth which had arrived in a spoiled condition and had had to be sold cheap. He sprinkled a little sand on the wet ink, blew it off when it was dry and turned the page. With satisfaction, he heard beyond the window the noise of another disturbance in the streets.

He then heard another sound, which irritated him. It was his wife's voice raised in altercation with the servant, Izzie. He wished Sarah would leave the girl alone. She was not very clever but she was willing enough and made a good rabbit stew, which was more than Sarah had ever managed. He had hoped for rabbit stew today but it had been mutton, which he did not like much.

He perused the next page of the ledger. He did not have to do this: he had a perfectly competent accountant. He was doing it because he was waiting for Rothmann, he did not like to waste time while he waited, and the ledger, with its orderly lists and firm arithmetic, calmed him. He often needed calming, these days. He spent a great deal of his time in a state of tension or nervous excitement. In fact he had not enjoyed himself so much for years, but it was in the nature of the situation that he could not admit it.

Once he had been one of the wealthiest men in Münster, a pillar of society and a councillor. He was still all those things, but now in addition he was their enemy. He was two people. One was the Bernard Dolling Münster had always known. The other was someone he still hardly knew himself. They appeared to have nothing in common. The first Dolling was hardworking, worldly, enjoyed business and the money it brought and took pleasure in expensive furs, good wine and a stove lit on a cold night. The second despised these things as vanities, and was working with Rothmann for the overthrow of everything that made business and the accumulation of wealth possible. He marvelled at himself very frequently.

So did many others. That afternoon he had addressed a meeting of clothworkers in the upstairs room of an inn. The air of that room, smoky, garlic-laden, beer-saturated, was still on his clothes, and he could still see the clothworkers' faces before him. Expectant, resolute, pinched. They understood what he was doing, but no-one else did. His former business associates thought he was mad. His wife belaboured him with questions about what would become of them when there was no more property. How would they live? Where would they live? He closed his ears. He had explained that when property was abolished everyone would have enough: that was the point of abolishing it. She didn't seem to have heard. Women exasperated him. (He made a mental exception here for that youthful paragon of female nature, his daughter.)

He had got into it in the first place because he was a businessman. In those days, the affairs of Münster had been run by the Chapter, a collection of high-born interfering clerics whose outlook was mired in the past. Restrictive legislation hampered progress, and unfair competition from the monastic workshops damaged the guilds, which had enough problems already with the introduction of more ruthless commercial practices. When Rothmann fired his opening salvo against the Catholic Church from the pulpit of St Lambert's, Dolling had been delighted. He liked the plainness and thrust of Lutheranism, too. It was about self-sufficiency, it gave a man more elbow room.

So he had offered Rothmann his support. Whatever was needed. Money, a friendly voice in the Council chamber, a place to run to when things got hot. As they did. Many times Rothmann had spent the night in Dolling's house because there were men with unfriendly intentions waiting for him outside his own. Dolling considered he was doing his civic duty. Münster needed Rothmann, and Rothmann needed a protector. At the same time, although he would not have said so, he found the plotting and manoeuvring exciting. He found he could address a crowd, and that it made his pulses race.

Even before Prince-Bishop Franz von Waldeck signed the treaty letting in the Reform as the price for holding on to his fief, Rothmann had moved beyond Luther. He had been in touch with the Anabaptists, many of whom, fleeing Catholic persecution in the Netherlands, had come to Münster. Within a short time he was preaching pure Anabaptist doctrine, from equality and the abolition of property to the Second Coming of Christ.

Dolling went with him. The momentum was too great to be stopped. In any case, he believed Rothmann was right. As a businessman, he could see exactly which way the wind was blowing and he had begun, with advancing age, to worry about his soul. And he had developed a taste for politicking which he could not give up.

He had never been without money and possessions and could not imagine it. He felt, however, that it would make no essential difference to him.

There was a woman kneeling on the cobbles of Salt Street with her face turned skyward and her hands clasped in supplication.

Rothmann recognised her. She was one of the nuns. All of them had rushed out together, weeks ago, under what they described as a divine command. They had thrown crucifixes down in the road for the townsfolk to walk on, and ripped their habits to shreds. After that they hadn't known what to do, since the illumination that brought them out of the convent gates had deserted them, and had wandered about the streets in a forlorn band before another wave of immigrants flowed into the city and lifted and dispersed them on its crest.

Somewhere, glass was being broken. He heard shouts. Behind them, he heard a deep, muffled, thrilling sound. Surely they weren't trying to take down the bells?

The Burgomaster stood at his shoulder, looking down. Tylbeck's breath was rancid with anxiety, and his blue eyes were more than usually protuberant.

"You must go down and calm them," he said. "Tell them to go home."

"I'll do no such thing. Why don't you send in the militia?"

"Damn it, Rothmann, you started this! Take responsibility!"

"I didn't tell them to riot," said Rothmann calmly.

"But what do you expect them to do? You preach against property. You preach community of goods. This to people who have nothing!"

"Whose fault is it that they have nothing?" Rothmann retorted. "All I've done is tell them the truth. What you see out there is the effect of the truth on people who've been kept in the dark for centuries. By their rulers, by the Church." He looked at Tylbeck's chain of office. "By people like you, admitting a little bit of light into the darkness and then shutting the door again out of fright."

"You would pull everything down," said Tylbeck grimly. "Where's the truth in that? It's revolution."

For a moment Rothmann saw it as the man standing at his side, the smell of whose fear plainly reached him in the overheated room, must see it. Of course these events must appear terrifying. Terrifying, the upsetting of order and hierarchy. Terrifying, the foreigners flooding into the streets with their handcarts, their tales of torture and their destitution. Terrifying, the things that were beginning to be seen in the sky.

He felt a certain sympathy for Tylbeck. Nevertheless, if Tylbeck stood in the way, he would be swept aside.

"You think this is my doing," he said, "but it's no-one's doing, it's the hand of God. We are living at the end of earthly time. These are the signs of it."

"Stuff and nonsense! Of course it suits you to say so. They believe the world is about to end because you have told them so."

"Someone of far greater authority has told them so. Read your Bible."

"You refuse responsibility."

"It is not you I am responsible to."

Tylbeck turned from the window to face him. "When the rule of law has broken down, Rothmann, what do you propose to replace it with?"

Rothmann laughed. "I am not going to replace it with anything."

"Then what are you trying to do?"

There had been increasingly loud shouting as they talked, and now a rabble burst into the street, yelling and capering around something swinging from a pole. Rothmann shuddered at the angle of the neck. But it was a dummy, made of sacks and stuffed with straw.

Tylbeck looked, and his features froze.

"It's just an effigy of the Bishop," said Rothmann.

"Have they nothing better to do?"

"What should they be doing?"

"They could work, instead of roaming the streets all day!"

"There is no work," said Rothmann. "The wonder is that they haven't cut all your throats."

There came another crash of breaking glass. Someone had started a fire: sparks were rising above the opposite rooftops, and as Rothmann listened he heard the hiss and crackle of flames.

"I am placing two alternatives before you," said Tylbeck. He hooked his thumbs behind his chain of office, as he always did when invoking his position. "Either you stop preaching this inflammatory rubbish, or..."

"You will run me out of town?"

"Yes."

"I won't stop preaching."

Tylbeck was not a stupid man. The last time Rothmann had been expelled from Münster, there had been disturbances considerably worse than any his preaching had provoked. On the other hand, Tylbeck could not stand by while mystics and beggars from half Europe took over his city. Rothmann smiled faintly: it was not his problem, it was Tylbeck's. He turned and began to walk towards the door.

"We stood shoulder to shoulder once," said Tylbeck.

A sentimental man, Rothmann thought. He reached the door, opened it and left the building.

There had been rain, and the street was puddling with an oily mud that sucked at his shoes. Something pale ran squealing past him. People kept pigs in the poorer quarters, and they were always escaping and running through the alleys.

The moon, a little short of fullness, was rising in a halo rimmed with watery gold. He walked briskly through the streets to Dolling's house.

"He threatened me with expulsion," said Rothmann.

Dolling laughed. "Again?"

"Should I go quietly, or defy the order?"

"If you defy it, he'll clap you in jail and you might not be out again so quickly this time."

"Why not?"

"Because if he's got any sense he'll have you taken to another town."

"Perhaps you could arrange for me to be abducted on the road," Rothmann said with a smile. It was always Dolling who got him out of prison.

They were sitting in Dolling's study. From the window, the ruddy glow of a fire was visible over the rooftops. The town felt strange. Bands of people were wandering streets which would normally be empty at this hour.

"Defy the order," advised Dolling. "The Council's hanging on to a branch by its breeches, and Tylbeck knows it."

He refilled their glasses. Rothmann found that, with the slice of plum cake he had been given, the sweet Portuguese wine went extremely well.

He said, "It's wonderful, and the Lord's doing, the way everything is coming together. The return to Scripture, the great upheavals in the world, the signs of the Last Days… "

"Yes," said Dolling absently.

The two of them sat for a while, absorbed in different thoughts.

Then: "They sound," said Rothmann, his attention recalled by a noise beyond the window, "as if they're waiting for something."

"They're waiting for someone to tell them what to do next," said Dolling. He spoke his mind a shade too quickly, on occasion.

Rothmann gave him a sharp look. "What do you mean?"

"I mean that they're at such a pitch that they're ready for anything, but they don't have a plan. All they can do is break things and riot."

Rothmann pursed his lips. Dolling leaned forward in his chair. He said, "Rothmann, if we act in the next few days I think we could take control of the town." He had been thinking this over, and it seemed to him the only course that made sense, however great the risk.

"Are you out of your wits?" said Rothmann angrily. "You want pitched battles in the streets? The Bishop riding in at the head of a thousand troops, and all our heads on pikes along the walls? Is that what you want?"

"It need not turn out like that."

"It certainly would." Rothmann drank his wine, and set down the glass with a hand that trembled slightly. Dolling looked at the hand, and then at Rothmann's face.

"You're afraid."

Rothmann blazed up at him. "How many times have I been in prison for what I preached? And each time I came out I went straight back to the pulpit. Do you think there aren't hundreds of people in this city who would like to see me dead?"

"I can't think why," said Dolling bitterly, "when all you're doing is sitting here drinking wine and eating cake."

A pause ensued. They had never quarrelled before. Rothmann felt a little shaken. In his relationship with Dolling he had always laid down what needed to be done, although Dolling was much the older. Now here was Dolling presuming to tell him.

But the worst of it was that Dolling was right. He was afraid. Not of dying, but of doing the wrong thing. He was afraid of misunderstanding God.

Dolling tried again. "You overestimate the opposition, Rothmann. They're very frightened. They're also divided. They won't put up much resistance."

"And the Bishop?"

"How you go on about the Bishop. If the Bishop counted for anything, things would not have gone this far."

"You are seriously suggesting we set up an Anabaptist city here, in defiance of the entire world?"

"Why not? What else has it all been about?"

He couldn't answer. Yes, he believed every word he had said. But to rouse the people to arms in pursuit of those words filled him with horror. He did not think he had the right. If God wanted it done, He must make His wishes clear.

"What I fear," said Dolling, "is that if we don't take the next step, someone else will take matters out of our hands. There are plenty of home-made orators out there, claiming to be inspired by the Holy Spirit."

"Some of them are."

"And some are inspired by nothing more than their own overheated brains."

"Then what are you going to do?"

"Unlike you, I trust the workings of the Spirit. I believe that God knows what He's doing in Münster, although I may not. By the time you find out, it may be too late."

"Where is your faith, Bernard?"

It had never been the most reliable part of him. Faith for Dolling was indistinguishable from feeling. It was his heart that rushed in and believed, or contracted with doubt. At the moment his heart was too taken up with frustration to believe anything much.

Rothmann said, "Why don't you lead them, if you think they need a leader?"

There was a subtle malice in this. Dolling would dearly have loved to put himself at the head of the levelling multitude outside his windows. But he knew as clearly as he knew anything that he was not the man for it.

3   What the Comet Meant

At the beginning of January, a comet appeared in the sky to the north-west. At first only a confused glow, where none should be, among the stars and planets, it grew in brightness until anyone could see it. The weather was cold and frosty that month, giving clear skies at night, and every night, until it grew too cold to be out and standing still, knots of people would gather and huddle, staring upward at this furnace in the sky.

What did it mean? The death of a king? The fall of an empire? War? All these and more, said Rothmann, whose reading consisted increasingly of the Revelation of St John. His sense of urgency was so great that at times he almost broke down under it. A huge responsibility rested on him. He must shepherd these souls into the one safe sheepfold before the storm broke.

"Repent!" cried Rothmann to his people. "Only God can save you! Turn to Him!"

Because such a conflagration was coming, such a mighty set of battles, that the earth itself would be consumed.

"Then I watched as the Lamb broke the sixth seal," intoned Rothmann to a huge congregation in the Cathedral square. "And there was a violent earthquake, the sun turned black as a funeral pall and the moon red as blood; the stars in the sky fell to earth like figs shaken down by a gale. The sky vanished as a scroll is rolled up, and every mountain and island was moved from its place.

"Then the kings of the earth, the rich and powerful, and all men, slave or free, hid themselves in caves and mountain crags. And they called out to the mountains and the crags, "Fall on us and hide us from the face of the One who sits on the throne."

He raised his eyes from the book. "The stars fell to the earth, like figs shaken down by a gale." He did not need to labour the point: they were wide-eyed with fright, and some of them had begun to rock backwards and forwards, moaning and lamenting. "It is coming!" thundered Rothmann. "Every day it comes nearer. Turn to God, and repent!"

That same afternoon, a group of former nuns from Hesse saw a lion wearing seven crowns stalking above the rooftops near the church of Our Lady. By the time the disturbance was quelled, there were hundreds of people who were convinced not only that the world was coming to an end very soon but that a special grace had been bestowed on Münster, where such things could be seen.

None of the Münster Anabaptists had yet been baptised. This was because only Matthys, the Dutch leader of the movement, and the apostles he appointed had the power to perform baptism. The situation was remedied in January, when two apostles arrived in Münster.

They arrived unannounced, immediately made contact with the Dutch who were already there, and then informed Rothmann of their presence. He had the impression, not for the first time, that he no longer knew exactly what was going on in the town: it had developed pockets of opacity. He consulted Dolling as to where the baptisms should be held. The thing had to be done secretly: the Bishop had just issued an edict which prohibited Anabaptism outright. They decided to hold the baptisms at Krechting's house. Dolling's was too conspicuous, being a big house in Highmarket, right in the town centre.

About a hundred people came on the first day. On the second, it was more like two hundred. It was clear that the strength of belief in the city was even greater than Rothmann and Dolling had thought. Rothmann's apocalyptic preaching, the feeling that the familiar order was about to break down, the signs and wonders seen in the sky, the constant influx of refugees with their tales of the cruelty of governments... all these combined to make the faith of those who had it fiercer, and persuade those who wavered that there was no time to lose.

The baptisms went on for almost two weeks. At the end of that time, a large section of Münster's population had committed itself to an illegal faith.

Everyone wanted to know about Matthys. Would he come to Münster? The apostles, however, had nothing to say on the subject. They had very little to say about Matthys at all, in fact. Perhaps this was deliberate, Rothmann thought. For Matthys to emerge from hiding would be very dangerous. The less people knew, the better.

The faces of the apostles were studied as if they could reveal something of the man who had sent them. If they did, it was not, of course, possible to tell what. Few people had seen Matthys, and a lot of those who had were dead.

When their task was finished, the two apostles left to travel to the next place.

Barely had they departed than another traveller arrived, in quite a different style. Dressed like a pilgrim, and carrying nothing but the traditional pilgrim's staff, this stranger entered the city through one of the northern gates shortly before nightfall. The first people who saw him were so struck by his appearance that they thought he must be Elijah, whose return to earth was expected as a harbinger of the Last Days.

The news spread quickly. Rothmann, studying his Bible, heard it shouted in the street. Tylbeck, locked in anguished wrangling in a back room of the Town Hall, heard it. Dolling heard it as he walked home from addressing a meeting. None of them, for different reasons, went to stare at the stranger. But a good part of the population did. People began to come out of their houses and follow him before he had even got as far as Cow Street.

A lot of the crowd, initially, consisted of children, but then the women came out to see what had become of their children and saw the little procession, and joined it, leaving the door open and a pot on the fire, until it was no longer a little procession but a very large one that was wending its curious way through the snowy streets under the deepening colour of the sky. The man at the head of this procession did not say anything, and did not look around except for the occasional glance at the tower of a church. He was walking towards the Cathedral, the roof of which was clearly to be seen above the houses, but in fact he had only once looked in its direction and everyone who followed him believed that he knew his way by holy wisdom. So far, hardly anyone had seen his face, either because they had joined the procession after it passed them or because they had lowered their eyes out of reverence. The only people who had really looked the stranger in the face were the children. So these found themselves the target of questions as the procession moved onward—"What does he look like? Is he like the carving of Elijah on the Town Hall?"—to which the children replied generally with the first thing that came into their heads; although the most truthful of them did try to say that he was not in the least like the carving of Elijah, they were immediately contradicted. By the time the procession reached the Cathedral there were about a thousand people in it, together with quite a number of dogs, cats, chickens and pigs. Considering all this and the general excitement, it was a surprisingly orderly and quiet procession, and when the stranger, having reached the Cathedral, finally turned to face the people who had followed him so far, a silence fell over the whole crowd.

For a little space nothing more happened: the stranger gazed at the thousand and the thousand gazed back.

Then Rothmann, standing alone on the tower of his church and straining his eyes through the gloom, saw an astonishing thing. It was like the wind bending a field of wheat. Rank on rank, people were starting to kneel in the snow.

He was not Elijah. His name was Jan and he came from Holland, and he said so as soon as he realised what a misunderstanding he had caused. The news was received with some disappointment. As Tylbeck sourly remarked, the more fantastic an event was, the more credence it received. No-one was interested in the ordinary, these days.

The newcomer sought out Dolling and Rothmann straight away, and told them that Matthys had sent him to find out at first hand what was happening in Münster. "And to see if I can help," he added, an apparently simple statement which became less simple as one thought about it. Dolling thought about it. Then he invited Jan to join them at a meeting at his house the following day.

The meeting had been arranged to discuss their next move. Dolling had no doubt what it should be.

"The elections for the Town Council," he said, passing beer, wine and cheese around the large kitchen table. "They're just a month away. That isn't long."

The Dutchman at once made a note of this. He was quite young, Dolling saw, in his early or middle twenties, and handsome, except that his nose was rather big.

Rothmann said, "A month is still quite a long time."

"It isn't if you're preparing for an election!"

"What I mean is that we can be moving forward on other fronts as well."

Jan nodded with approval. "Agitation. Work on people's feelings."

"It's connected," said Dolling. "The more the disturbances increase, the more easily we'll gain control of the council."

"Unless there's a reaction against the disturbances?"

"They aren't united," said Krechting. "That's our strength."

Dolling explained that the Lutherans, who controlled the council, were so paralysed by their fear of a return of Catholic rule that they couldn't act, while the remaining Papists were too few to be a threat, but were very useful as a reminder to the Lutherans of what they had escaped from.

"In other words," said Jan, "they can't act, which means that we can."

It was a little too pithy for a man who had barely been in the city twenty-four hours. They all looked at him. He shrugged, smiling. "When the time comes, I mean."

He had charm and tact, Rothmann thought. He knew how not to tread on people's toes. That was as well, since all the toes in the room were highly sensitive.

For the next part of the meeting the Dutchman kept his horns in. He restricted himself to the role of the stranger seeking instruction. That was perfectly agreeable: they were happy to instruct him. He asked who was entitled to vote in the elections, how many councillors there were, how many members were elected by each district, where the wealthiest residents lived and where the poorest lived, and so on. Then he asked where most of the people who'd been rebaptised, and came to Rothmann's sermons, lived, and that was more difficult to answer.

Dolling went upstairs to his study and came down with a large sheet of paper. On it he drew a rough map of the city. He put in churches and public buildings, major streets, the river. At the centre was the Cathedral: he drew the twin towers and put a few trees round it. He drew in the curve of Highmarket, skirting the Cathedral square to the south-east and with St Lambert's at its shoulder. He pointed with the nib to a spot just across Highmarket from the church.

"This is where we are now," he said. "And our friends live... here, here... here... and here." The pen moved widely over the map, describing circles, lingering more in the southern outskirts but visiting most parts of the city.

Jan studied the map and nodded. Then he asked, "And where is the armoury?" There was a startled silence. Dolling then moved the tip of the quill so that it pointed at a spot on the river's course where it wound between the Cathedral and the Church of Our Lady.

"There's a look-out tower there. The main armoury is housed inside it." The pen moved to the city's perimeter. "More weapons are stored in some of the fortified towers along the wall."

"Where's the gunpowder?"

"In the cellar of the armoury."

"Who has the key?"

"Tylbeck, the Burgomaster. And for the past few weeks he's been wearing it round his neck."

Rothmann said, "Are you suggesting that we… arm ourselves?"

The Dutchman laughed. "I just want to know where everything is."

His face was unreadable. They looked hard at him, and then again at the map.

After they had left, Dolling sat nibbling walnuts and drinking Rhenish in his kitchen. He was in no state of mind to go to bed, where his wife had summoned him as soon as she heard the street door bolted. Before him he saw the young Dutchman's face, intelligent, following everything that was said with close attention, giving nothing away.

Why was he here? What instructions did he have from Matthys?

Dolling's thoughts would have been simpler if he had been able to feel hostile towards the newcomer, but he did not. There was a liveliness and humour about the man which was very attractive. Perhaps the truth of the matter was merely that Dolling had been spending too much time with Rothmann, who had never had much lightness about him and these days had none at all, obsessed with the end of the world. Dolling did not expect the world to end. He realised that it would have to end in someone's lifetime, but could not imagine it ending in his. He was a merchant.

Upstairs, his wife called fretfully. He walked to the window and peered out. Pitch darkness was broken by, here and there, a tiny candle flame burning in a lantern. There was one about fifty yards away, dimly illuminating a small area of carved stonework. It was hanging from the porch of St Lambert's. Rothmann might be trying to pull the world down, but he was scrupulously observing the Council's regulations about street lighting.

Dolling capitulated. He went upstairs, peeled off his boots and clothes, put on his nightshirt, performed briefly and without enthusiasm the act his wife was demanding of him, and fell asleep.

Sister Agnes was very happy in Münster. The people were friendly. It wasn't at all the way she had imagined a city to be. But then, she had been in the convent a long time, and in the convent they were taught nothing about the outside world, only that it was a wicked place. Sister Agnes had not found it so.

She was surprised by the number of people who were like her. In the convent she had constantly been reprimanded for not being sensible. She had tried to be sensible, but it didn't work. She would listen very carefully to what was said to her, and a minute later it would all have gone out of her head and she would be doing something silly again.

A city, Sister Agnes had assumed, would be full of sensible people. But here she was, and it was full of people who had visions of Heaven and spoke the angelic language. All her life she had been told there was something wrong with her because she saw the things she saw and heard the things she heard: either that she did not see and hear them, or that if she did she shouldn't because they came from the Devil. She should have been in Münster all the time!

Her family had taken her to the convent as a girl. They didn't want her. The only things she could remember about her home were her mother's blue dress and her father being angry. They had called her Crazy Kate and said the nuns would know what to do with her. The Lamb had started to come to her by then.

She called him a lamb because he was a lamb the first time she saw him. He was lying in a field full of daisies with his front feet tucked under him and a circlet of daisies plaited around his delicate horns. She knew at once that he was not just a lamb but the Lamb. She was so happy to see him that she began to sing. After that, she saw him often. Sometimes he wasn't a lamb, but she could always recognise him. He was like the sun. He was like music that comes into your head a moment before you can hear it.

She was in the convent for ten years. There were some things she liked about it. She liked the smell of herbs in the convent kitchens, and the way the roses in Reverend Mother's garden filled with light when the sun touched them. But the thing she liked best was going to get the milk from Brother Ignatius. Going across the fields she would run and skip, and the rabbits would sit up and watch her with their soft faces. She had been told not to run, but she couldn't help it. She didn't run on the way back, though, because she was carrying the pail of milk.

Brother Ignatius had looked after the cows. He milked them and cleaned out the barn and took them their fodder in the winter. He had names for all of them. He ran his hand over their great damp sides and waved the flies away. When they saw him come into the field, they would stop their grazing and run towards him, frisking their tails and making little sideways jumps for pleasure.

He had made Sister Agnes frisk and jump, as well. Perhaps that was why she ran when she went to fetch the milk, knowing his hand would touch hers on the pail handle, although running was something that seemed to happen to her feet anywhere. His hand would touch hers on the pail handle, and his foot would nudge her smaller foot, down there in the bright yellow straw that was splashed with glistening dung. Then often she did not take the milk back to the convent straight away, and when she returned Sister Martha would scold her for daydreaming and tell her that Satan kept a special place in Hell for idlers.

One day at the convent, without any warning, everything was changed. Sunlight streamed through a barred window into the refectory, which had always been in shadow. A door which every day for ten years had been shut and bolted stood wide open. Sister Agnes went through it, and found herself in a little yard where garden tools were kept. She wondered what had happened, but there was no-one to ask.

She wandered through the silent cloisters, and sat for a while in the rose garden where the nuns were not allowed to sit because it was Reverend Mother's. No-one reprimanded her. A sparrow came and pecked in the earth around the roses.

After a while she got up and went inside again. She walked through the stone corridors and thought how strange it all was. Then she went into the chapel. Reverend Mother was there, kneeling. When she heard Sister Agnes's footsteps, she turned round. She got to her feet.

"Oh, you're still here, Sister Agnes," she said.

Sister Agnes said that she was.

"Well, they've all gone," Reverend Mother said. She looked at Sister Agnes as if expecting her to do something. "Don't you want to go?"

"Go where?" said Sister Agnes.

"Goodness, I don't know," Reverend Mother said impatiently. "Why don't you go to Münster? It seems to be the place everyone is going to."

She blessed Sister Agnes rapidly and went back to her prayers. Sister Agnes found an apple on a table, and took it with her.

Before dawn on a morning when the snow lay thick, Dolling, Jan and Krechting, at the head of a silent band of men, broke into the armoury. The snow had muffled their feet as they came through the streets, and anyone who saw them closed the shutters again quickly, but the sound of splintering wood, Dolling knew, would give them away at once.

A boy pushing a load of hay on a cart stopped with his mouth open, took in the scene—the determined faces under the flickering lanterns, men posted with a weapon at the ready in case someone should interrupt them—and took to his heels. Dolling stepped through the wreckage of the door and held his lantern up. The place smelt of earth and steel.

He half-groped his way, and found the pikes in a rack that ran most of the way round the wall. Manouevring the long shafts and wicked blades carefully in the narrow space, he began to hand them one by one to Jan, behind him, who handed them to Krechting through the door. After the first few he got quicker at it, and felt a warm trickle of sweat crawl down between his shoulder blades. He was surprised how calm he was.

He worked his way round the wall until there were no more pikes. He picked up the lantern from the floor and held it to the bare stone. There were cutlasses in here somewhere.

He found them, gleaming coldly on a wall behind him. He called Jan, and together they began to take the cutlasses down and hand them through the doorway. Hands grasped and took them, and other hands were thrust into the gap. Outside, Dolling could hear footsteps and quiet talk. He hoped their people were doing what they'd been told to do, and not hanging round waiting for further instructions.

"What about the firearms?" asked Jan when all the weapons in the lower room had been distributed.

"Upstairs. But we don't have anyone who's trained to use them."

"Then we'd better set a guard on the place."

Dolling left some men to guard the armoury and followed Jan to the Cathedral square. The Dutchman moved at an easy stride, a bare cutlass in his hand. The cutlass looked at home there, it looked like part of him. Dolling had the Italian sword that had been his father's. He hadn't wielded a weapon since boyhood. He hoped he had not forgotten how.

The Anabaptists occupied the area around the Cathedral and took possession of the Town Hall. Dolling positioned their solitary crossbowman at a first-floor window overlooking the lower end of Highmarket and facing the alley which led to the Cathedral. The church bells were ringing by now, the sky was lighter and people were milling into the streets.

It wasn't long before the first body of Lutherans made their attack.

They had armed themselves from the collection of weapons held in the Buddentower on the north wall. Dolling had forgotten that weapons store, and cursed himself, but at least they'd got hold of no firearms and they were not any more experienced at street fighting than the Anabaptists were. They came rushing down Horse Lane into the Cathedral square looking—Krechting said later—frightened half-out of their wits but none the less dangerous for that, and they engaged fiercely with Krechting's group. The sides being fairly evenly matched, the fighting was inconclusive. The Lutherans retreated under the trees and waited for reinforcements.

Dolling, in command at the Town Hall, waited for the challenge to his own little force. It did not come. The morning wore on. He sent messengers across to Krechting to find out how he was faring and what was going on. Krechting sent back that his men had seen off the first assault but that he had no idea what was happening elsewhere.

Dolling fretted. He must have information.

"I'll go," offered Jan. He was gone before Dolling could stop him.

He was away for roughly an hour. During that time, groups of people gathered in the street, staring at the windows of the Town Hall and at the men stationed outside it. At one point Dolling heard shouting and the clash of steel. It came from behind him, in the direction of St Servatius.

Jan came back with his eyes dancing. "They're at each other's throats."

"Who are?"

"The Papists and the Lutherans. There's skirmishing everywhere. It's utter confusion, and Tylbeck's in the Guildhall wringing his hands."

He laughed, and laid his cutlass on the long table around which the Council, in calmer days, had debated the affairs of Münster. Dolling's eyes dwelt on it in fascination.

"Good. That's just what we want," he said, recollecting himself.

The battle for the streets went on for two days. It was fought with cutlasses, cudgels and fists. The fighting was disorganised and often seemed random. Some old grudges were paid off. By late afternoon on the second day, fourteen men had been killed, an uncounted number injured, the Anabaptists were still in control of the Town Hall and the Cathedral square but had not gained any ground, and nothing at all had been decided.

It was at this point that news was brought that the Bishop was on his way with a large troop of horsemen.

The fighting stopped at once. Wherever they heard the news, people stopped what they were doing and looked towards the walls, as if they hoped to see through them.

Jan wiped his face and sheathed his weapon. He had exchanged the cutlass for a good Spanish sword with a filigree handguard. Dolling did not ask where it had come from.

"Where is Tylbeck?" said Jan. "We have to see him."

Tylbeck's role in the fighting was unclear. Some people claimed to have seen him laying about him with a sword in a melee; others said he had done nothing but wring his hands and send messages. Presumably one of the messages he had sent was to the Bishop.

They found him on the steps of Clothiers' Hall, besieged by a turbulent crowd of people who an hour earlier had been trying to kill each other but were now united in a desire to avoid the arrival of Franz von Waldeck.

Tylbeck no longer looked like a Burgomaster, although the chain was round his neck and from time to time he touched it with a finger. Perhaps he needed to assure himself it was still there. In the past two days his face seemed to have collapsed away from its bones; he looked both flabbier and less substantial.

The men around the steps were flushed from fighting, and some had not yet sheathed their swords. They had no interest in Tylbeck's delicate position. They shouted that he should send at once to the Bishop refusing his aid, in the name of the city authorities, and should close the gates.

Tylbeck protested that he could not close the gates against the city's legal prince; it was tantamount to declaring war. Impatient voices wanted to know what the arrival of cavalry meant, if it didn't mean war.

"How can I refuse von Waldeck's help if you go on fighting?" shouted Tylbeck. "If you won't accept the Council's authority, he has every right to intervene and you have only yourselves to thank."

They saw he meant it. That he had given up, and would let in the Bishop, and they would have Popery, saints and indulgences back by nightfall.

There was angry muttering. Many of them had enjoyed the scrap and were not ready to stop. As far as they were concerned, matters were still far from sorted out. However, if the Bishop was the only alternative...

"We'll call a truce," a stocky man who had been prominent in the fighting said from the front of the Lutheran ranks.

Tylbeck cast his eye over the dishevelled, sweat-stained citizens before him. "Will you agree to a truce?"

Yes, the Lutherans would agree to a truce. They didn't like it, but they grumbled assent.

Tylbeck turned to Dolling's group. "Will you agree to a truce?"

Dolling felt Jan's hand press hard on his arm.

"No," said Jan.

The surprised silence was followed by a growl of anger, and a drawing of swords which had not been long in the sheath. All eyes turned towards the Dutchman.

"And who are you," grated Tylbeck, "to answer?"

"A servant of the Lord."

"But not a citizen of Münster."

"Soon I will be, and you won't."

This calm, insolent and incomprehensible reply was all that was needed to unleash fury. A pack of Lutherans flung themselves at Jan, who moved like lightning and was up on the steps beside Tylbeck, defending himself with an impressive display of swordsmanship. As Dolling and other Anabaptists shouldered in to help him, Tylbeck raised his voice half in rage and half in despair above the din of steel.

"What do you want?" bellowed Tylbeck. "A truce or the Bishop?"

The reply was incoherent and came from fifty throats.

Into the fraction of a pause that followed, Dolling shouted, "We want freedom of religion!"

"You want to destroy government!" yelled the Lutheran leader.

"Silence!" Tylbeck thundered at him, which so surprised the man that he said nothing further. Tylbeck's eyes moved to Dolling. They rested on Dolling with something close to resignation. Certainly they held a complete understanding of the stage the game had now reached.

"Freedom of religion," Dolling repeated, "or there is no truce."

Having sent his message to the Bishop, Tylbeck convened the Council in the most extraordinary of extraordinary meetings and told it that it must accept the practice of Anabaptism or face civil war. He then resigned as Burgomaster. The Bishop withdrew his cavalry, but quartered them in a nearby town. Peace, of a kind, returned to the streets. The Council had lost the last shreds of its authority.

In the weeks following the Council's submission, the trickle of families leaving the city swelled to a steady stream. They were those who had something to lose. They took what they could, piled on carts and horses, and left what they couldn't. They told anyone who was interested that they intended to come back when things had returned to normal and reclaim their property. They hurried out of the gates, jeered on their way by the street urchins who, as soon as they were out of sight, would break into the abandoned house and race through it with wide eyes and whoops of derision, break the vases and piss in the fireplaces and cram their mouths with whatever remained in the larder.

No-one put a stop to this because there was no-one in control any longer. The Town Council had abdicated. If it knew what orders to give it did not give them, and if it had no-one would have listened in any case.

They listened now to the preachers, and anyone could be a preacher. On any corner you could find a man or woman who claimed to see visions and interpret them, and the visions were always of the same kind. Battles. Not earthly battles, with their siege cannon and earthworks and confusion; no, something both vaster and simpler. The battles of the Last Days. A sword of light cleaving the sky, cleaving Creation into good and evil. The final raging of those opposites, followed by the irresistible triumph of the Elect and their rule for a millennium in the New Jerusalem.

"It is written," said Rothmann. "It must come to pass."

As the propertied citizens flowed out through the gates, a quite different-looking crowd flowed in. Dutch, Brabanters, Frisians. Ruddy-faced from the cold, heaving boxes on their backs, looking closely at the departing emigrants. Hundreds of these people came in every day. They went to the Town Hall, where Rothmann had set up arrangements to help them. They were given food, clothing, a little money (all contributed by the better-off Münster brethren), and somewhere to stay. They settled down quickly: wherever they'd come from, they would find someone else from the same place. The streets were full of different dialects, not all of them mutually comprehensible. Some of the self-styled prophets who were reported to be speaking in tongues were in fact doing nothing of the kind.

"Everything's going very well," remarked Jan to Dolling.

He had written to Matthys: it was the first thing he had done after the rising. He told Dolling and Rothmann he had done it, but did not tell them that he expected Matthys's arrival any day. However, he did not discourage speculation that Matthys would come. He never showed all his hand.

He was taking some trouble to make a friend of Dolling, whose knowledge of the city would be invaluable to them.

When the new Town Council was elected, it was Anabaptist to a man. Dolling was one of the Burgomasters. The other was Krechting.

Münster's Cathedral had been built in the Middle Ages. A massive structure of pale stone roofed in copper, adorned with an oddly delicate spire, it dominated the city and could be seen for many miles, its green roof seeming to float above the battlements. It was the symbol of Münster, or had been until Popery was abolished. Then it became the symbol of a tyranny.

But that was not why they sacked it in celebration the night the results of the election became known. They sacked it because of its images.

The main entrance to the Cathedral, the porch known as the Paradise, was thronged with stone carvings. From above the doorway, Christ enthroned looked down on creation, his right hand resting on the *Book of Life*. Around him were the four sacred beasts. To right and left, on facing walls, the apostles stood in niches, each head haloed, each surmounted by a crown that was also a tiny building in stone, a representation of the Holy City. High up on the north wall of the porch reclined the Lion and Lamb. The thin, stern face of St Paul looked on.

By the time Rothmann arrived to see what was going on, enthusiasts had already begun attacking these idolatrous works with iron bars and anything else they could find, and others had gone into the main body of the church and were busy there. Men were bringing ladders, lanterns and armfuls of iron tools which must have come from a forge. Carrying these, they ran laughing past Rothmann, their faces shining in the light of a fire which someone had lit and on which more fuel was being thrown every moment. They had started to rip out the choir stalls.

He walked up the south aisle. People were swarming everywhere. He had a dreamlike impression, seeing the frenzied activity illuminated in the fitful light of lanterns, that they were building a cathedral rather than trying to demolish one. He picked his way over jagged timber and made his way towards the transept. He was greeted by the people who noticed him, but most of them were too occupied. They were pulling the pretend-saints out of their niches, ripping off the silk and velvet robes and putting them mockingly around their own shoulders. They were trying on the tin crowns. With kindling axes they hacked at wood carvings and poked the pretty coloured glass, paid for by rich men to buy a place in Heaven, out of the windows. They slashed hangings and canvases and ripped the cloth from the altar. The gold ornaments, naturally, had already disappeared.

Onto the bonfire outside the south door they were piling the hangings and the altarcloth and whatever vestments they had found. People passed Rothmann with their arms piled high with white and gold silk, cambric and linen, richly embroidered fabrics, the work of hundreds of hours. Exquisite, irreplaceable. This, too, was part of what had to happen, Rothmann thought. A boy had climbed up to the top of the high altar, using the niches as handholds, and was trying to dislodge the figure of the Virgin Mary. As Rothmann stood watching, the boy, with a mighty wrench, tore the Queen of Heaven from her throne and sent her crashing to the ground. Her painted plaster broke and scattered, revealing the plain wood at the core.

Several people who were carrying things to the fire stopped and stared at the broken Virgin. A man said wonderingly, "I never knew that that was all she was."

Matthys arrived the next day.

4   The Baker of Haarlem

He had a bony frame: you might call it emaciated, Dolling thought, looking at the plainly-dressed figure before them. It was a bony face, too, a hardened face, the face of a man who had seen his companions die. The eyes were deeply set and fierce.

Words were tumbling out of him. Most were words of fervent thanks and praise. To God. So far he had not said much about Münster.

He was thanking God for His great mercies. That the time of suffering was over, that the wicked, and all kings and princes, were about to be submerged in a tide of their own blood, and that the Kingdom of Heaven would shortly arise on earth.

"Praise God!" cried Matthys. "For He shall redeem His people! He has promised to do it, and He *will* do it! We shall eat and drink His salvation!"

"Praise God!" echoed everyone in the room.

"His salvation will come to us here on earth! Here in this city! Praise God!"

"Praise God!"

"None here shall taste death before the Son of Man comes in glory! This is written in Scripture!"

"Praise God!"

"And when will He come? Brothers, He will be here in the twinkling of an eye! We must purify ourselves, because we are not yet worthy. We must purify our city so it is fit to receive Him! Praise God!"

"Praise God!" Was it, this time, slightly muted?

"And therefore what a great mercy it is that I have been led to you, and that you have been brought to this state of understanding. For there is not a moment to be lost. I beseech you, brothers, to throw yourselves into the task with all your will, all your God-given strength. For He comes to judge and to save, to throw down and exalt. And He must find us ready! Praise God!"

"Praise God!"

Dolling shifted on his seat. He tried to catch Rothmann's eye, but Rothmann did not allow him to. He then studied what could be seen of Jan's face a few feet away, but Jan was raptly attentive.

"He calls us to purge this city called Münster. He calls us to do away with everything which cannot be made a vessel for Him. He calls us to turn the sword against the unbelievers in our midst, who defile His temple. He calls us to slay them, brothers, so that his dwelling place may be made clean."

A stillness fell on the audience as the import of these words sank home.

"For this is no earthly city you inhabit, brothers. Open your minds to a miracle! In a vision I have seen this city transformed and streaming with light, and the people who walked in its streets were without sin. Brothers, *this is the New Jerusalem about which the prophecies were written!* Christ shall come to it, and shall reign in it with His chosen ones!" He flung out his arms and cried at the top of his voice, *"Praise God!"*

There was no massacre. In the wild enthusiasm which Matthys's announcement about the New Jerusalem generated, it was possible to persuade him that a massacre would not help their cause. It would, Dolling said, turn the outside world against all Anabaptists so surely that no more of their friends would be able to make their way to Münster: they would simply be killed on the road. This was an argument which even Matthys could not ignore. (It was the first and last occasion on which he allowed his mind to be changed.) It was agreed to expel the unbelievers from the city instead. This was done the next day.

Arms were distributed at first light. Dolling had already visited the men on duty at the gates and told them what was going to happen, and that they must close the gates again as soon as they were ordered to, whatever the hour.

Matthys had been abroad since before dawn, a spectral figure hurrying through the dark streets with a bobbing lantern, banging on doors to alert the preachers to their tasks and crying aloud in every street the need for repentance. As soon as the sky began to lighten, the preachers emerged from their houses and went to the districts that had been assigned to them.

The unbelievers lived mainly in the better part of town, away from the river and the marsh and the smell of the tannery. The preachers went up and down the snowy streets, putting marks on the doors of the houses of those who did not accept the Anabaptist faith. They, too, called on the unbelievers to repent and turn to God. They warned that the day of reckoning had come. Those who did not repent of their hard-heartedness would be driven from the city.

The wind was rising, and it blew their voices about and muffled the words. Not that it would have made any difference, Rothmann thought, because although, when the armed men came, the people in those marked houses did not understand what was happening, how could they have understood it anyway? There had been no warning that the bleak toleration that had been extended to them was about to be withdrawn. He thought the way it was done was unnecessarily brutal. Two or three times he intervened when he saw actual cruelty, but he could not be everywhere. He had decided that his role was to persuade as many as possible to convert before it was too late. But for most of them it was already too late.

The armed men went from marked house to marked house, breaking in doors where their banging and shouting did not bring them instant admittance, and ordering families into the street. By this time snow, driven on the wind, was coming almost horizontally between the rows of houses. Half-blinded by the snow, and nearly senseless with fright and cold, the dislodged occupants blundered about, tried to get back into their houses and were prevented by pikes and sword blades, pleaded to be allowed to cover themselves more warmly, take food, a few possessions, pleaded for some recognition that this was monstrous and nothing like it had ever been heard of, and were struck in the face and laughed at, were pushed headlong and driven through the bitter streets with blows and curses until they reached the city gates, which, having been opened from an early hour, were shut and barred behind them when the last of them had gone through.

As the last gate closed, and the word was passed, a shout went up from all over the city. Matthys, standing alone on the watchtower of St Lambert's, from which all Münster could be seen, raised his arms to the leaden sky and called on God to witness that the city now was clean.

Snow continued to fall all day, obliterating the blood in the streets and erasing the footprints of the unbelievers as they wandered away from the walls, until it was as if they had never existed.

The war started the next day.

An urgent message reached Dolling at home, where he was indulging in his favourite occupation of listening to his daughter play the harp. She had made excellent progress under a new tutor. A boy with his hair plastered all over his forehead from running knocked thunderously at the door and gasped that Jan wanted him by St Ludiger's Gate. Dolling sighed, donned his coat and went to the ramparts.

Jan was there with Rothmann. In silence the three men strained their eyes towards the south-east. There, faint but distinct on a low rise of land, like scratches on the yellowish sky, were a line of pikes. Over the tops of the pikes, something fluttered. The Bishop had arrived.

"What are they, do you think?" asked Jan.

"Mercenaries, probably," said Dolling. "Perhaps he's borrowed some Catholic pikemen from Jülich-Cleves."

"Hasn't he got his own troops?"

"Peasant levies. They won't want to fight. They'll probably go home at sowing time." He surveyed the great double circle of walls and moats which had protected Münster since medieval times and was the pride of every Münster man. "Fortunately, these defences are impregnable."

Jan laughed. "No defences are impregnable. There is always a weak spot."

"I've yet to see the weak spot here."

Dolling spoke pugnaciously, but his heart had sunk into his boots. He had not really believed it would come to a war. War had threatened for so long but never happened: they had always been able to avert it. They had always been able to talk their way out of it. Scheming, manipulation of the enemy's weaknesses: he had been good at that. Now there was coming something he wasn't at all sure he would be good at.

"What's the matter?" asked Jan.

"We don't have any professional soldiers here," said Rothmann, the diplomat. "Well, perhaps a handful."

"That's enough. We just need a few men who know something about gunnery and can teach the others."

Dolling frowned in doubt.

"We're defending our lives and homes," said Jan. "People don't need to be soldiers to do that, they just need to be organised."

"Who's going to organise them?" asked Dolling.

Jan looked him over. "I think you should."

"I'm a merchant!"

"Well, the buying and selling is finished. What are you going to do instead?" He smiled at Dolling's consternation. "You are exactly the right person for it. *Why* were you a merchant?"

"Because my father was," said Dolling stubbornly.

"But why were you good at it? Because you have a talent for practical matters."

Beside him, Rothmann smiled.

"Everyone will have to take part in this defence," Jan said. "Every man, woman and child. And everyone will need to be absolutely clear what their part is. We'll need to build earthworks, we'll have to organise a round-the-clock watch. We'll want to get stone and other materials ready to repair any breaches in the walls. We'll need to think about where to site our cannon, and build emplacements. That's just the start. Is the water supply secure?"

Dolling gazed mutely at him.

"I'll help you," said Jan. "But *you* have to do it, because *you* know the city and the people."

Dolling still said nothing. He looked over the inner rampart and its encircling moat towards the outer wall, which rose sheer from the top of a steep embankment and was protected in turn by the second moat. A long stone's throw in front of him, where the road through the countryside entered the city through St Ludiger's Gate, this second moat had been dug outwards in an arc to allow for a widening of the embankment into a projecting, flattish apron of land on which artillery could be sited. Dolling saw all this and peopled it with men, Münster men, some standing watch, others toiling to move a heavy cannon on its carriage. Further back, squads of citizens made their way to the ramparts with stones for the repair of the walls and lead for melting down. In the forges the smiths beat out weapons, and in the masons' workshops cannonballs were chipped from blocks of stone to save the precious iron for other uses.

A familiar impulse stirred in him. An impulse to see that it all worked efficiently.

He walked the circuit of the walls with Jan, and returned home just as it grew dark. He went at once to his study, and worked, stopping only to eat a plateful of cold meat which his wife sent up, late into the night.

He went to bed not much before dawn, and slept for two hours. Then he rose, breakfasted on a slice of bread and went to find Jan, taking with him a sheaf of papers.

The earthworks behind the gates were begun at once. Rothmann, taking a brief rest from his labours in the Cathedral square, walked to Our Lady's Gate to see what the noise was about and found gangs of men breaking the wintry ground with pickaxes. A rope had been stretched between staves, and, beyond that, another length was being paced out. The air was loud with the brittle chipping of axe heads on rock, the slithering of earth on shovels, the hollow knock of stone on stone. The men worked willingly, grunting with exertion. Rothmann walked for some way along the line of the trench, and then back through the streets where stone from a demolished building was being taken away in carts. It all seemed very well organised, and was being done with an energy which impressed him.

He returned to his post. Hundreds of citizens had chosen to be rebaptised rather than leave the city, and Rothmann, with the help of two preachers, was baptising them. His arm ached, and his right hand was numb from constant immersion in the tub of cold water. From time to time his attention wandered from the shivering converts in front of him. He forced it back to the matter in hand: this was very important, it was the saving of souls.

But the converts mumbled their confession of faith and avoided his eyes, and he knew that most of them were not sincere. They had chosen conversion in order to stay in Münster, in order to keep their homes and perhaps their businesses. Some were his own hasty converts from the day of the expulsion. He could only pray that they would in time come to believe what they professed. And hope that there would be time. He sprinkled water into the last chilled face that offered itself to him, and said, "Go in peace, brother."

The man muttered a "Praise God," and took himself out of the square at an unseemly pace, pulling his hat down over his dampened head. He was a furrier with a large house on Salt Street; he had been a member of the Lutheran council. Rothmann knew him well.

The books were burnt within a few days of Matthys's arrival. Although a start had been made with the contents of the Cathedral library, the clearing-out had stopped there and books were still to be found in many houses. Matthys ordered them all to be taken to the marketplace, and himself put a torch to the pile.

Everyone was surprised at how slowly the books burnt. After all, they were just paper. But they burnt slowly, very slowly, from the edges inward, the fire gnawing and not knowing how to vanquish them, and finally discovering it could do it page by page, as first the cover and then the inside leaves stirred and lifted in the hot wind. Then each topmost leaf would shrivel and shoot upward in a black ghost which floated above the fire before disintegrating into fragments, some of which rose high above the buildings and treetops, to be found, sodden but inscrutably intact, in somebody's garden a week later. And while this was happening the fire would be searing the leaf which had just been exposed, until it, too, rose up in its last agony and was at once annihilated. And so it went, with volume after volume, with their Latin and Greek and German, their Gothic script and woodcuts, their fine bindings made by craftsmen all over Europe, and their words, which nobody wanted, living with a more intense blackness on the blackening page for a last instant. Then gone.

Now there would be only the Bible.

Those in charge of the fire—in fact no-one was found who would accept responsibility—had underestimated their task. Next morning, a great number of books were found at the centre of the bonfire, covered in ashes, which had been only partly consumed. The weight of many other books on top of them had protected them. The fire had bitten their edges, but at the core of them, on blocky islands of barely yellowed paper, large tracts of print could still be read.

So it all had to be done again.

One morning there was a great heap of bedding in one of the rooms of the Town Hall, and in another room were piles of clothes. Men were sorting the clothes out into smaller heaps of coats, hats, doublets, shoes, women's things, and so on, but their work was hampered by the fact that people kept arriving with armfuls of more clothing, so that the original heaps never got more than half-levelled before they were restored to their original height.

"What's going on here?" asked Dolling, on whose lists this activity did not feature.

He was told that all the useful property left behind by the unbelievers was being brought to the Town Hall. If he went further down the corridor, he would come to the kitchenware.

"By whose order?" asked Dolling.

"Matthys."

On his way home he passed a procession of people carrying furniture.

What Matthys proposed to do with the abandoned property was soon clear. It would be distributed to those who needed it. They must apply for it, in person, at the Town Hall. It would be allocated by seven officials, called deacons, who had been appointed for the task.

Dolling asked who the deacons were. He was given six Dutch names and one German one.

It was true that the people most in need were the immigrants, and that by far the majority of the immigrants were Dutch. Nevertheless he did not think it was right. He went to find Matthys.

The prophet was in the armoury, supervising the stowing of the weapons which had been found in the unbelievers' houses. Dolling asked if he might have some private words with him.

Matthys appeared not to understand the request. He stared at Dolling with his sharp unblinking eyes.

"Brother, I would like to discuss with you the choice of deacons," said Dolling.

"What is there to discuss?" said Matthys. "They have been chosen."

"There is only one Münster man," said Dolling. The others in the small cave-like room had stopped what they were doing and were listening. He felt sweat on his skin although the air was cold enough. "I could suggest the names of several good men who know the city well."

"The names have been *chosen!*" exclaimed Matthys violently. "They can't be changed."

Dolling persisted, with as much calm as he could muster. "Why can't they be changed?"

"These names," enunciated Matthys, as though every syllable were costing him blood and he would have Dolling's blood to replace it, "*were vouchsafed to me.* Do you understand?"

There was a silence.

"There is no tampering with these names," said Matthys. He turned back to what he had been doing.

Dolling walked away. His heart was thumping as furiously as if he had just escaped death.

As he stepped out into the ordinary air of the street, he heard Matthys's cry behind him. "This is not Münster, but the New Jerusalem!"

Jan was constantly distracted from his work of assisting Matthys and helping Dolling organise the defence by thoughts of Devera, and of how soon Matthys would send for her. On his arrival in Münster there had been so much to occupy him that he had had little time to think about her, but Matthys's arrival changed everything. Every time he saw Matthys he saw, glimmering behind him, the form of Matthys's wife.

From the first he had been drawn to her. From the first, seeing her in Matthys's cold hideout in Haarlem, he had been roused by old-fashioned (and unaccustomed) chivalrous feelings. He had wanted to be her rescuer. He had imagined being faithful to her unto death, even if he never saw her again and despite unimportant attachments to other women.

He would rescue her from what? From Matthys, of course, whose chilly, bony embraces he imagined with fascination and horror. Matthys's snakelike hand on her creamy flesh. Matthys's snakelike member bumbling its way about her loins.

Yes, he was jealous. Women had never been difficult for him to obtain, but then he had never met one like this. Her smile enslaved him, her eyes pierced him. Her silence tantalised him. So did her purity, which naturally he wanted to defile. She seemed to him made of different stuff from other women. And *Matthys* had got her!

On the other hand, it made him just enough of a man. Meeting his wife, you knew that at least he recognised beauty when he saw it, and at least he must know what pleasure was, although everything else about him denied it.

Why, Jan wondered, had she accepted him? Circumstances, perhaps. He understood that a woman's choice could be limited in any number of ways. But in his mind was a picture of Matthys haranguing her about the will of God until she simply gave in from exhaustion.

When Matthys arrived in Münster alone and threw himself into the creation of his fancied New Jerusalem, Jan was afraid he would not send for Devera for months. He thought it was quite possible that Matthys did not even notice her absence. Often it was on the tip of his tongue to urge Matthys to send for her.

He managed never to say it. With strenuous self-control, he asked once, on Matthys's arrival, after his wife's health, and never mentioned her again. It was a daily torment but it was necessary. Matthys might be unworldly, but he had a terrifying intuition.

In the first week it was possible only to redistribute the goods of the unbelievers and survey about half the housing in Münster. In the following week Matthys appointed deacons to visit all the houses and list the food stocks. The intention was to take from those who had a surplus and give it to those who didn't have enough. Everyone approved of this in principle, but then, later, the deacons came back with handcarts and lists to take away the "surplus," there were some angry scenes. For days, Rothmann was called in to one house after another as peacemaker. Not that he could make any difference, but the Münster people trusted him. It was unfortunate, he thought, that Matthys appointed his own people to everything and even went about the streets surrounded by a crowd of them, so that it looked as though he had a bodyguard. Matthys was not a diplomat.

But then, he was setting up the Kingdom of Heaven, and how could you expect him to be? He worked as if possessed. Issuing instructions in that uncomfortable voice, poring over lists, arbitrating between squabbling underlings, listening to problems, visiting houses with the deacons, constantly exhorting everyone to greater efforts of unselfishness…he couldn't let anything out of his hands, Rothmann thought. Except the defence. The military defence of the city he regarded as a task almost beneath contempt. God would see to that, was his reasoning.

He had now announced the Day they must look to. This Day would witness the deliverance and justification of the city. It was Easter Sunday. Easter was just a few weeks away. Why bother with siting cannon and forging armour when Heaven was about to manifest itself?

Rothmann was privately sceptical about Easter. His experience of the ways of God was that they were not so tidy. He was tempted to quote Revelation 16 to Matthys—"Behold, I come as a thief in the night"—but he held his tongue. Matthys had been told about the Day in a vision, and had preached at length on it. You did not question Matthys's visions. His authority rested on them.

By Easter, therefore, everything had to be accomplished. Five weeks to turn the world upside-down. All property to be held in common. All housing to be at the disposal of whoever needed it. *Money abolished.* Wage-labour also, therefore, abolished and buying and selling abolished. Complete equality. No rank, no deference. No priest. No prince. Only God.

"Does he mean it?" Dolling asked Rothmann.

"Does he mean which part of it?"

"Oh — any of it."

Dolling spoke with a certain impatience. These days he was busier than he had ever been. He did not want the men whose labour he was organising, and whose loyalty the whole town depended on, confused by prophecies or disheartened by impossible demands.

"I think he means every word of it," said Rothmann.

"It will be difficult to enforce, particularly the money."

"We have to persuade people. It may take some time. In the end they will see the rightness of it. Bernard, you *wanted* this."

"Yes, I did. But it's the wrong time."

"It is *always* the wrong time!"

"What I mean is that the start of a siege is not a good time to sow disaffection."

Rothmann looked at him keenly. "I wonder who is disaffected."

"Are you suggesting that I am?"

"I suggest that you keep your thoughts to yourself, and particularly in the presence of Matthys. He will have no hesitation in getting rid of anyone who crosses him. Even you."

Dolling, who knew this, pretended he had not heard it. He said, "You were never very interested in money, Rothmann. You never really understood what people saw in it. You underestimate what it means to them."

"You underestimate what is happening here."

"I am telling you there will be a revolt."

"No," said Rothmann. "What there will be when we have done this, and I admit the difficulty of doing it, is a united people. United as no people has ever been since property was first established. Thus united, we shall be invincible."

"I hope you're right."

"What's more, it's an inducement to others to join us, if they see that we mean what we say about community of goods."

That was true. Believers were still coming to join them. The encirclement was far from complete—he Bishop could not muster enough troops, and the ones he had were incompetent—and it was not difficult for new recruits to slip through the gates. All were welcomed joyfully. Dolling had noticed that women greatly outnumbered men, but at Jan's instigation he was including them in the defence plans. The more defenders the city had, the better. One day the siege would start in earnest.

Unless Matthys was right about Easter.

The first step towards outlawing money was taken when proclamations were nailed to the church doors, the brewery, the guildhalls and Town Hall and the blacksmiths' shops saying that, from now on, the Elect would begin living without the exchange of coin. Those who could read, read the proclamation to those who couldn't. Preachers began expounding the theme the same day.

The response was mixed. For many people, joy that the Kingdom was come a little nearer was mingled with plain fright. Sharing their worldly goods was one thing, it was something anyone could understand, but if they had no *money*...if *never again* could they have money...why, that was different. They were not sure they could survive it. And it seemed to cut them off by a vast and uncrossable void from the rest of mankind.

But they were already separate from the rest of the mankind! That was the point of their community! Living under the new law, in the radiance of the Last Days, what did they need with money? This was how the preachers encouraged them to think of it. And on the following Sunday, Matthys himself preached on the subject in the Cathedral square.

The whole city gathered to hear him. He stood on a table so they could see him properly, wearing his invariable homespun tunic belted at the waist and, hanging from the belt, his sword. His voice, as ever, rasped like a saw on green wood.

He preached as if the world were on fire and he had five minutes in which to tell them how to save themselves. He thundered and threatened like Jehovah, promising that the sky would rend, the earth quake and the stars fall to punish mankind for its sins. He drew an unforgettable picture of the torments of Hell, the knives that would flay, the flame that would gnaw flesh that could not die. This, for rejecting the salvation that was offered. Yet how simple to claim it! A single act of loving submission was all that was needed. A single repudiation of everything that kept them from God.

The rasping voice sweetened. That repudiation, which they were now called to make, would seem hard because it went against everything they knew. But its hardness was a proof of God's love for them. Once they had passed this test, they would come instantly into their reward. The Father in His mercy had seen to it that every sacrifice brought joy to the sacrificer. Once they had renounced money, they would find themselves freed from the greatest burden mankind had ever invented for its own tormenting. They would thank God on their knees for it.

The treasury room in the Town Hall would open at eight o'clock the following morning so that people could begin bringing in their money and valuables. Four weeks would be allowed for the settlement in money of all existing business: after that, money would cease to circulate and there must be none left in private hands.

"Praise God!" cried Matthys.

Jan stepped up beside him to add a few words. The money brought to the Town Hall would belong to the whole community, he explained, and would be used for communal purposes. It might be used to buy provisions for the city, or arms.

Matthys shook his head. "The need won't arise," he said. "Look to Easter! After that, we shall want for nothing!"

Rothmann had kept his distance from Jan. The Dutchman rang false with him, and he had not forgotten the theatricality of his arrival in Münster.

Other people praised Jan's readiness to listen, his ability to come at a problem from a novel angle and solve it, his knack of dissolving tension by a joke. Rothmann disliked him for these very qualities. They smacked too much of the world. He had said as much to Dolling, who laughed at him.

Jan came to his house one day, to Rothmann's surprise.

"We need your literary talents," he said.

"Mine? I have none."

"Nonsense. I've read some of your publications. I admire them. You write eloquently."

"You flatter me."

The Dutchman sat down, without invitation, on the bench. "I know what I'm talking about. I used to write plays."

"Plays?"

"I had quite a reputation in Holland. Until I met Matthys and was converted: then, naturally, I gave it up. But, you see, to write speeches and to write a pamphlet, they aren't so very different." He looked at Rothmann earnestly.

"I suppose not," said Rothmann. He was astonished.

"I want you to write a pamphlet we can send out to the Bishop's troops. With the object of disheartening them, persuading them to desert. It must be short and simple, the kind of thing anyone can understand."

"I imagine I could do that. What do you want it to say?"

"Use your judgement. But since he probably isn't paying them, we might be able to induce them to come over to us. In which case it wouldn't hurt to make quite a lot of the communal ownership of property."

Rothmann recalled the recent "cleansing" of the city of its unbelievers, and wondered that Jan did not see any inconsistency in trying to lure more unbelievers in through the gates. Perhaps he thought that as soon as they changed allegiance they would change their ways.

"What about the abolition of money?" he said. "Do you want me to mention that?"

"No, I'd leave that out," smiled Jan.

Stefan Wald reckoned himself a plain man and as good a Christian as most. He had never been outside the town he was born in, and had no wish to. Quite recently, he had found a wife there. They lived together happily enough in a room behind the forge.

Stefan took things as they came. He saw no point in making problems for yourself, when life presented an unending succession of them anyway.

He was a blacksmith, and would one day take over from his father. It was a solid trade in more ways than one; you didn't find many blacksmiths out of work. And he was an Anabaptist, like everybody else he knew, having first, like everybody else he knew, been brought up a Catholic and then gone over to Luther because the way Rothmann preached it, it was the obvious thing to do.

His faith was grounded, ultimately, in the conviction that what he believed was common sense. It seemed quite clear to him that adult baptism was right and infant baptism was wrong, that mankind had been created without kings and princes and that the goods of the earth should be held in common. He did not exempt his own. He made no objection when the deacons came and took some of his flour away. He did not even complain when they came back the next day and took away a keg of beer.

It was when he listened to Matthys preach about the surrendering of money that a protest stirred within him. Even then it wasn't really the money, because theirs had never been a household in which there was money to spare, so they had no savings to protect, and he fully understood that it didn't mean they were going to starve, because everyone would be paid for their work in kind, and moreover if you didn't have any money you couldn't pay any taxes. No, it was the way it was done. This Matthys was beginning to stick in his throat. Him and his flock of Dutchmen. Who, it crossed his mind unpleasantly, had brought nothing into the town, *did* nothing (except preach), and in a few days would be sifting through its accumulated gold and silver with their long fingers.

Weren't they all supposed to be equal now? Well, where was the equality in this, that a Dutchman should tell them what to do and should go everywhere surrounded by a cluster of other Dutchmen wearing swords? Rothmann had never behaved like that. Even when the Town Council were plotting all sorts against him, he had gone round alone and unarmed. Unfortunately, since Matthys had arrived in Münster, not very much had been heard from Rothmann.

Stefan turned this over and over in his mind, and the more he thought about it the less he liked it. In the end, he said something.

He said it first to a customer at the forge. He had shod a mare. She stood lifting her feet and whuffling beside the wall. The lad who collected her dropped a coin in his palm: money was still changing hands, and would for a while yet.

Stefan held the coin up in his fingers. Bitterness filled him. He said, "Reckon in a few months' time we'll still be using these, but they'll have Matthys's head on them."

The boy grinned nervously and led the mare away.

The following day, under some obscure compulsion, as he was finishing his dinner in the communal dining hall which had been set up for the men on watch and in which they *had* to eat whether they wanted to or not, he said it again. He took a coin out of his pocket and, turning to his neighbour at the table, said "You know what? We'll still be using these come Martinmas, but they'll have Matthys's head on them."

The table went quiet, and no-one said anything in reply.

They came for him when he was beating out a piece of iron on the anvil, the sparks showering like gold in the gloom, and he saw them hesitate just inside the entrance, because he could have turned the tongs with his wrist and flicked the incandescent metal at any one of them. He pretended to think that they'd come to see his father, and said, "He's in the house." But one said, "It's you we want, Stefan," and they waited while he plunged the glowing iron into the water and laid it aside. They let him get his jerkin, and then they took him through the streets.

Matthys was surrounded by a crowd of people. He looked, to Stefan's frightened gaze, supernaturally tall and skeletal.

He bent down, and in a breath that stank of garlic, said, "You slandered me, little smith."

"I meant no harm," stammered Stefan.

"You said I would have my head on the coinage. Is that a harmless thing to say?"

Stefan in his panic could think of no better course than to deny that he had said it.

"There are witnesses," insisted Matthys. "Either they are lying or you are."

"I swear…"

"Oh, you swear, too, do you? I think the sooner we are rid of you the better." He turned and announced to the crowd, "This man must be cast out."

"Ask him to repent," said a familiar voice.

"How can he repent, Rothmann, when he says he did not do it?"

Stefan tried to look around him. To every side, his view was blocked by Matthys's Dutchmen. He did not know why all these people were here. Indeed, so frightened was he that, in a city whose every stone he thought he knew, he did not know where he had been taken.

"He must be cast out!" repeated Matthys. "It is not just me he has slandered, he has slandered the Work we are engaged on, he has slandered God Himself!" His voice had risen. It had a terrible sound to it, as if it was being pushed up by something beyond his control.

Stefan now became aware of a dispute. Rothmann was arguing with Matthys, other voices were joining in. At one point Rothmann called out urgently, to someone, "Confess it!" but Stefan did not know what the words meant. He could hear Matthys's voice with perfect clarity, but he didn't need to know what Matthys was saying: he could see into Matthys's mind. He knew exactly what Matthys wanted.

The voices wrangled and snarled. Then they fell silent.

The onlookers saw a blade flash in the Baker's hand. Out tumbled the pitiful entrails, the well of blood.

Matthys screamed. But it was the smith that died.

5 Easter

Martin the printer stood watch on the ramparts.

He spent more time on watch these days than he did in the print shop. Master Eck, having been elected to the Council, now hardly ever put in an appearance on the premises, which in a way was a relief because they would have had to call him brother Eck instead of Master Eck, and that might have been difficult. In any case there was much less work for all of them. After books became things nobody wanted to be seen in possession of, it was obvious that no-one would want any printed. This had put Martin at war with himself, because he thought a well-printed book was a beautiful thing and he had wept when the books were burnt. On the other hand, he understood the reason. A book was a powerful thing, too, and its power to mislead and confuse was deadly. Matthys had preached a whole sermon about it. In the end, Martin told himself that everyone had to give up something to be worthy of the Kingdom of Heaven, and this was his particular sacrifice. He was quite pleased with this answer: while in a sense it answered nothing, it did put the question in a frame which he found helpful.

Since there were no books to print, they were reduced to doing pamphlets and ordinances. Of which there were quite a number; Matthys was fond of issuing ordinances, and they were usually backed up by lengthy quotations from the Bible. Even so there was not enough work to keep a printing shop occupied, so it was as well everyone had other things to do, like standing watch and weapons training.

With all this, his understanding of what work was had changed. Appropriately, because everything was changing. He saw now that if an activity wasn't done for the good of everyone, then it was worthless. This meant that keeping watch on the walls was more important than any work he'd done before in his life. Everything now was for everybody. This was a wonderful thing, and he still exulted in it. They were all brothers, all equal, all had what they needed. Here was dignity at last, here was the world as God had meant it to be.

No "mine and thine" of houses, or anything else. Oddly, just as he was getting really used to it, Jakob had moved out to live with a Dutch family who had been given a house down the road. He and Susi had the place to themselves again, although not for long. There was going to be a baby.

He stood on the ramparts as night fell, feeling the living city at his back, its streets and squares, the steepling churches. In the houses, fires burning, people settling down for the night. Love for it filled him. Love also for his companions, standing the watch with him: he would trust any of them with his life.

Lights flared in the Bishop's camp, less than a mile away. Sometimes you could hear laughter and music from it, and sometimes you could see the women arriving for the soldiers. Martin scowled into the darkness. The Lord would come and find them all insensate with drink and sprawled in a bed of lust, and they would have lost not only their useless lives but their immortal souls as well, all in the twinkling of an eye. He could hardly wait for it. But if the Lord was kind, he thought, He would allow them to mount just one attack on the walls first.

Martin longed for battle. He longed for some of the wickedness that was burdening the earth to spill his way, so that he could mop it up with his sword.

Two days later he had his wish. A troop of horsemen appeared in front of the walls, their mouths full of uncouth insults. They loosed off a volley of arquebus fire at the defenders, hitting no-one, and the defenders jeered and fired back with equal inaccuracy.

Martin had just arrived at the printing shop. The officer commanding his district rushed in and ordered him at once to the western gate. When Martin arrived, breathless, he found the area in front of the gate swarming with men and horses. Rudolf, his neighbour of the watch, was in the crush, lowering a helmet on to his head. Then hands grabbed Martin, strapped a steel breastplate to his chest and hoisted him on to a nervy black gelding. A helmet was passed up to him and, while he was still struggling with it, a sword. Moments later, Rudolf was beside him, horsed, leaning over and fastening the helmet. Martin barely had time to thank him before they were riding out through the opened gate, spurring their mounts (he did not have to spur his, the beast was so eager for movement he had to rein it back) and shouting their battle cry, "Jerusalem!" A pungent rush of leather, horse and sweat flooded his nostrils. It didn't occur to him to be afraid.

The rhythm of the trotting hooves quickened to a canter and there, astonishingly close, were enemy faces. He raised the sword and struck at a helmet. The blow glanced off, jarring his arm. He was unhurt. He wheeled his horse round and saw confusion. A pike lay on the ground; its owner sat beside it with a surprised look on his face and his hands cupping his ribs. A little way away a dense knot of riders strove to bring down swords on each other's heads, but were impeded by being so closely pressed together. Two horses were wandering the field riderless. Martin urged his mount towards the tangle of riders, but the noise of hooves behind alerted him and as he swerved to the left an arquebus ball whistled past his right cheek. He wheeled and rode yelling at his attacker, and to his amazement saw the trooper put spurs to his horse and gallop away.

He broke off the pursuit. For a few moments he sat his horse, feeling its warm musculature and its faint trembling, feeling the sun on his face and himself alive.

Then with a rush it all started again, the knot of riders loosening as if someone had found the end and tugged, and out they all fell, striking at each other and missing because the horses were going all over the place. Only a few moments later it was over. The enemy was riding off. A distant cheer went up from the battlements high above them. They rode back through the gates, smiling and joking. Someone had caught the bridle of one of the loose horses, and was bringing it in.

Martin rode under the arch of the gate, his heart swelling.

Dolling had chosen helpers and sent them into every corner of the city to make inventories. From the information they brought him, he had compiled lists.

He made lists of names, arranged by street and then by district. On one piece of paper or another, he believed he had the name of every adult in the city. He made lists of the weaponry and equipment in the armouries and those in private hands (many of the immigrants had brought their own). He made lists of tasks, divided into those that required to be done only once and those requiring to be done regularly. Finally, in a large blank ledger he mapped out days and hours, and to them attached tasks and names which rotated in an orderly progression. He was creating a huge clock, a timepiece the size of a city with ten thousand living parts.

He thought it would never be completed, but then one day, quite suddenly, it was done, and he set it in motion. It worked. Even he, who had created it, was astonished at its smoothness. However, there was no time to contemplate his success: other tasks at once crowded in on him. The mechanism needed to be maintained, it needed constant checking and oiling.

He complained occasionally, without really meaning it, of having too much to do. Jan told him to choose a deputy, but as soon as he did, the number of things he had to see to promptly doubled. He was rarely home at mealtimes, but ate frequently in one of the dining halls Matthys had had set up for the men on watch. He found he enjoyed that. Male company was much easier at meals. He could have done without the accompanying Bible reading, however.

He kept out of Matthys's way. The Baker had an instinct for divining what people were thinking, and Dolling in his presence was usually thinking something he would not like. If Dolling had a problem, he took it to Jan. He was more and more impressed with the man. It was his quickness that Dolling particularly admired. He would almost jump at a difficulty sometimes, wanting to solve it before it was properly out of Dolling's mouth. And his solutions were bold.

There was the culverin, for instance. It was their most powerful weapon and they couldn't find the right place to site it. When the siege began it was on the outwork in front of St Lambert's Gate, where it threatened four tents, a windmill and a thornbush. Its range was wasted, too. It needed to be moved back half a mile, and if possible put somewhere where it could be turned through a hundred and eighty degrees.

It needed, in short, to be sited right in the centre of the town, where all space was fully occupied.

Jan looked up at the Cathedral. At the two great towers, the immense copper roof. His eyes ran along the sea of copper, and back again.

"Take that down," he said, pointing at the thin spire which rose from the ridge just where the transept joined the nave. "It's resting on a platform, or supports of some kind. Whatever it's resting on, we can rest the culverin on."

Dolling stared upwards, and felt vertigo.

"You've got men here who can do it," Jan encouraged him. "Just find them." He looked at Dolling. "What's the matter?"

"How do we get it up there?"

Jan laughed. Dolling flushed and glared at the spire.

"We get it up there on a hoist, like anything else." Jan put an arm round Dolling's shoulders. "I'll design one which will do the job. I know quite a lot about hoists."

"Do you?"

"I used to have to design them for theatrical productions. You need something strong enough to lift a person but light enough to be carried from place to place. It's quite an art."

They levelled the spire, and put the culverin on the platform where it had rested.

The earthworks were finished by now, and not too soon. There had been several assaults on the walls. The first had alarmed Dolling, not so much because he feared the enemy would break through (weren't the defences, if properly manned, impregnable?) as because this was the real test of his planning, the weeks of organising, the careful accumulation of stores, weapons and ammunition, the compulsory training sessions in the handling of weapons and the strengthening of the fortifications. His efforts were vindicated. The skirmishes that took place were invariably won by the defenders.

It was partly, of course, that the Lutheran soldiers sent against them had no very clear idea what they were fighting for, which was understandable since they were fighting the war of a Catholic prince and probably would get nothing for it. Even so, in the midst of the gunsmoke and shouting, rushing from one part of the defences to another encouraging his men, directing fire, ordering rocks to be thrown down on to a party bold enough to put ladders against the wall, in the midst of all this Dolling had found himself once actually *laughing* because it was all working just the way it was supposed to.

One of the men throwing down the stones was wounded in the left shoulder. Arquebus ball. It was their only serious casualty in that attack. Dolling went to see the man, who had survived the attentions of the surgeon and was being cared for by his wife. Matthys was there. He was telling the poor fellow how greatly favoured he was to be a martyr in the wars against the New Jerusalem, which wasn't well received by either the martyr or his wife, but you could see that at least on this occasion Matthys had meant well. You could not accuse him of cowardice, either. He'd been laying about him fiercely enough with that sword of his.

There was nothing to be done about Matthys. He was at the same time an inspiration and a catastrophe. What worried Dolling more than anything was the gap in him between belief and common sense. All manner of necessary precautions could fall into that gap and never be thought of again. Though he did not think many people listened to Matthys in that sense. They listened to him for something else. He had his finger on the pulse of the future. He was the only one who knew the road they had to tread, and he would not shrink from shepherding them along that road with whips and scorpions, if need be.

That was why the people obeyed him. No-one loved him. Except his wife, perhaps.

Jan, fortunately, was quite a different matter. Wherever he'd come from—and nobody seemed to know—he was human. No gap in him. Common sense? Thank God, he overflowed with it. This was a man you could get along with. The evening of the discussion about the culverin, Dolling invited Jan back to his house to eat with them. It was an invitation he didn't often extend except to close friends (which meant, in effect, Rothmann), not because he didn't like company but because he was reluctant to expose the lack of marital harmony in his home to outside gaze. On this occasion he decided to risk it. He directed Jan to make himself comfortable in the study, and went to tell Sara that they had a guest. (She said nothing, merely lifted her head in what might have been a nod.) When he went upstairs again, he found Jan talking to his daughter, Lisabeta.

Dolling saw that he had charmed her, but that she was also a little frightened of him. That was natural, and he tried to reassure her with fatherly enquiries about how she had spent her day.

Doing not very much, he privately thought, as she prattled about embroidery and the pet squirrel he'd bought her and sewing dried herbs into muslin bags. Perhaps she was saying what she thought would please their visitor.

Dolling dismissed her with a kiss on the forehead and sent her to help her mother.

"You're very fortunate in your daughter," Jan remarked when she had left the room.

"She's the consolation of my life."

"All the same, you will have to let her go, one day."

A little stab of pain went through Dolling. "One day, no doubt."

"How old is she?"

"Only twelve. You must hear her play the harp. She has a wonderful touch."

Jan was supervising the construction of some lead pipes as part of the defensive works when he heard that Matthys's wife was in the city. She had arrived the previous evening. The men who were beating out the lead grinned slyly. They would watch their words in his hearing, but Jan knew that as soon as he left them they would speculate. What kind of wife would a man like that have? Did he say "Praise God!" after he'd bedded her? And so on.

He thought with bitterness that every man in the world had the right to talk about Matthys' wife except himself. He was even the last to hear of her arrival.

He went on with his various tasks mechanically, unable to concentrate. He devised, and discarded, reasons for visiting Matthys at home. Then when he went back to the place where he was staying, he found that Matthys had left a message inviting him to dine with them.

It was seven weeks since Jan had seen her. His heart threatened to suffocate him as he walked down the cramped street in Jewry (the poorest district: it would be, wouldn't it?) where Matthys lived. He knocked at the low-lintelled door and waited. His ears strained to hear Devera's footsteps, but those he heard were Matthys's. It was Matthys's hand that grasped his, Matthys's voice that welcomed him.

The house was familiar: he had visited it on several occasions. Now he saw, in a rapid glance, small and deeply-affecting signs of her presence: the hearth swept bone-clean, a vase of rushes by the window, fresh bread on the side. Warily he stepped forward and allowed his eyes to investigate the depths of the room. She came towards him from the kitchen.

"Welcome," she said, and his blood leapt.

He had an impulse to bow low over her hand. He had done so with countless other women and here, for the first time, the gesture would have been heartfelt. Naturally it was unthinkable. Instead, he murmured something and clasped her hand in fraternal greeting. He wondered if she could feel the heat of his skin. Would she think he had a fever, or would she know its cause?

At the table he took his seat facing her, abashed, triumphant but outwardly calm. He dared to look for an instant directly into her eyes. It was a terrible mistake. For he saw there only the mirror of his own demeanour: a correct degree of sisterly warmth, and the deference due to her husband's chief helper. Nothing else.

What else could he expect?

But his heart plunged into a pit, and he felt a flash of anger as if she'd spurned him.

Matthys had invited one of the Dutch preachers to share the meal: a stupid man and a garrulous one. Jan resented his presence and detested his conversation, which began as soon as Matthys finished saying grace. He took a piece of bread and crumbled it in silence. He would not think of her again. She had clearly not thought of him once in the past seven weeks. She was not worth his trouble.

Some time later he became aware that Matthys was asking him a question. It was about the conditions he had found in the city on his arrival. The question was for Devera's benefit. Grudgingly, Jan stirred himself and began to talk. Her eyes dwelt on his face, she seemed to drink in his words. His resolve began to melt like snow in the sun. Before long there was no trace of it left.

Not think of her again? She filled his trembling, dread-tuned senses. And how could he think of abandoning her, when in Münster she would need him more sorely than she ever had in Haarlem, where she had been among fellow-countrymen and friends? A painful remorse smote him. Lastly, how could he expect her to acknowledge his devotion, when to do so was infinitely more dangerous for her than for him? He was a man, he could defend himself against what came. But if *she* was accused, if even a breath of suspicion touched her, they would stone her and Matthys would not lift a finger to prevent it.

He stopped talking, powerfully affected by his feelings and hoping that it had not been noticed. After that he was glad of the insufferable preacher, who distracted Matthys's attention by his barrage of nonsense. This allowed Jan to recover himself, and towards the end of the meal he felt sufficiently emboldened to steal a few covert glances at Devera.

"You should send for your own wife, Jan," said Matthys kindly. "A man shouldn't live alone."

"Yes," he said, "I'll send for her soon."

Sister Agnes had been offered shelter by a dyer's family, and had a pile of straw to sleep on in the kitchen which was perfectly comfortable. She went often to hear the preachers. Her favourite was still Rothmann, whose voice thrilled her and always built up a thundering climax (after a while she knew what he was going to say, but it didn't matter). However, Rothmann preached less often now that Matthys had come.

Matthys, she thought, was like a man who can only see out of one eye, and has to stare very hard to make up for it. But the other one, Jan, she liked. He was handsome and had a spring in his step.

Exciting things were happening in the city these days. They were getting rid of money, which was good: she had never understood it and thought everyone would be much better off without it. People weren't always pleased when she told them this. And she was delighted with the earthworks.

The earth had been thrown up in great banks around the city gates. Sister Agnes enjoyed the softness of the earth and its brownness, and the smell, the damp uncovered secret smell of it. But most of all she enjoyed the enormous *size* of the workings, how they rose up and up like a mountain almost between one night and the next. She used to visit the earthworks as often as she could, and climb up to the top although you were not supposed to, and at first she was shouted at and told to get down but in the end, when she went on doing it and explaining that she couldn't help it (because she couldn't), they got used to her and would leave her alone.

However, there was no time for such excursions after she was put on stone duty. Everyone now had a job to do because of the war, and many of the women were put into gangs to carry stone up to the walls. The stone usually came from a building that had been knocked down: there was quite a lot of knocking down, because room had to be made for the guns and the earthworks. The women had to go every day to collect stone and carry it to the walls. It was quite a laborious walk, picking their way through the defences and then climbing the steep stairway to the top of the ramparts, holding the stones.

Often the stones were so big that the women could only carry one at a time, holding it against their bellies with both hands. The edges of the stones cut into their hands and the coldness and the weight numbed them. The fabric at the front of their dresses wore thin where the stone was constantly rubbing, and their shoulders ached so badly by the end of the shift that their necks and faces were aching as well.

But they didn't mind. Certainly Sister Agnes didn't mind. The women sang and talked as they carried their stones. Sister Agnes learnt a lot of things that way. The women talked about this and that, but what they talked about most was their husbands.

Once a week Sister Agnes went with Ruth, the dyer's wife, to help her carry the provisions from the store. You were given wooden tokens, and exchanged them for what you needed. Sister Agnes enjoyed going to the store because of the mixture of smells from the cheese, the flour, the ham, the dried fruits if there were any, the honey and vinegar. It reminded her of Brother Ignatius and the smell of milk.

On the day when someone told Matthys that people were burying money in their gardens, Rothmann was there in the Town Hall. Money was being counted: it was tipped out of the bags, packages and purses in which it had been brought in, on to a long table at which the tellers sat. The amounts were entered in a ledger and the coins, sorted into denominations, put into leather bags in a deep chest at the back of the room.

The counting went on every day. People had started to bring in their money almost as soon as the first proclamations went up, but it was only after Matthys made it clear that failure to surrender one's money would be regarded as an offence against the community, and therefore heavily punished, that it began to arrive at the Town Hall in a steady stream. Rothmann came to the Town Hall for an hour or so every day; he would talk to the deacons and whoever else was there, and watch, as discreetly as he could, as people filed past the reception table to give their gold and silver to the city. He marked great differences in the way they did it. Some quietly proud, some joking. Some wordless, dumping a cloth bag on the table and turning away with a closed face. He was sorry about the last ones and would have liked to speak to them, but that would have exposed them to public gaze.

It was as he stood a few feet away from the table where people were handing in their bags of coins and thought how fast things were moving, that he heard a shout of giant anger from Matthys at the other end of the long room. His feet took him dutifully to the spot although the rest of him would much have preferred to remain where it was.

Matthys, fist doubled, was towering over a white-faced youth called Joachim who almost anyone in the town could have told him was a professional sneak. His tales generally had some truth in them, so he got a hearing. On this occasion, he had aimed higher than usual when looking for a suitable ear. Perhaps he would stop doing it now, thought Rothmann.

Matthys was ordering him to repeat what he had just said, so that everyone could hear. The frightened boy's voice swooped up and down like a bird which has lost its nest.

"Some people are burying gold and silver in their gardens instead of bringing it here, brother Matthys."

The Baker glared round at them all with a sort of furious triumph, as if he had always known this was a place unfit for his vision.

"Have you seen them?" Rothmann asked.

"No." The boy knew he had gone too far, and wanted to get out of it.

"Then how do you know?" asked Rothmann.

"I...I've heard people talking."

"Who are they saying has buried gold?" Matthys demanded.

The boy shot a look at the reception table where there was normally a line of people waiting to leave their money, but no-one was standing there. They had all fled.

He quavered out some names. Rothmann's heart sank. They were all late-baptised, the people who had converted at the time of the expulsion.

"Rothmann," said Matthys savagely, "do you know who these people are?"

"Yes," said Rothmann, since, if he had said no, it would not have been believed.

"Then you can take us there. We shall visit these children of Ananias." He laid his hand on Joachim's shrinking head. "Bless you, my son, for your uprightness."

He strode towards the door, summoning the armed Dutchmen who were never far from him, and sweeping up a cluster of preachers in his wake.

"We'll collect some shovels on the way," Matthys was saying. "The town must be full of shovels, to judge from all the earthworks that have been dug."

They visited each house and dug in the garden. Nothing was found, except some old spoons wrapped up in sacking under the roots of an apple tree, on which Matthys seized, although it was obvious that they had been there for years.

The following day, all the late-baptised were rounded up and taken under guard to St Ludiger's church. Rothmann asked to be allowed to see them, but was refused permission.

Jan had heard rumours about gold being buried, and thought they were probably true. Matthys, however, was distraught. He said to Jan that he did not know what to do with these people. How could he open their eyes when they simply *refused to see?*

He decided to make an example of the late converts after a night spent in prayer. He had them taken to the church, then summoned Jan to accompany him there. It was cold and gloomy in the church and there was nowhere to sit because the seating had been ripped out. You could hear rats scuttle. The converts huddled, holding their children. Two guards stood by the door with pikes.

Matthys harangued his prisoners. He told them they were nothing, worse than nothing, were just stumbling-blocks to the chosen people. He called them ungrateful beyond belief. He said they complained when a scrap of food was taken from their larders to feed the hungry. That which the Father had given to all his children, they could not share. When the rest of the city had given its copper, silver and gold to the common chest, they had buried theirs in the ground. Where worms and other vile things were. Where *they* deserved to be.

His face a mask of disgust, he went away, ordering the door to be locked. They were left there all day. Darkness fell.

About an hour after sunset, Jan, going the rounds of the walls as he normally did, was summoned again to Matthys's side. This time Matthys had with him twenty-four men carrying swords and lanterns.

To Jan, as they re-entered the building, it seemed that a change had occurred at some profound level. A decomposition, as it were. He noticed the smell first, both fetid and rank: they had soiled themselves. Then the noises crowded on him, rushing back to fill the silence into which the door had opened. Moans, sobs, a high wailing. All coming out of the dense obscurity beyond the ring of lanterns carried by the guards.

The armed men took up position around the nave, encircling the prisoners. Matthys walked to the chancel steps.

When he spoke, his voice echoed in the church with an oracular hollowness.

"Make what peace you can with God, because you are going to die."

There was a short interval before anything happened. Jan then saw with amazement that there was nothing Matthys could not do. For they were all going down on their knees to him, from the oldest to the children, and crawling towards him with cries and pathetic gestures of self-abasement and submission. Matthys stood and waited.

The sobs and cries became more desperate. A woman began to bang her forehead rhythmically on the floor. The man kneeling beside her tried to stop her, but she pulled away from his hand and went on doing it.

"I see that you repent," said Matthys. "In that case, I will intercede for you, as best I can."

He turned his back on them and went to kneel in front of the bare altar. He prostrated himself. He began to pray. They heard the drone of his voice but not the words, apart from an occasional loud "Father, if it be Your will…"

Time passed. The cold in the church increased. In the lanterns, the candles were burning low.

Matthys ended his prayer at last, and lay motionless on the stones of the sanctuary. In the body of the church, the weeping had stopped. Someone took off a shawl and wrapped it round a child. The silence of exhaustion fell.

Matthys rose from the floor. Now he would come back and kill them.

His skin glistened and his voice shook from the effort he had made. "I have wrestled with the justice of God," he said. There was not a sound in the building. "Praise Him," ordered Matthys, "for He has forgiven you."

Tumult broke out. Grown men, still on their knees in the filth, were babbling thanks like babies. Everyone was weeping, and on every face was the same idiot smile.

Matthys had broken them and put them together again. But they would be broken for ever.

The spring was advancing. The green shoots of early onions appeared in the gardens of those brethren who had been provident enough to plant them. Birds sang from branches which had begun to bud, greeting the longer days. As the sun rose higher in the sky, the spirits of the townsfolk rose also.

The siege as yet was causing no hardship. If anything, it had been a good thing, Rothmann remarked to Dolling, in that it brought them together. A tangible threat, to put beside the spiritual goals set by Matthys.

Dolling lifted his glass ironically. "To the Bishop!"

Rothmann would not allow him to drink to that.

"Very well. To the Providence which has given us something else to think about while Matthys has been wringing the last drop out of us," said Dolling. He had had several glasses of Rhenish. And if he couldn't trust Rothmann, whom could he trust?

Rothmann looked worried. "Is your heart not in this, Bernard?"

"Of course my heart is in it! I spend all day and half the night labouring on its behalf."

"I am not sure you do. I am not sure on whose behalf you are labouring."

"What?"

"I only mean that you seem to be enjoying yourself a lot."

"I don't see the need to be miserable because we're led by a man who believes in suffering."

"He has experienced suffering," pointed out Rothmann.

"Yes, and it has unbalanced his mind."

The atmosphere changed subtly.

Rothmann said, "If you believe we are led by a madman, what are you doing here?"

"This is my city. I have no intention of abandoning it."

"I see."

"I don't say he's mad. No. Just not human. He expects perfection of us."

"He has visions," said Rothmann. "He can't adjust his sight."

"Ah. Is that what it is."

"Don't mock what is beyond you, Bernard. Do you have visions?"

Dolling said, "Do you believe in this miraculous deliverance at Easter?"

Rothmann hesitated. "Does it matter what I believe?"

"But do you believe it?"

"No."

"Nor I. And I wish he would stop talking about it, because if people believe they're going to be saved by an act of God then why should they bother to take the normal measures to defend themselves?"

"I see," said Rothmann again. After a moment he added, "But you get on well with Jan?"

"One can *talk* to him. He's a man of many parts, in fact."

"He told me he used to write plays."

"Something of the sort." Dolling became defensive.

"He didn't seem to see a difference between writing plays and writing pamphlets against infant baptism."

Dolling reached for the wine. It seemed better not to reply.

Easter was only a week away. Then only three days away. Then it was Good Friday.

As they had in the days before Jan and Matthys came, people took to standing in the streets staring upward, trying to read the riddle of the sky. What would happen on Easter Sunday was virtually the only thing anyone talked about. The preachers, having initially whipped up the speculation, then became afraid that it would get out of control and tried to dampen it down, but the argument they resorted to, that it was impious to guess at God's intentions, had the effect of pouring oil on a fire.

Since the only guide to the coming events (indeed, the only guide to anything, since all other books had been burnt) was the Bible, it was pored over for clues. There were plenty, but they gave no reassurance. The Book of Revelation was terrifying. The mind could not take in its landscapes of devastation. Moreover, amid the lakes of fire, the horned beasts and the earth brimming with blood, there was scant reference to the Elect who were saved. When they made their brief appearance, there was nothing to show who they were. A doubt grew in some quarters and quickly ripened to panic. Suppose after all the men and women of Münster were *not* the Elect?

Several hundred people took to the streets, wailing with despair. Their cries mingled dangerously with the other feverish currents that swirled about the city. Matthys, who had withdrawn to his house, took control just in time. He summoned the entire population to the Cathedral square. They must leave whatever they were doing and come at once to hear him. This was the afternoon of Easter Saturday.

It was the strangest speech anyone ever heard him give. Normally, his speeches were an assault on the listener. On this occasion he spoke without anger, without passion. He seemed to have resigned his will.

He told his audience of a beautiful vision he had received. He had been lifted up to Heaven and shown the whole earth "subdued to God's will." At the centre of the glorious scene had been Münster, the holy city, "shining like a jewel" as was described in Revelation, and with its people thronging the battlements and singing hymns of praise. He described the transfigured streets, the divine light that bathed the ramparts, and the people, spotless and incapable of sin.

"You will see this with your own eyes," Matthys told the listening multitude. "This was not a dream, but a sign of what is to be! And I was shown how it will come about. Tomorrow, the Day of Our Lord's rising, I shall ride out with twenty men from this city and our enemies will flee. The wretched army at our gates will melt away when it sees the angels hovering above us. We shall ride on invincibly, the vanguard of the Lord..."

"I've already spoken to him," Jan told Rothmann and Dolling when they went to see him later. "He won't listen to any words of caution."

"He is going to charge the enemy camp at the head of twenty men?"

"Yes."

"They'll kill him," said Dolling.

"I hope you will keep your unbelief to yourself, brother. People are looking to you for leadership."

Rothmann intervened carefully. "Jan, he *may* be mistaken. Anyone can misinterpret a vision. We're all human. What if they capture him, or…" He was unable to finish the thought.

"Why should he be mistaken?"" Jan gave a ghost of a smile. "I think it very likely that the Bishop's army will take to its heels at the sight of Matthys bearing down on it accompanied by a host of angels."

Rothmann stared at him. "Suppose they can't see the angels?"

The smile that was not quite a smile was still on Jan's face. "That won't mean the angels aren't there."

Dolling was straightforwardly angry. "Don't ask me to help you pick the troop. I won't send twenty good men to their deaths."

"They will have to be chosen by lot," Jan told him, "because every man in the city wants to be one of them."

About the middle of Sunday morning, in a festive atmosphere, Matthys and his twenty companions rode to St Maurice's Gate. A group of women had got up early to gather rushes, and strewed them before the horses' hooves.

Matthys had given instructions for a hymn to be sung. The singing began as the mounted troop was seen coming down Stoneway towards the gate. The inner battlements were thickly crowded with people, and at the outer rampart, too, men and women stood three or four deep on the wall of the embankment. They would be lucky if no one fell to his death, thought Dolling, never mind riding to it. He forced a "Praise God!" out of his lungs as he gave the signal for the culverin to be fired. At once all their other guns fired and the gate swung open.

The little company rode out across the drawbridge. They crossed the second line of defences, the wide outwork with its embankment and wall, and waited while the bridge was lowered over the second moat. As they passed under the outer gate, Matthys lifted his spear above his head. It had been forged for him only the previous day, a virgin weapon. He rode a white horse and he wore a polished steel breastplate which, as it caught the sun's rays, dazzled the eye. He had refused a helmet, saying faith was his helmet. For the first time since they had seen him in the city, his face wore a contented smile.

Matthys spurred his horse and the troop made directly for the Bishop's camp. There a line of cavalry had mustered, alerted by the firing of cannon and the commotion on the walls. To the onlookers crowding the battlements, the charge of Matthys and his men seemed irresistible: it would carry them through that feeble line of horsemen, through the camp fires and unclean tents and the women who would soon be wailing, and on through the plains and hills and the cities beyond, where every force thrown against them would be trodden into clay in the sun-filled advance of the Lord.

So that when that uncertain line of horsemen suddenly consolidated itself and rode to the attack, and was joined by another troop of cavalry spurring from the camp to cut off God's soldiers from behind, when it became clear that Matthys and his men had ridden too far, were outnumbered by opponents whom mysteriously they did not at once slay, when the supernatural radiance that had hung above the battlefield faded into the common light of a mortal disaster and they saw their leader the prophet flung from his horse with a lance through his throat, they understood none of it and they went on singing for quite a long time.

Perfection

The dead were left lying on the field. One man crawled home under cover of dark. The following day, the Baker's head, no longer smiling, was found stuck on a pike facing Our Lady's Gate. His legs, arms and trunk, wrapped in portions of his bloodsoaked tunic, turned up in various places around the outer walls in the course of the week.

6   Seed

Jan had been standing a few feet from Dolling on the battlements when Matthys fell. Dolling saw his face turn as white as curd. He turned and pushed his way back into the crowd, which was three or four deep on that part of the wall, and disappeared from sight.

When Dolling looked for him, no-one knew where he was. No-one had even seen him leave the battlements. It was as if he had been Matthys's shadow, and vanished with him.

When the realisation of what had happened began to sink in, the city became a vault. A great silence descended on it. Dolling went to the walls in the evening and found not a man on watch. He visited the homes of the watch captains to tell them to organise their men, and was told bluntly that the men would not come, they thought there was no purpose in it.

What if the Bishop attacked? asked Dolling. Let him, they said. He realised that they wanted the Bishop to attack because then they would know what to do. What they were afraid of was not dying, but living. Matthys had taken not only the future with him, but the past and present as well, and they did not know who they were any longer.

He did manage to round up a party to bring in Matthys' head. It had been set up facing the east, so that the rising sun conjured a baleful glare in the glassy eyes. The beard was a clotted mass of blood, around which flies already hung in a moving sphere. By the time Dolling's men got to it, the eyes had gone. It had been a hard winter, and the crows were hungry.

Dolling called at Rothmann's house, and found him huddled over his Bible. He looked as if he hadn't slept.

"What are we going to do?" Dolling said.

"I was hoping you would suggest something."

"You're the man of God," said Dolling unkindly.

"God?" Rothmann repeated, in a tone which made Dolling wonder if he had started thinking wild thoughts, such as that God didn't exist.

"What does your Bible say?"

"'Once again I will act against you, to refine away your base metal as with potash and purge all your impurities.' Isaiah, chapter 1, verse 25."

"Really?"

"I opened it and that is what I read."

Dolling sat on the bench beside his hearth, in which the fire was laid but not lit, Rothmann's house being always cold.

"It is the only possible explanation, isn't it?" Rothmann said.

"That Matthys was taken because he was 'base metal'?"

"What else can it mean?"

"But we all followed him," Dolling said. He did not need to elaborate this thought. There was a heavy silence.

"Did you think he was wrong?" Rothmann asked after a time. "I know you didn't like the way he went about things, but did you think he was wrong?"

Dolling reacted fiercely. "Did I think he was wrong? I am not a theologian!"

"You have your conscience. I am sick to death of the way you hide behind your worldliness, Bernard. You organised the defence of his people, his creation, so you must have thought he was right."

"I organised the defence! You preached everything he told you to!"

It became clear to both of them at the same instant what was happening.

"Now he's dead, we betray him," said Rothmann. "Soon, the fact that he's dead will be all that matters about him."

"But meanwhile," Dolling said again, "what are we going to do?"

"God knows."

"Will He tell us?"

Rothmann pushed the Bible across the table. "Perhaps He will tell you."

Dolling opened it. His eye fell on the following: "A night watch passes, and Thou hast cut them off. They are like a dream at daybreak, they fade like grass which springs up with the morning but when the evening comes is parched and withered."

"What is it?" asked Rothmann.

Dolling read it to him.

"Oh yes. Psalm 90. Three times I have opened it at that."

"Where do you believe Jan is?"

"Gone," said Rothmann. "Fled, or dead. Who knows? They have left us on our own."

After two days, Jan came back. He did not say where he had been in the interval. He appeared among them grave, but also smiling, and with a frightening pallor. He said little, but clasped their hands and looked into their eyes. It was all so strange, and there was such a brightness in his look, and they were so overjoyed to see him, that several people tried to kneel to him, but he laughed and at once lifted them to their feet.

He went all round the town that way, greeting people and touching them. Then he went home—to rest—he said. He would speak to the leaders of the city at Dolling's house in the morning.

No-one who was there ever forgot that meeting. There were about thirty of them, councillors and district leaders, as many as the room would hold, sitting on seats brought in from elsewhere or on the window ledges. Dolling had had a fire lit in the grate: the crowded room was cheerful, there was almost an air of gaiety, simply because after all he had not deserted them.

Jan took his seat and for a few moments said nothing, but looked into the fire.

Then he said, "Until brother Matthys was taken from us, we were all rather pleased with ourselves, weren't we?"

The crackling of the fire became suddenly very distinct.

"Look at what we'd done! Driven out the unbelievers so there was no-one who disagreed with us. Baptised everyone who said they agreed with us, without enquiring too closely into what their reasons were. Opened our houses to people who had nowhere to live, and shared our food with people who had nothing to eat. What generosity!"

His scorn was terrible. Dolling felt himself shrivelling under it.

"And we'd given up our private hoards of wealth, hadn't we? Or some of us had. Some of us had to be persuaded very vigorously. Six weeks it took, for the children of God to give up the earthly goods they should never accumulated in the first place. Some of us probably still have a little bag of coins buried two feet down under a tree in the garden, where I can't see it but God can."

Dolling suddenly remembered, with horror, a gold seal ring of his father's in a hidden compartment of his desk upstairs.

"And we'd organised ourselves to defend our town, hadn't we? Well, there's no great spiritual merit in that. That's no more than anyone would do, with an enemy at the gates. What else? Oh yes." He laughed. "We had a new town council." After a pause, he repeated with scalding contempt, "A town council."

The logs shifted downwards in the fire, and the leaders of Münster looked at the floor and fleetingly, if they dared, at each other. They did not dare to look at him.

"We haven't even begun," Jan told them. "The very first thing we have to do is rid ourselves of our pride and complacency. They were the reason why Matthys was taken from us." He allowed a little space for them to absorb this. Then he said, "We must look in our hearts. That is what God commands us to do. In the time I was away from you, that is what I was shown."

He raised his hand and pointed towards the nearest section of the city wall. "Out there, they see only the husks and rinds of things. Where a journey ends is all that matters to them, but never where it starts. They apply the crudest measurements. A thing is done, or it is not done. There is an oak tree, or there is not. But suppose what we have is an acorn?"

Unexpectedly, he smiled. "Suppose you want to kill someone. You want it very badly. You brood on it, plan it, you buy a knife and keep it sharp. You keep your hatred sharp. You frequent the company of the man you are going to kill. You watch him, and think about how it will feel when you slide the blade into him, what the look on his face will be, what his last words will be, what you will say to him as you kill him. You dream about this. It becomes more real to you than your daily life. You have created his murder in your heart. Meanwhile you are murdering your own soul, which is a piece of eternity and belongs to God. What will be your punishment for all this, out there? Nothing. They will not even notice it. They will only notice that something has happened when you finally kill him, and then of course they will hang you. As if the killing did not grow out of anything. As if the oak had had no acorn."

He picked up something tied in sacking which he had brought in. He unwrapped it and held up an oak seedling for them to look at, complete from root-tip to leaf.

"At what moment," he said, "did this become an oak tree? Or if you say it is not yet a tree, what will make it one?"

Rothmann coughed. "If you're saying we must strive to improve ourselves, surely there's no-one here who will disagree with you."

"I am saying much more than that. Until now we've been content to rule ourselves by the same kind of laws as the rest of the world, which is doing its best to destroy us. And we don't have the excuse that the rest of the world has: it is blinded by Satan. Here we see clearly by the grace of God. We have a duty. It is to judge, not the action, as the world does, but the thoughts of the heart."

A sense that they were about to embark on something entirely unknown and extraordinary filled Dolling with a mixture of exhilaration and dread.

"Surely," said Rothmann, "we aren't going to bring back Confession?"

"No. It smacks too much of Popery, and there are dangers in it. What we have to do is recognise the impulse from which the wicked act springs, and punish it. So, since murder springs from hatred and anger, we must punish hatred and anger."

Every tiny movement in the room, every tap of a finger or sway of a foot, stopped.

"Since theft springs from covetousness, we must punish covetousness. We must punish not only lying and slander, but the idle gossip which leads to them. We must punish blasphemy, of course, and also disobedience, by which I mean disobedience of any authority including that of a husband or father, since one kind of disobedience leads to another. And we must punish discontent."

Dolling was startled out of his daze. "Discontent?"

"This is no ordinary city. This is the New Jerusalem. And it is surrounded by its enemies. Discontent eats away at the bulwarks. A man who kills his neighbour has despatched one soul to God and his own to Hell, but a man who grumbles in a besieged city is endangering ten thousand souls. In this city he is endangering the work of God."

"So how will these crimes be punished?" asked Dolling.

"I'm glad you asked that question, Bernard, because you are the right person to answer it. What sentence would you pronounce on a deserter in face of the enemy?"

"Death," said Dolling without hesitation or reflection.

There was a silence after he said this. It deepened and continued.

It was done. He was cold: he wrapped his coat around himself and went to his bed and lay down. He was exhausted. His pulse was racing. It would pass.

He remembered that when he had been a touring player he had sometimes felt, after a difficult performance, as if a great wind had come along and blown him inside out. What an existence that had been! Playing in tithe barns, marketplaces, churchyards. Come rain, come sun. The audience, smocked yokels who had cowshit on their shoes and slept with their sisters, or drunken apprentices who wanted to hear no voice but their own. To get their attention he had had to pour himself out like a pitcher of wine, out and out until there was nothing left for him, only the sour air at the neck of the flask and the black dregs at the bottom.

But then there had been the other times, and that was why he had gone on doing it. The times when, as he walked to the edge of the rickety stage and held the crowd with his eyes, a silence fell over them. Then he knew he could do whatever he wanted. Something magical had happened, and the leading strings of their hearts had been put into his hand.

That was exhausting, too, but in the way that riding a half-wild horse was exhausting. You had to go on doing it because it would not let you go, because you were drunk with the power that flowed through you, which was and was not yours.

Afterwards, indeed, you did not quite recognise yourself. This figure on the rushing horse. You wondered at your transfiguration. You tried to learn from this person who on these occasions you were, to borrow some of its glory, but you couldn't. You could only be it, or not be it.

He would see how far he could go with this.

He lay still. Warmth was returning to his body. His pulse slowed. The weakness was over.

He swung his legs to the floor and stood up. His head nearly banged the ceiling. The room was too small: he must find a house of his own. There would be people coming to see him, meetings. A house on Highmarket, like Dolling's, would do. And he must get a woman in to cook for him. He couldn't go on eating at the communal dining hall or wherever he was invited. It was unsuitable, and he would need time to himself, he would need to guard himself against intrusions.

There was something else he needed to think about. Delay could lose him everything. But so could haste.

He regarded himself in a glass. All were there, the long, pale face, curling hair, high brow, full and well-shaped mouth, the nose that he had once feared was too long, and, gazing straight at him, the eyes which of course had only seen what he had seen but sometimes surprised him by their look, as if they had seen something he hadn't.

His beard needed trimming. He tested the edge of his dagger, and found it sharp enough. As he trimmed he turned his head from side to side, inspecting the effect in the mirror.

There was no doubt about it, he needed a wife.

Everything, and nothing, had changed, Dolling thought. As before, they carried powder, stones and lead up to the walls, stood guard, ate together in draughty halls while preachers read to them from the Bible. But something had changed as surely as music changes when another instrument joins the consort.

It bewildered him, that new instrument. Its range was unfamiliar, it went far beyond what he was used to. Its high notes were so high. Its low…perhaps he only thought he heard them.

Then Jan gave him an additional duty, one he did not like at all. He was very angry.

"Public executioner?"

"That's right."

"When I was a boy, the public executioner was more despised than the criminals he despatched."

"You were a boy in a different country, Bernard. We have started again. The last is first, and the first last. I am giving you an honour."

"Oh. Forgive my slowness."

"It is part of your defence duties. I hoped you might see that."

It took days for his anger to subside.

One morning he was supervising the resiting of a cannon. It had to be taken up a steep incline to the top of the earthworks, with ropes and pulleys. The ground was soft and the clumsy wooden wheels sank into it; the men laboured and sweated. Dolling put his hand to the thing as well, and was surprised to touch warm metal, for the sun had been on it although in the shadow of the walls the frost still lingered. As five of them strained, slipping in the mud, to move the huge contraption, a cannonball struck the outer wall and a great cloud of dust and bits of stone rained on their heads. Dolling was filled with mingled rage and happiness. Rage at the enemy, happiness to be in the company of these men, to be one of them. There could not be anything better, he thought, than to be doing exactly what he was doing at that moment. He saw what a huge privilege it was to be entrusted with the defence of their little nation from its enemies. And then he saw in a sudden flash of understanding that there was no point whatsoever in defending it, that it could not be defended, if its heart was not pure. In other words, that what Jan had said about the inside and the outside being one was quite true, for there was no place at which you could insert even the finest knifeblade between one and the other.

Dolling went to see him after they had moved the cannon, and said that he would be glad to accept the post of public executioner. Jan said nothing, only smiled.

By that time, the Town Council had been abolished. Jan said that it was inappropriate, having been created "under the old order," before Matthys had come to the city. Moreover, it was elected, and every elected body had the faults of the people who had elected it. He pointed out to them, amid rather subdued laughter, that both the Emperor and the Pope were elected. He proposed to replace the Council by a congregation of Elders, on the Israelite model. The names of the Elders were given to him one by one, by a Voice which spoke to him in the spirit.

When the full list was announced, it turned out to consist equally of Münster men and immigrants. Dolling was greatly relieved to be one of the Elders, and to be told that his duties had not changed. He had a new title: Master at Arms. Perhaps it was to make up for the loss of Burgomaster.

Rothmann was an Elder, too. That also was a relief.

"Much of what we're doing is symbolic," Jan said to Dolling. "That doesn't mean it isn't real, of course. Symbols are very real." He looked at Dolling searchingly. "Aren't they?"

"Symbols? Yes, I suppose so."

"What do you think of the new laws?"

Dolling was unprepared for this.

"Speak your mind," Jan said. They were alone.

"They're very far-reaching."

"Yes. Yes, they are. They are impossible to keep." Dolling stared at him. "They are symbolic."

"Does that mean...?"

"That we shan't enforce them? Of course it doesn't. They must be seen to be real. But they must also be understood to be symbolic. After all, any law is symbolic if you consider that it is only framed on the assumption that it is going to be broken."

He was turning over in his hands a huge crossbow bolt which had been brought to him. It had embedded itself in one of the gates, with the head of the bolt protruding a good three inches on the far side of the wood. Dolling tried to understand what he was saying.

"Our laws are symbolic," Jan went on, "in the sense that all we care about is the heart. If our hearts are right, everything we do is right. The laws indicate that. It's so simple that anyone can understand it. Is it your impression that there's anyone who doesn't understand these laws?"

"No."

"But just so that the symbol is taken seriously, we may occasionally have to enforce the law in its literal sense."

"With a literal execution?"

"Which will also be symbolic, in that it will stand for many others."

"Jan," said Dolling, "I'm just a merchant. If I execute a man both literally and symbolically, is he going to die?"

"I would think so, unless you make a particularly bad job of it."

In fact he never executed anyone at all. The executions were all carried out by the sergeant of the armoury. Dolling assumed in time that Jan had been testing him, or something of the sort.

Every evening, Jan went to the little house in Jewry.

When Matthys was killed, he had not immediately thought of Devera. It was several days before he remembered her. Afterwards this astonished him.

Even then, he did not go to see her at once. He had a sudden and disgraceful failure of nerve. It seemed to him that he should not visit her so soon, that it might be talked about. He was sure she wouldn't lack for visitors. The city was full of widows and unattached women. Among all these women, he reasoned, Devera must have many friends.

But of course she did not. Matthys had taken care that she did not. When finally he did go to that house, he found that no-one had been near it for a week. She had been quite alone. Alone with that dreadful image of her husband's head stuck eyeless on a pike.

He fell to his knees in contrition. He saw from her astonishment that she really had not known that he loved her until that moment.

So now he went to see her every evening. For the sake of propriety, she always received him in the company of a widow whom he had persuaded to move into the house. After an interval, the widow would find something to do in another room.

He pursued his courtship by subtle means. He could afford to do this because Devera now knew what he was about. He could play the protector, her late husband's friend, indefinitely and know that her feelings were being worked on by the knowledge that he was not, that he had fallen to his knees before her like a lover.

Caution was necessary, in any case. Thanks to Matthys and his blabbing, not only Devera but the whole city knew that he had a wife in Leyden. He had not managed to think of a way around this problem. He thought of declaring all marriages to unbelievers invalid, which would get him out of the legal difficulty, but it would not do his standing any good because people would ask why he had not sought to convert his wife, why he did not send for her. He had been asked the latter numerous times already. And his goal could only be attained by marriage. He could not make Devera his mistress. Not only because it was far too dangerous, but because she would not allow it.

He would find the solution. It would present itself.

He enjoyed their conversations. She had a woman's mind and sympathies, but she was intelligent and sometimes she noticed things which had escaped him. She was not all seriousness, either: she liked to laugh.

He could not imagine how such qualities had got along with Matthys.

"Did he talk to you?" he asked one evening.

"About what?" She was sewing something; she raised her eyes from the work and looked at him quizzically.

But he had not meant "about" anything in particular. He had meant, did Matthys talk intimately to her, did he unlock his mind?

"About himself," he said.

She considered. "I don't think he ever talked about himself. I don't think he would have thought of it."

"Well, did you talk to him?"

"Of course I did. He was my husband."

"Some husbands don't like their wives expressing opinions."

"I never did, unless he asked for one."

"Did you often have an opinion which you didn't express?"

She snapped the thread with her teeth. "Sometimes I must have done, I suppose."

"Such as?"

"Jan, what are you trying to make me say?" She smiled, but the smile contained a reproach.

He let it go, but he would return to it. He needed to know what Matthys had said to her, what she had said to him, in what tone it had been said, whether the candle was lit on the table, and a hundred other things. He could never get enough to fill up the ravenous maw of his curiosity, because it was not really curiosity but hate. He wanted to hear her betray her husband. At the very least, he wanted her to have thought a thought that was not licensed by him.

He asked her how they had met. She said that, after leaving the convent, she had found work mending linen for a large family. She lived at the top of the house. One night, about a dozen people arrived at the house for a meeting. She was intrigued by the secrecy and the lateness of the hour, and, when she judged the meeting had started, she crept downstairs to listen.

"He opened the door and saw me," she said.

"Did he know you were there?"

"He said he did, although I'd been as quiet as a mouse."

Jan could believe that he had known.

"He said that now I knew what they were doing, I must join the meeting. So I did. Afterwards, he asked me what I thought of the things I'd heard. I said I thought that a lot of true things had been spoken, but there were some I would need to think about. He seemed very pleased with this answer."

Jan loved listening to her voice. But as he listened, he stored up in his memory the image of her creeping downstairs to eavesdrop.

"I went to the subsequent meetings, and he baptised me," she said. "Then one day he told me he was looking for a wife, and asked me to marry him."

"And did you marry him straight away?"

"What was the point of waiting? He was already being hunted, anyway."

"That didn't weigh against it, for you? A life of danger?"

She seemed surprised. "Did it weigh against it for you?"

He laughed it off. "I'm a man."

"I don't see what that has to do with it," she said quietly.

So there he was, having gone right up to the thing that tormented him and grasped it by the throat, and he had gained nothing. He still didn't know why she had married Matthys.

"You must be pleased," Rothmann said after Dolling's title of Master at Arms was announced.

Sunlight bathed the pale stonework of St Lambert's. It would soon be summer. Dolling smiled a smile of unwise complacency. "I've made myself indispensable," he said.

"Don't be a fool," said Rothmann. "No-one's indispensable to him."

Dolling was prevented from making a sharp rejoinder by noticing that Rothmann seemed preoccupied.

"What's on your mind?" he asked.

"Nothing particular."

He means, thought Dolling, nothing he wants to tell me.

The distance between them which had been growing almost imperceptibly since the evening when Dolling accused Rothmann of cowardice was now palpable. It was linked to the change in their respective positions. As Rothmann's influence had waned, Dolling's stature had increased. Jan depended on him for the smooth running of the defence and many other things. He seemed unable to put a foot wrong. Rothmann, by contrast, was perpetually out of step. He had picked away in public, for weeks, at the new code of laws, unable to see that he had no support and that the new laws would never be strictly implemented anyway, because they couldn't be and (as Jan had explained) they were symbolic.

All of this was embarrassing to Dolling, and he wished that Rothmann would show a little more sense. Both for his own sake, and because Dolling was beginning to have doubts about the wisdom of associating with him.

It was not possible to say any of this, of course, and since it could not be said Dolling frequently found it was the only thing he could think about when he was with Rothmann, which led to awkward conversation.

"I'm wondering how far he'll go," said Rothmann suddenly. "That's all."

"I don't know what you mean by that," said Dolling. "He will go as far as God calls him to."

"Rubbish," said Rothmann. "He has never heard the voice of God in his life."

Dolling's first reaction was panic. He did not want to be in the room in which this had been said. After a moment he asked as calmly as he could, "Are you calling him a fraud?"

Rothmann shrugged, as if names were not important.

"The other day," said Dolling with vehemence, "he was up on the battlements inspecting some damage when an arrow was fired at him from the camp. I was there. It missed him by this much." He held his thumb and forefinger an inch apart. "Will you tell me why he should be risking his life if he doesn't believe?"

"I didn't say that. I have no idea what he believes."

"You as good as called him a liar."

"Did I? I think he does not hear the voice of God. What's more, I think he knows very well that he doesn't. Unlike Matthys, who was sure it was always the voice of God, when clearly on the last occasion, at least, he was deluded."

"You're too subtle, Rothmann, do you know that? The books have been burnt."

He regretted it at once: it was a terrible thing to say to an old friend. Too late to unsay. In any case, Rothmann had badly upset him.

"And you think I should have been on the pyre with them, is that it?"

Dolling listened to a blackbird sing outside the window. In the end, attempting to recover the situation, he said, "You've no idea how hard he works. Just as hard as Matthys, only he does things differently."

Rothmann grunted.

"He never rests. He's constantly looking for improvements we can make, better ways of doing things. Everything from the penal system to new weapons. And what does he get out of it? He lives like a hermit. If he doesn't hear the voice of God," said Dolling, "then what on earth is he doing it for?"

Rothmann offered no ideas.

Brother Ignatius had smelt of the cows, of milk and hay and cowshit. Sister Agnes couldn't get enough of this smell: she sniffed and lapped it off his skin. Afterwards, in her cell, she would smell it on her own skin and it would excite her again.

She never understood why the friars thought it was a sin, what she and Brother Ignatius did. Not that she ever confessed it: why confess something you know isn't wrong? And how could it be wrong when no-one thought the worse of animals for doing it?

It was the animals that started it.

She had gone to fetch the milk, and Brother Ignatius came across the field to meet her, which he had never done before. He put his finger to his lips and led her a different way to the barn, across the stream and behind the hedge. The bull had been brought for the cows, he said, and he pointed through a gap in the hawthorn at where the biggest animal she had ever seen was standing helplessly while a mass of scarlet flesh erupted from below its belly.

Sister Agnes was astonished and rather frightened. However, Brother Ignatius took her hand and reassured her. They stood together and watched. The bull tried to get on top of a cow, holding her with his front legs, but he slithered off. He tried again, and Sister Agnes could see the red thing waving about and butting its head against the cow's hindquarters. This went on and on. The bull would heave and struggle, and seem to be achieving something, but then the cow would move a pace forward to pull up another tongueful of grass and the bull would slither off again. But he went on trying, and at last Sister Agnes could see the red thing disappear inside the cow and the two of them were locked together, almost motionless, but staggering a little.

Sister Agnes could feel her eyes as wide as plates. Then the strangest thing happened. Brother Ignatius, who had been standing quite close to her all this time and was still holding her hand, now moved her hand sideways and put it on something she didn't recognise at all, and was sure had not been there before, something which was as hard as rock and was sticking straight out under his habit like a schoolmaster's pointer.

Sister Agnes was bewildered. She began to understand when, there behind the hawthorn hedge, he showed it to her. It was like the bull. Then he lifted her clothing and with his thumb he gently touched her between the legs, in a place she didn't know existed, and she felt a great shock go through her, not of pain but of something completely new. After the first moment she wanted him to touch her there again, and then again. And the more he did, the more she wanted him to. Only she had no idea where this was leading or what to do next.

Then he showed her. He placed her hand on his pole of flesh, and she moved it as he showed her, and suddenly out of it there spurted a fountain of stuff like milk, and she laughed because it seemed that everything about him was to do with milk. He had his eyes closed and a look on his face that was neither sad nor happy, but was like the perfect stillness of water when there is nothing to disturb it. She thought, this is beautiful, this is the most beautiful thing God has given us.

There had been some heavy bombardment of the north-east wall. A section of stonework had given way. On his walk to Devera's house, Jan passed a long line of women toiling up to the ramparts with blocks of stone for the repair. Each woman carried a single stone against her belly as if it were a child. It struck him that, for many of them, that was the only child she would ever have. The pathos of this first occurred to him, and then the inappropriateness of it. For if this was the community of the Elect (and he sometimes found himself assuming that it was, since everyone around him assumed it was), it should be producing as many children as possible, instead of producing fewer than its enemies were.

"How many women do you reckon there are in the city?" he asked Devera.

She looked at him in surprise. "What a strange question."

"It seems to me there are about three times as many women as men."

"That's possible. I wonder how it happened."

It didn't matter how it had happened. The question was what to do with them. He had drafted them into the defence as far as he could, but there was a limit. You could not train them to wield a sword. The only thing to which they were perfectly suited was childbearing, which brought him back to his previous reflections. Waste displeased him.

Devera sent him off on a different track.

"In a way, it's a pity you made the law more severe," she mused, and turned her sewing so that the light from the window fell on it.

"What law?"

"About...what may be done in marriage."

Fornication was already a capital offence, but he had widened the definition of it. He had included in it any act between husband and wife in which seed was spilt which could not result in conception. Men could not now have relations with their wives when the wife was pregnant or menstruating. He had done this because it was logical and a further exercise in seeing how far he could go. Somewhere in his mind had lurked the thought that if he could not have what he wanted, there was no reason why anyone else should.

He played with a small animal carved out of pearwood that had been left behind by the owners of the house. A pretty little thing.

"It must make things more difficult for the men," Devera said. She shocked him by adding, "And the brothels have been closed for months."

They had been closed by order of the old Council, and it had not been a difficult order to enforce because the women had by then mostly left town in a panic, seeing the way things were going, and those who hadn't had overnight discovered a talent for embroidery or making pies.

"What do you know about these things?" he said roughly. "A nun, and then married to Matthys."

He turned the carving in his fingers. It was a monkey. Held at a certain angle, it revealed an erect phallus striving upward over its belly. He closed his hand on it, startled. Matthys could never have seen that, or he would have thrown it in the fire.

The worst of it was that she was right about making things difficult. In his fascination with playing with the law he had turned a problem into a catastrophe. He had ended up with a city whose men did not have legitimate outlet for their seed, and a city of women who vastly outnumbered the available…

He stood up quickly.

"What is it?" asked Devera.

"My dear, I must leave you. Things to do." He slipped the monkey into his pocket.

"Have I annoyed you?"

"On the contrary." He clasped her hand, heroically resisting the urge to kiss it.

He went home, locked his door and plunged into the Bible.

He used the Bible which Matthys had brought with him from Holland. Oh, Matthys, what riches there were between those heavy covers! But there were also swamps of who begat whom, and deserts of "Thou shalt not." It took him many days to get out the nuggets of gold he wanted. During that time he saw no-one, not even Bernard, not even Devera, because he did not want distraction and he was afraid that someone might glean from a look in his eye what he was thinking of.

He knew that he must look first in the Old Testament. The evidence was scantier than he would have liked, but it was clear enough and it could not be dismissed. Abraham, Jacob… these were not names you could quarrel with. He came to Solomon, and was dazzled. Solomon was excess made flesh. To the sober folk of Münster, he realised, Solomon might not be much of a recommendation. All the same, the Lord had smiled on him and he must be added to the list of proofs.

Emerging weary from the Old Testament, he gave himself a day's rest before he dived into the New. This would be more difficult. He was looking for small signs that had never been picked up because they went against the grain of orthodoxy. Chinks which could be used to prise apart the practice of fifteen hundred years. At first, what he was scanning seemed a smooth and unbroken surface. Forbidding, even. But he went on reading, at night by candlelight while his eyes ached, trying to keep his mind at the same time wide open and flint-sharp, as if he were interrogating a Sphinx. He read the Acts of the Apostles over and over. St Paul. For days he pored over Paul. He knew it was there, somewhere. It had to be. The scorner of women, the enemy of carnal delight. It had to be there, and it had to be Paul.

Then he found it. The first epistle to Timothy. "A Bishop should not have more than one wife."

He laughed aloud, rose from his seat and did a solemn dance of celebration. After that, he delayed only to eat a mouthful of bread and wash his face. Then he ran and skipped, watched by wondering citizens who thought he was seized by the Spirit, all the way to Devera's house and asked her to marry him.

7 The Law of Turks and Rabbits

This time, Rothmann noted, there was no play-acting with seedlings dug up from the garden. This time, Jan walked into the meeting room carrying the Bible.

"I have received a revelation of the greatest importance," he said.

At first they could not believe what he was saying. Then they were so outraged that they could not find words to express themselves. Then the arguments began.

The arguing went on for weeks. Rothmann stood out stoutly against the proposal, and had, of course, all the theological arguments at his command. However, Jan had studied thoroughly that massive Bible to which he made constant reference, and came back with the custom of the patriarchs by which Abraham had had three wives, Jacob four and Solomon seven hundred, and a strange and quibbling reference to Paul. They spent a long time on Paul, who had not really thought a man should marry at all, let alone marry several wives. But then, as Jan pointed out, Paul had been addressing himself to Corinth, a sink of worldly iniquity, and Münster was quite a different matter.

The picture he drew of the lonely, husbandless women of Münster, empty-wombed and denied the joys of a man's company and protection, would have wrung tears from a stone. On the other side of the picture he placed the virile Münster menfolk, wanting nothing more than to sire children for the glory of God and denied by an outmoded law the opportunity which God Himself had given them. A law whose worth could be judged by the fact that it was scrupulously observed by the licentious soldiery outside their walls.

Despite the vehement protests, the issue was not seriously in doubt. It was already decided on the third day, when certain Elders, led by Krechting, announced that, having reflected deeply and prayed, they believed they were being called to take a second wife and live with her in a godly manner. Although the Congregation continued in session on the subject for several more weeks, it was clear that Jan would have his way. The opposition continued mainly for the sake of appearances, thought Rothman.

When Jan finally declared the debate over, it was proclaimed, and the preachers began to preach, that a man might have as many wives as he liked, and that women married to unbelievers who had fled Münster were to be regarded as single. This was so that there would be no confusion about who was eligible for marriage. It was emphasised that women must not be forced into marriage. On the other hand, they were all expected to have a husband within three months.

Many had one within the next three days. Jan had reduced the formalities to a minimum, foreseeing that there would be a heavy call on the services of the preachers who would perform the ceremony, but it soon became obvious that other measures were needed. Special marriage deacons were appointed and given offices in public buildings. The offices were easy to find: there was always a line of prospective couples waiting patiently outside them from early in the morning until they closed at dusk.

"I suppose I shall have to make way for some new woman of yours any day now," Dolling's wife remarked to him.

He was eating a pickled herring, a thing he was fond of, and herring wasn't so easy to get these days. He was enjoying it, and at the same time thinking about a meeting he had to go to directly he'd eaten, and he was so used to the sound of Sara's voice complaining about something or other that at first he didn't hear what she'd said. All he registered was the tone of voice: it was one that generally accompanied meals.

Then he heard in his mind the words "new woman of yours."

She was sitting across the table with her mouth pursed in the way he detested. He was instantly furious. The Elders had not even finished debating the matter!

"Are you referring to the proposed new marriage law?"

"If that's what you call it. It's a proposed adultery law if you ask me."

"Fortunately no-one is asking you. God forbid we should have to consult our wives before we pass a law."

"You don't pass laws," she said contemptuously. "He tells you what to do, and you do it. You'd all rush out and hang yourselves from the battlements if he told you to."

"Be careful, Sara."

"Why? Are you going to tell someone I said it?" She picked up a herring from the dish with her fingers, laid it on a slice of bread and bit into it.

"I don't plan to take another wife," he said, "if that's what's troubling you."

"Don't tell me you haven't thought about it."

"I haven't."

She laughed.

"I tell you I haven't. I have enough to think about."

"You mean one wife's enough? I give you enough trouble, is that it?"

He had never managed to teach Sara respect. When they had guests, he lived in fear that they would hear her say something to him from which his standing in the town would never recover.

She put down her piece of bread and herring, licked her lips and said, "Too many piglets make the gruel thin."

"What?"

"It's a saying that's going round. I thought you might have heard it."

"I certainly haven't."

"Well, it bears thinking about, doesn't it? It's not every man would be up to having a lot of wives." She looked at him meaningfully.

He had never heard anything like this from her before. He had always credited her with a womanly delicacy of mind.

"Perhaps that's what you're worried about," she went on. Not believing his ears, he then heard her add, "I'm not surprised. The gruel in this house has never been anything but thin."

He rose, abandoning the pickled herring, and went to his meeting.

Jan married Devera on the first day of the new law. He took her home after the brief ceremony, kissed her lips for the first time, and then laid her on the bed. He lay down beside her and unlaced, slowly, the white ribbons of her bodice with his left hand, while he leant on his right elbow and smiled into her eyes. When the last ribbon snaked free of its tiny restraining loop, he slid his hand beneath the crisp fabric and rested it on the cool, firm flesh of her breast. That coolness! How it astonished him, and he raised his fingers and settled them on that smooth cream swell a second time in order to taste it again. He moved his hand downward then, and felt the nipple rise with a tiny hardness into his palm. He held his hand there, cupped and tenderly teasing over that nipple, which, emboldened, seemed to thrust upwards into his palm with stiff purpose.

He wanted to delay. He had lived so long for this moment that now it was here he wanted to postpone it further, to dip his tongue into it and then put it away, safe, in the future, where it could always be enjoyed in prospect and where the end of it would never be reached. But he had kept himself away from women, under the iron discipline of Matthys and the eyes of Münster, for half a year. He could not delay. As he caressed Devera's nipple with the curve of his palm, with the very tips of his fingers and finally with the merest brush of his lips, he wondered if he could even take the game through to its end, and he reached down and unlaced himself, letting the caged beast out.

He fed on her breast. He took it whole into his mouth, all its round vulnerability crowned with that tough pink nut, and sucked on it like a monstrous child. His member grew huge. He knelt on the bed and removed her clothes. Then he had to move back from her, stand on the floor and gaze, because of the complete beauty of what was revealed. Her breasts – one slightly inflamed now — were small, perfect globes, full without heaviness, set above a ribcage which showed itself in faint indentations as it rose and fell with her breathing. In the narrows of her waist a navel like a jewel made its smooth inverse pyramid. Her hips flared out like summer, and at the base of the silky plain between them a dark, downward tapering triangle held his eye captive and vanished into the deeper mystery between her thighs.

His gaze moved up slowly to her face, where he read uncertainty. She was not sure how to behave with him. Perhaps she was even a little afraid. Then he saw how her gaze also travelled over him, and realised that he was still wearing, not only his clothes and his boots, but also his sword, which he had been in too much of a hurry to unbuckle as he came in through the door.

Quickly he took all of these off until he was standing there naked, and as stiff as a lance. He saw her looking sideways at it, and he told himself with triumph that this was a feat Matthys had never equalled, if the astonishment in her eyes was anything to judge by.

He spread her legs and knelt between them. Then, feeling the chill of the room, he went and got a coverlet and spread it over them so that it rested on his head and back and made a tent for their bodies. He began to worship her with his lips and tongue. He began with her hairline, that musky, moist region of contrasts, and moved down over her white forehead, the slender arcs of the brows, the sweet hollow between them from which the nose took its graceful rise, and the eyes themselves, forest pools which he sealed shut with a kiss on the lid of each. He parted his lips along the nose and kissed its tip, and returned to graze on the mouth, to which he had given too little attention. Her mouth tasted of spice and wine. He swallowed its warm breath and chased her tongue with his, sliding his along it, playing serpents. Lightly, he nibbled her lips. He discovered her ears, miraculous and intricate, and paid homage to them with the lightest touch of his teeth. He fell like a famished man on the warm, yielding curve of her neck.

He traced with a finger the line from the hollow of her neck to the hollow between her breasts, and then in reverse traced the same pilgrim's path with his tongue. With his tongue he explored the odorous forest of her armpits, and then he ran his tongue downwards, lapping the edge of the left breast, grazing it with his lips with a promise to return, his tongue moving stealthily down over those precious springing ribs, to the point where the ribcage ended and was succeeded by that wonderful and frightening expanse of softness, the innocent stomach, on which he laid his head with a groan, and beyond that again, just beyond it, where his beard lay, its hairs mingled with her darker, secret, nether beard.

He raised his head and sniffed her scent. Then, kneeling, he touched her on the inside of the thighs, first one and then the other, right at the top where the flesh was slightly tough and was luxuriant with hair. It was hot there, and he felt the heat and the moisture and darkness drawing him in. She gasped when he touched her there, and he leaned forward and kissed her on the mouth, feeling his sex knocking at the lower gate as he probed the cave of her mouth with his tongue.

He could not hold back any longer. He was burning. He felt her with his finger, and then he plunged into that other, sacred cave that was waiting for him, and which he had waited so long to enter, and it was like entering a river of silk, or Lethe. Up it he swam, hearing the current ever louder in his ears, and seeing the walls of the cavern fall away and become a mouth to the sea. Then the sea became the sky, in which he was flying, and he flew over the edge of the world.

Sister Agnes lay watching a globe of light in the room grow larger. Starting at about the size of her fist, it grew until it was as big as she could just have held in her hooped arms. Not that she could have touched it. It came from another world, and could not be touched. In any case, she couldn't move from where she lay.

Inside the globe was an angel. The cloudiness of the globe, which was like the sun shining through mist, cleared, and there was the angel sitting cross-legged on a cushion. He was looking at her earnestly.

"Sister Agnes, you are living in a state of incompleteness," he said.

Sister Agnes said she was sorry.

"You must go down to the riverside," he said. "To the house which is next to the house of Otto the cane-weaver. There you will find people who will tell you what to do."

Sister Agnes tried to speak again, but there was something stilling her lips, like a finger laid on them. The angel began to fade. His earnest expression had softened. By the time he flickered out, she fancied he was smiling.

When the strength came back to her, she got up. She washed her face, put on her Sunday gown and bonnet and went down to the riverside.

It was the middle of the afternoon and there were several people about. She had no difficulty in getting directions to the house of Otto the cane-weaver. It was a small wooden house with a thatched roof and an earth yard full of tubs in which cane was soaking. About twenty yards further along the path was a rather larger house which had an entirely different air. The windows were obscured—by soot or paint or some dark material, she couldn't see—the yard was littered with rubbish in which a pig was contentedly rooting, and the roof looked as if it let in more rain than it kept out.

Sister Agnes made her way through the yard and knocked at the door. After an interval it was opened by a man in a dirty smock.

"Yes?" he said. He looked her up and down. A waft of warm air and ale came from the dark interior behind him.

"I am Sister Agnes," she said. "I was told to come here."

"Oh yes? Who sent you, then?"

"An angel," she said.

His expression did something complicated. Then it righted itself, and he pulled the door back for her and said, "You'd better come in, sister."

She went into a big, dark room in which benches and tables were set against the walls and people were sitting at them. A stove burned in the corner, and a long-bodied, pale dog was stretched out in front of it. Lidded flagons of beer stood on the table, and here and there a plate with hunks of dark bread on it.

Sister Agnes sat down at a table. It was warm and comfortable in the room. She folded her hands and waited.

The man who had let her in brought her a tall pewter mug. It was filled with beer. She drank a little of it, and ate a bit of the bread that was on the table.

Two men were sitting on the bench on the other side of the table. They had been watching her in a friendly way. They now opened a conversation.

"It's good bread, that."

"Yes, it is," said Sister Agnes.

"His brother makes it," said the second, nodding towards the man who'd brought the beer.

"He's a baker, see."

"Oh, I see," said Sister Agnes.

"Come here before, have you?"

"No."

"We don't often see…ladies here."

Sister Agnes looked around. There certainly weren't any here at the moment. Apart from her.

"Waiting for someone, are you?" asked the first.

"I suppose so."

"Do we know him?"

"I don't know who it is." She laughed, thinking how odd it was, really, and that they would think it even odder. "It might be anyone. It might even be you two." She didn't know why she said that. It just seemed the right thing to say.

Their eyes goggled. They began to drink their beer more quickly, and soon were calling for more.

When it came, she found her own mug replenished as well.

The conversation became livelier. They introduced themselves. They were Georg and Karl, and they were boatmen. At least, they had been boatmen until the city was closed and the river with it. Now…

"The council said it would keep us on as ferrymen," said Karl. "Taking goods from one side of the city to the other by boat. But who wants anything taken by river for that sort of distance? Doesn't make sense, two lots of loading and unloading. So we're carters instead."

"Aye."

"Of course, 'tisn't the council now, 'tis called something else."

"'Tis the same thing."

"Aye. Well. And what about you, my sweetness? Do you have a husband at home?"

"Don't be daft," said Georg. "She wouldn't be here if she did."

"No, I don't," said Sister Agnes.

The two men exchanged a look. Then one of them — it was Georg — turned to her and started telling her a long story about a journey he had made as a boy all the way down the Rhine to Strasbourg, with his father.

The beer was strong, Sister Agnes was not used to it, and she became aware that little intervals of time were occurring in which she had, as it were, been absent. This didn't perturb her. She was enjoying herself and she liked Georg and Karl.

They seemed to like her, too. One of them came and sat beside her. She thought it was Karl. Then she saw Karl opposite her and realised it was Georg. He—Georg—had a hand on her breast. She had no objection to this. In fact it was very nice. She wished he would put his hand on her other breast as well.

After a while, there was indeed a hand on that breast. It was Karl's. He was sitting on the other side of her. Both men were talking to her. She had no idea what they were talking about. It didn't matter in the least. She felt extraordinarily peaceful. She seemed to be floating. Her breasts felt warm and cared for. A tiny stab of pain as the left nipple was squeezed interrupted these pleasant sensations, but was succeeded almost at once by a quite insistent sensation between her legs.

She knew what this was. It was what had happened in the cowsheds with Brother Ignatius, and happened a number of times, too. They had both enjoyed that very much. Thinking fondly of Brother Ignatius, she placed a hand—she had two, how convenient—on the groin of each man sitting beside her on the bench. There was a startled silence, and then the talking began again in a manner that was even more difficult to follow.

Then all at once they were getting up. The two men, lifting her carefully between them. They were going somewhere, it seemed. She didn't mind. It was time for a walk. In any case, she had drunk quite a lot and she needed to empty her bladder.

So did they. A short distance up the lane, they turned their backs to her and pointed to a gap in the hedge a little further on. So she walked to it and squatted down among the reeds and grass, thinking how beautiful everything was, how tranquil, in the evening light. Georg and Karl came up as she was pulling her skirt down and picking some bits of fern off it, and the three of them walked on together to a cottage which had a hawthorn tree right outside the door.

It was getting dark by now. They went into the cottage, and Georg lit the lamp and threw a log on the fire. Karl led her to the bed. He helped her take off her Sunday gown, and laid it over a chair for her. Then he unlaced his breeches. He stood there, and looked at her without a word. She went to him and took the thing in her hand. Lovely, it was. Warm, stirring and big. Then Georg came to the bed and undid his, and she did the same for him. Then for a little while they all stood there, she holding one of them in each hand.

Georg said in a voice full of wonder, "What did we do to deserve this?"

"Don't ask," said Karl. "Just be thankful."

After that they finished undressing her, and sat her on the bed. Then they stood before her, erect, like two princes.

"Oh, you're beautiful," she said. "You're both so beautiful."

They lay down on the bed, and she with them. In the midst of it all, she had a moment of great clarity in which she saw that the angel had intended all of this and that she must marry both of them.

It took a while for Dolling to realise that he did in fact have a choice. It took him even longer to admit that he wanted what was offered him. He was a merchant, and he did not believe that you ever got something for nothing.

When Jan asked him if he had taken another wife, he expressed surprise, as if he had thought that the ordinance did not apply to him. Then he laughed and said no. He was content with his arrangements, he said, uncomfortably aware that the whole of Münster knew otherwise.

"We have a duty to have more children," Jan reproved him. Jan had started talking a lot about this, as if the plans of Heaven depended on there being a sufficient number of souls inside the city. It was a sign of faith to have children. Dolling did not see the point. For one thing, he did not believe the end of the world was imminent. He had wrestled with himself over this point, and sometimes had almost reached the point of believing it, but he had never quite got there. He accepted now that he would never believe it, but would always have to pretend that he did. He occupied himself daily with things to do with the defence of the city—with guns, explosive, steel and stone—that is, with death. Sometimes in the midst of his labours the clear realisation came to him that they were all going to die. In which case he did not want to beget another baby so that some Catholic peasant could put a pike through it.

Yet he loved life, too. Food had always tasted good to him, wine delicious. And the bodies of women, when he was a young man, how they had haunted him! When you married and took on responsibilities, you had to learn to turn your eyes away. Or there was trouble. And trouble...well, it wasn't worth the candle. Not for a busy man, respected in the community, financially important and as time went by a mover in political affairs.

But now...

Yet there had to be a price. In this case he knew very well what the price was: it was open warfare in his home. He was tempted, yes, but he had decided that the price wasn't worth paying and that he wouldn't think of it again when one day Jan said to him, "Bernard, you must take a second wife. It doesn't look good. You have to set an example."

He grasped at a straw. "I don't have time to look for one."

"Make the time."

He felt terror, and a huge relief.

He went to see a man he knew: a soap manufacturer who had a small factory by the river. He had done well under the old order and employed four men. However, it was months now since he had taken anything out of the vats at all. There was some ingredient he couldn't get.

Dolling walked with Josef through the deserted factory. The smell of soap seemed to cling more fiercely to the walls than it had when the place had been turning out barrels of the stuff every day.

"There's a time for everything," Dolling said, putting an arm on Josef's shoulder. "The time for soap is past."

"I never thought I should see the day."

"We should consider using the premises for something else." Dolling was thinking of gunpowder. It was a good solid building, well sited.

Josef said, "If I could find a way of making soap with what we have…"

Dolling changed the subject. He said he was receiving excellent reports of this neighbourhood: two weeks in succession it had come first for punctuality on watch. This reflected credit directly on Josef as neighbourhood leader.

Josef smiled wryly. "Don't worry," he said. "I know what you've come for."

They went up the lane to his house. Herbs were drying in a roomy kitchen and there were jars of pickle on shelves. A dog got up from the floor as they went in, approached to sniff at Dolling's knees and then retired under the table. Dolling was offered a mug of beer, which he accepted.

As he sat sipping it, Josef's wife came in. She greeted him warmly but, he thought, apprehensively, and took her place in the corner with some sewing. Josef, who had gone into the garden for something, came back and sat down heavily on the bench. The two of them looked at Dolling.

"I would like to marry your daughter," he said.

The girl had been virtually hidden by her family as soon as the proclamation was read. Dolling knew they thought her too young to marry, but she was fourteen and it was a foolish idea born of over-fondness. She could not be kept out of sight indefinitely, and the longer they hid her the worse it would be for them when she was discovered. And one thing was certain: if Dolling didn't marry her, someone else would.

Anna burst into tears.

"The last thing I want to do is cause you distress," Dolling said. "But you know the laws, and Marianne can't be exempted from them."

"It's just that we'd hoped for a bit longer," said Anna.

"She's only fourteen," said Josef.

"It's old enough," Dolling said. The dog whined in its sleep under the table.

"I'll fetch her," said Josef, and started to get up from the bench. Anna rose. "I will." She left the kitchen, carrying her head high.

Dolling found nothing to say. He and Josef sat listening to Anna's footsteps receding into the house, the opening and closing of a door, a stifled cry. At length, again footsteps.

A child stood in the doorway. No, she was a woman, it was just a trick of the light.

Dolling rose from his seat. "Marianne, I have the honour to ask you to be my wife."

She was pale. Her eyes travelled up and met his. He felt the tiny shock of the meeting, and how much courage this required of her. He was moved.

She nodded without speaking.

On reaching home, Dolling went straight to see Lisabeta.

"I shall be bringing home a sister for you," he told her.

She was playing with her squirrel. She had taken it out of its cage and was feeding it nuts. The creature was quite tame and would perch on a chair back with its curiously long feet, or stand on the tablecloth and nibble something you gave it.

"How can you bring me a sister?" she laughed.

"Ah, well, you'll see."

"When will she be here?"

"Tomorrow."

"Is she older than me, or younger?"

"Two years older."

"What's her name?"

"Marianne."

"Does Mother know she's coming?"

He hesitated. "Of course she does."

"Who is she really, Papa?"

He sat down. He handed her another nut, and she placed it carefully in front of the squirrel on the tapestried cloth, withdrawing her hand not too quickly so as not to startle it. The animal stooped, seized the nut in its flexed paws and straightened up again in a single flow of movement.

"She will help your mother," he said. He had been going to start off by talking about the law, but decided that she would think that an evasion.

"How?"

"This is a big house, and there's a lot to do."

"Is she a servant?"

"No."

"And I know she isn't my sister, because you've never mentioned her before. And in any case I know she isn't my sister because of the way you said it. Papa, I'm not a child. Who is she?"

He swallowed something in his throat. "She will be my second wife."

A great wail came from her. The squirrel vanished.

"And she will be your second mother. And a sis…"

"I've got a mother!"

She stamped her foot, weeping. He took hold of her and clasped her in his arms.

"Listen, darling, we have a new law now, and people have to do things…"

"You don't have to!"

"Yes, I do."

"I don't believe you."

Some men, he thought, would not tolerate this from their daughters.

"I knew as soon as you told me! I knew as soon as you came into my room!"

The squirrel had reappeared on the curtain pole. He rocked his daughter in his arms. "I didn't want to hurt you. I didn't know how much you knew…"

"Everyone's talking about it. And do you think I can't hear what goes on downstairs when you have a meeting?"

He wondered why one even tried to keep a secret from women.

"It won't make any difference to us," he said. "You'll see."

"Of course it will. How can you say that?" She broke away from him and went to the Flemish chest of drawers he had given her for her last birthday. It had a pretty beading of carved vine leaves around the top. She took a square of cloth out of it and blew her nose.

"Whatever difference it makes," he said, attempting to settle the matter, "it is going to happen."

She was about to cry again. He had had as much of this as he could stand. Besides, he had something else to do.

He kissed her hot, damp head, and left the room. He walked along the passageway and down the stairs to tell Sara.

Martin and his wife faced each other across the narrow board.

"For pity's sake, Susi," he said, "it is not my fault."

Without taking her eyes from his face, she dug her knife into a strip of cheese, so hard that the wooden plate unbalanced on the table's uneven surface and skidded to the floor. Silently, and still looking at him, she bent to pick it up.

"Susi, I have done nothing," he said.

She had not spoken to him since he got home. He had come through the door to find her seated by the fire, motionless, with a piece of sewing in her lap. As he closed the door behind him she had risen to her feet and fixed her eyes on him. Wordlessly she had backed away as he moved forward to kiss her. She had turned and busied herself at the stove, every movement and angle of her body forbidding him to come near her. He had not, he was not so foolish.

Now they sat over their meal. She had not eaten, beyond a mouthful. He had forced down the food, and now it lay in his stomach like a stone. All the time, she had watched him. He would have thought she had lost her mind, were it not that her gaze was entirely lucid.

He said, "I shall not take advantage of this law." He was ashamed at once. He wiped his knuckles across his mouth, tasting the gunpowder he had been handling. It had parched his skin.

She watched him as he reached for his tankard and took a draught from it. "Won't you?" she said.

He was greatly relieved that she had spoken. But the voice was strained and distant, not like her voice. He smiled at her; there was no answering smile.

He looked down at his powder-stained hands. "What can I do?" he said. "I didn't make this law. Lord knows where it'll all lead. And us having a child soon."

Her hands were clasped over her belly, as if his last words had put them there, and her eyes remained fixed on his face.

"This need not make any difference to us," he said with sudden resolution. "Others can do what they like. They can live like animals and pretend God has given them leave to do it."

He saw, with astonishment, her small hand move to rest on his. "Be careful, Martin," she said.

"Careful?" He was confused.

"Mind what you say." Her eyes moved to the door.

He clasped her hand between both of his. His heart expanded with devotion and gratitude. It was all right. It was again the two of them against the world, as it had been when they were just married and had to leave his parents' house because his father thought he had married beneath him. Two, he thought, and soon to be three.

"I'll make a cot for the baby," he said. "It won't be long, now." With one hand he cut a slice of cheese and gave it to her. "Eat."

She smiled a little.

"It'll be a boy," he said.

"You know, of course."

"I do."

"It had better be a boy," she said, "because only boys are worth anything now."

"Susi…"

"Too many women. Like too much of anything, the price goes down."

"Susi, I love you."

"You're a kind man, Martin, and you're a good husband, but you will stick a knife in my heart all the same, because that is the way things are going here."

He went on his knees in the rushes that strewed the kitchen floor. He said, "As long as you live, I will not take another wife."

Rothmann had a visitor one evening. It was a man called Mollenbecke, whom he knew but not well. There was something in Mollenbecke which discouraged intimacy. He bore himself with a stiffness which suggested pride but was probably just extreme reserve. Before the rising he had been a member of the Town Council, and a strong Lutheran.

He came to see Rothmann after dark. He shut the door with a glance into the street behind him and, shaking rain from his hat, walked into Rothmann's flagged kitchen.

Rothmann offered him refreshment. Mollenbecke refused it and sat down at the kitchen table. He put his head in his hands for a moment. When he raised it again, Rothmann saw his cheeks glisten.

He came straight to the point. "Rothmann, you've always been a man one can speak plainly to. Are you still?"

"I am still."

"Well, then. I don't think it's right, marrying more than one wife."

Rothmann waited. He had known this would happen.

"I don't believe it's in the Bible, whatever that Dutchman says. No-one will ever convince me it's the will of God we should marry like Turks and breed like rabbits. And what's going on is a scandal."

"What is going on?"

"Men who used to be respectable citizens behaving like a pack of wolves. This is not the New Jerusalem. He's turned it into Sodom."

"The marriage edict has the support of the Elders and the weight of law."

"Whose law?" Mollenbecke said with contempt. "There's only one person whose voice counts in Münster now."

Rothmann let this pass.

"It's said you don't agree with it," said Mollenbecke. "That you argued against it. Is that true?"

"I argued against it at the time. Now that it's law, I accept it. Why have you come to see me?"

"You're the only person who can help us."

Rothmann knew he should get rid of the man at once. But he went on sitting across the scrubbed table from him, held by a kind of fascination.

"Us?" he repeated.

"Myself and a number of like-minded friends."

"And you are like-minded to what purpose?"

Mollenbecke's features stiffened even further. "We are agreed not to accept this law. We will resist it with our lives."

"And you want to take me to the scaffold with you?"

"There's a lot of feeling against this godless tyranny. If we have your help, the people will support us."

"Do you think so?" Rothmann ran his fingers along the clean grain of the table top. "You seem to forget we're at war."

"I don't forget that. I love my city and I want to serve it. But I no longer know what we're fighting for."

Not a day passed when Rothmann did not ask himself the same question. The answer he found was that, as long as they could hold the city, the path of truth was still open. If through stupidity or weakness they let go the one place where the Gospel had begun to be practised on earth, there was no hope for them, and perhaps none for mankind. This answer still, just, sufficed.

"We're defending ourselves," he said, "against the rest of the world, and specifically against Franz von Waldeck, who wants to reclaim his diocese."

"As far as I'm concerned, he can have it."

Rothmann felt a reluctant stirring of admiration for the man.

"Once I would have laid down my life for this city," Mollenbecke said. "But I can't live like this. There's no holiness in it."

"You don't seriously expect to involve me?"

"You're the leader the people want."

"I don't think you know what the people want, Mollenbecke."

Mollenbecke got to his feet. His movements were heavy. He picked up his hat, said that he was sorry to have disturbed Rothmann and made for the door.

"Mollenbecke, forget this, whatever you're doing," said Rothmann. "Leave it to God, I beg you."

Mollenbecke opened the door and went out.

8 War

Dolling was awoken at about three o'clock in the morning by a sound which disturbed him by its stealth. It was a muffled footstep under his window.

He was wide awake instantly. He swung his legs to the floor and felt under the bed for his father's sword. He had it in his hand when they rushed the outer door and came storming up the stairs.

He stepped out of the bedroom to meet them. They were below him on the stairs and he had a chance if there were only a few. But he saw in the lantern-light that there were perhaps ten.

"Drop your weapon," said the man at the front. Dolling recognised him: he had had a saddler's shop in, appropriately, Horse Lane. "You don't want your wife hurt, do you?"

They were frightened. They looked as if they'd run him through for the slightest unexpected movement. Dolling let the sword clatter on to the floorboards. Behind his back he could feel Sara peeping in terror around the bedroom door. They began to hustle him out of the house half-dressed. He protested that at least he must have shoes, and one of them went back to get a pair and flung them at him. He thrust his feet into them clumsily, feeling the prick of the swordpoint in his back.

In silence they went through the empty streets. It was a clear, starry night, a bad night for a conspiracy. Dolling searched the darkened houses with his eyes for signs that they were being watched. He was trying to work out who was behind the plot, and how much of the town the conspirators held. He thought it could not be much, or they wouldn't be so jumpy. An armed group was waiting at the entrance to Vintners' Hall. He glimpsed a few faces he knew. Well-to-do Lutherans. He was marched up the two shallow steps and inside. They took him through the assembly room and then through a small door at the back. He was hurried along a narrow passageway and down a flight of stairs.

There were stone flags underfoot, and the air was close. A narrow door was unlocked and opened; hands pushed him inside. As the door slammed, cutting off the lantern-light, he was plunged into pitch darkness.

He waited for his eyes to adjust, and took in the heavy smell of wine and wood. At least he would have something to drink. He groped around, and after a couple of steps encountered barrels. He groped further, found one at a height he could sit on, and sat.

A small, barred rectangle of grey began to define itself at about shoulder height in the blackness. Dolling was looking at it when there came a tramp of feet in the passageway, the door was flung open and another prisoner was thrust inside. He did not need to hear the voice to know who it was. He was flooded with relief.

"Who's there?" said Jan as the key turned.

"Bernard."

"Ah!" He laughed. "They got you, too. Well, what are we going to do, my friend?" He seemed in a remarkably good humour considering the circumstances.

Shortly afterwards they were joined by Rothmann, which answered a question in at least Dolling's mind.

It was getting light.

"Who's behind this?" Dolling asked.

"Some fool called Mollenbecke," said Jan. "Do you know anything about him?"

Dolling was surprised. "He was a town councillor. Lost his seat in February. He was a Guildmaster at the same time that I was."

"We should have made him an Elder, and then he would be quite content." Jan had been sitting on a barrel; he now got up and began to prowl the cellar. "Does either of you have a knife?"

No, they didn't. Or anything else either.

"They won't pull this off," Dolling said, unconvinced.

"It seems to me they have," said Rothmann.

"They haven't succeeded until they've killed us," said Jan. "They should have done that first." He pulled a small barrel off a stack, laid it on the floor and rolled it experimentally with his foot.

The door opened again to admit Krechting, fuming at the indignity of being in his nightshirt. In the end, there were about twenty of them in the wine-cellar with the barrels and it had become very crowded.

The morning began to pass with excruciating slowness. From time to time the prisoners heard quick footsteps in the street outside, and raised voices. Once a group they presumed to be rebels rushed past with a great clatter of weapons, but it must have been a false alarm because afterwards everything was quiet. The men in the cellar tried shouting, pressing themselves close to the little window, but no-one shouted back. There was nothing to be seen through the window but a brick wall a few hands'-breadths away, with a trail of ivy growing up it.

Then, at last, there came to Dolling's ears a sound that was different from all the other sounds they had heard, and on which he fastened with the first hope he had felt that day. It was like a river in spate, and it was the sound of hundreds of running feet, coming closer.

A man was standing on the stone horse trough between the Cathedral wall and the trees, making a speech, when Martin came off watch. Around him had gathered a large crowd, mainly of women, which was held back from the speaker by a ring of men with drawn swords.

Martin strained his ears to hear what the man on the trough was saying. He could get only snatches of it. Something about marriage.

"What's going on?" he asked the woman next to him.

"That's what we'd like to know," she said. And indeed it was an unfriendly-looking crowd.

The man on the trough was not an orator. He looked ill at ease and his gestures were stiff. He started to say something about their freedoms being restored to them, but angry voices in the crowd demanded to know what he was talking about.

He shouted, "I am talking about true Christianity, sisters."

This incensed the woman standing next to Martin, who yelled back, "We've got the Christianity we want, thank you very much, and we don't need any of yours!"

"Papist!" began to be shouted. Also a number of other names for Catholics which Martin was surprised respectable women should know. The men guarding the speaker looked uneasy and fingered their swords.

The man on the trough made a renewed effort. Pitching his voice so it could now be heard right at the back, he cried, "The Dutchman has tricked you! He is a liar, a fraud, he is leading your souls into perdition."

"What are you going to do about it?" jeered a woman somewhere. "Open the gates to the Bishop?"

At this a great roar of anger came from the whole square, and the man on the trough went chalk-white. Suddenly — Martin did not know where the movement had begun — the crowd was surging down the narrow alley into Highmarket, abandoning the speaker to gesticulate on his perch. Everybody was running, the women hoisting up their skirts and running over the cobbles as if the town were on fire. Martin ran with them, not having any idea where they were all going or why. As the crowd rushed down Ludiger Street, women staring from the doorways of houses lifted up their skirts, too, and joined it.

A cluster of armed men standing outside Vintners' Hall threw down their weapons and flattened themselves against the wall as the tide rushed down the street. The vanguard of the little army checked only for a moment at the steps before pouring through the entrance into the building.

It took two days to crush the rebellion. Not because of the size of it—the core of the conspiracy involved only fifty men—but because of the desperation with which the conspirators fought once it became clear that the townsfolk would not follow them. After fierce skirmishing in the streets, they barricaded themselves in one of the massive siege-towers which reinforced the north wall. Its stonework was five feet thick. From its embrasures they fired a stream of arrows and shot at anyone who approached them. Towards the end of the second day this stream diminished. They were running out of ammunition.

"Leave them there to rot," said Dolling. They had no source of water. But Jan wanted it over and done with. He sent men up to the top of the tower with grappling irons at the same time as others were ramming the door with a tree trunk. It was soon done.

The rebels fought as if they wanted to die, but Jan had given orders that they should be taken alive, and most of them were. They were executed over a period of days. The bodies were displayed along Highmarket. It was a warm summer and the stench soon became very unpleasant.

Rothmann, who lived at the top of Highmarket, could hardly avoid using the street and deemed it unwise in any case to make an obvious detour. He held his nose and averted his eyes as he walked past the meat-shop of bodies. But he felt he owed it to Mollenbecke to look at him. The Guildmaster's limbs hung horribly after his racking: he could not have walked to his death. He had been garrotted with an iron collar which, as it closed, drove spikes into his neck. Around the caked blood the flies buzzed eagerly. His wax-white face was already sunk and blackening.

Rothmann wondered if Mollenbecke had betrayed him. If Mollenbecke had talked, the fact that he had not betrayed Mollenbecke was quite enough to make him one of the corpses on display. Therefore Jan did not know that Mollenbecke had come to see him. But perhaps he did know, and for some reason was biding his time.

Well, after this there would be no more rebellions. Mollenbecke had been a fool, Rothmann thought: the rising had had a patrician flavour which nobody liked, and most people in Münster still believed themselves to be freer under the new regime than they had been before. Moreover, men with several wives were not going to give them up again. Nevertheless the part played by the women in rescuing the leaders from the cellar surprised him. He was forced to admit that plural marriage might be more popular with the women than he had imagined it could be. "Women who have no hope of a husband will put up with a great deal," Jan had said to the Elders when they protested that no woman would be content to share a man. Rothmann had thought this unpardonable cynicism, but perhaps he did not know very much about women.

A state which would have to be rectified. Jan had ordered him to marry. Not one wife, but two. Following Mollenbecke's revolt, which had been openly directed against the new marriage arrangements, failure to marry a second wife was now regarded as disloyalty.

Rothmann took refuge from all this in an activity he knew. He was writing a short book, which he thought of as a series of connected sermons or pamphlets, explaining Anabaptist beliefs. Among other points, it defended community of goods and the abolition of money and rank as these things were practised in Münster. It declared its faith in the New Jerusalem (without claiming that perfection had been reached there), and it called on Anabaptists in other regions to throw off the shackles of worldly government and wait for the coming of Christ.

It would be entitled "Restoration," and it would be his testament. He had had to seek Jan's permission to write it, but Jan to his surprise had encouraged him. Fortunately not all the printing presses had been destroyed after the book-burning. The book would be smuggled out of the city and taken, he hoped, far afield. He was not sure how to deal with the issue of wives. He was leaving it for a later chapter.

Sister Agnes's new life had begun the day after her arrival at the cottage by the river. She got up early, washed her face under the pump and set to work. She riddled out the stove and laid the fire. She had a look in the larder and there didn't seem to be much, so she made some bread with the flour that was there and put it in the warm. There was a bit of smoked fish and some cheese: she thought, with the bread, that would do for breakfast. Then she swept the house with a broom she found in the corner, and washed a couple of dirty shirts and hung them over the bushes to dry. Georg and Karl were still snoring, so she put the bread to bake and went for a stroll.

When she'd come to the cottage the evening before, the lane, the riverbank, the hummocky roof and the hawthorn tree with its straggling branch reaching out to the door had been like the shadowy drawings of a picture that still had to be finished. Now, in the early morning light, it was all complete and every inch of it full to bursting with life: the ground so thick with blades of grass, and every blade quivering and dew-beaded, and home to scuttling ants and beetles; the river thick with fish, and green with luscious weed and scum; the air thick with birds and thistledown, and more birds atwitter in the trees and flashing faster than sight between the thorn bushes, and everything so joyfully the thing it was, the grass so green, the mud so slippery and brown, the birds so quick and feathered, and all of it praising God, and so did she.

She wandered along the path a little way, and then went down to the riverbank. She didn't mind that her skirt was soaking wet from the dew and her thin shoes had turned into boats of mud. The grass was very high and lush at the bank's edge, but a few feet from the bank it was trodden short in a narrow, muddy path which she began to follow.

The river meandered. It was very quiet. She drank the quietness in through her skin. On the opposite bank she could see some large, empty-looking buildings, factories she supposed, no longer making anything, and behind those she could see housetops and treetops and the steeples of churches. Smoke was rising from the roofs in long grey ribbons. It went up and up into the pale sky, getting more and more like gossamer, until it wasn't there any more.

On her side of the river she couldn't see any houses at all for quite a long way. What she could see were some low stone buildings without windows which she couldn't imagine the use for until suddenly, climbing over a low wall that came right down to the river's edge, she came upon a field of horses. All tethered and peacefully grazing the rich grass.

She wandered through the field, talking to them and touching their noses. She thought how Brother Ignatius would have loved to see them. He was always happy in the company of creatures, but especially of the big ones. It was their feet, he had said to her once: he loved animals with big feet.

The thought of the bread came to her. She picked up her skirts and ran, greatly startling the horses, who were just getting used to having her in their field. She ran and skidded and slid all the way back to the cottage, thinking what a terrible way to start her married life, burning the bread.

When she reached the cottage, Karl and Georg were sitting at the table, and between them, done to perfection and with the steam still rising off it, was the bread.

"We thought you might have gone," said Karl.

"I didn't," said Georg.

"I went for a walk along the river," she said. She turned round and there were a trail of muddy footprints all across the kitchen floor she'd just cleaned.

"Is that bread ready to eat?" asked Karl.

"No," she said.

"Yes," said Georg. He took the knife out of his belt and cut it.

They ate hot bread and cold cheese. A bird sang on the hawthorn branch.

"D'you reckon you'll stay, then?" asked Georg.

"Tell me what he was like as a husband," Jan said.

"What a strange question."

"I don't think so."

She got out of bed, pulled a coverlet around her and went to the window, which was half-shuttered.

"What are you doing?" he said.

"There's something happening in the street."

"Why won't you answer me?"

"Because what can I say?—Jan, two men are fighting!"

He could hear it. Running, blows. It had become quite common.

"Aren't you going to stop it?" she asked.

"Someone will. Come back to bed."

She lingered at the window.

"Come away before you're seen, Devera."

She obeyed him, then. He wondered if she had ever disobeyed Matthys. She came back and sat on the edge of the bed.

"Tell me what he was like," he ordered.

"What do you want to know?"

"Everything."

"Then you must tell me where to start."

"What did he call you?"

"Wife." She pulled the coverlet around her and added, "But at the beginning he called me 'Sister'."

Jan laughed. "Presumably his relations with you were those of a husband?"

A blush rose on her cheek. "Yes."

He slid his hand under that convenient coverlet and found the warm nest at the top of her thigh.

"What did he do?"

"Just the act which babies are born from."

"Was it what you expected?"

"Jan, I was in a convent from the time I was twelve. I knew nothing about men."

"That is not what they say about convents."

"I don't know about other convents, only the one I was in. The nuns were kind to me. I was happy enough."

"Why did you leave, if you were happy?"

"I wanted to know the world. No-one asked me what I wanted when I was put in there."

"Was Matthys kind to you?"

"I don't know what you mean."

"I mean, was he kind to you? Like the nuns?"

"He was a man" She paused. "And he believed he was sent from God."

Jan caught her wrist tightly. "Wasn't he?"

She looked a little frightened. "That's not for me to say. If he was, I don't understand his death. If he wasn't, I don't know where he got his strength from."

He could not have given a better answer himself. He relaxed his grip. But then the next question began to hurl itself at him, like an incoming sea at a cliff, and he could not stop it.

"Do you think I am sent from God?"

An indrawn breath. Then, steadily, "Only God knows that."

The perfect reply. Too perfect: a rebuke. He felt his blood gathering. Then he recalled that he loved this woman and loved her passionately.

He drew her towards him and kissed her on the mouth. The kiss drew him down and down into a dark softness like the heart of a flower.

He pulled himself away, seeing on her face the dreamy smile that women have when they are kissed, as if something deep, deep in them is being fed. He would not ask her where she had learnt to kiss like that.

"You still haven't really told me about Matthys," he said.

She sighed. (He would make her pay for that sigh.)

He took her hand and guided it under the blanket to his towering flesh. "Was he like this?"

The blood flooded her face. She said quietly, "Jan, why can't you leave him in peace?"

He flung the blanket aside and made her lie down. He parted her legs and entered her without gentleness.

Later, he walked through the streets. Where the fight had taken place there was a pool of blood seeping into the dirt of the road. He touched it with the tip of his shoe.

Things had got out of hand.

With the proclamation of plural marriage, a feverishness had taken hold of men. It was as if, once the iron rule of one-man-one-wife was lifted, they could accept no further constraint at all. There were brethren who demanded in marriage the hand of every unattached woman they saw, and within days had a household of wives who fell over each other, bickered, refused to do the household chores since there were so many others to do them, and did not accept the authority of the first wife. This example stimulated other men, rather slower in taking advantage of the law, to sudden frenzied efforts of wife-getting when they saw what was happening, lest in a short time there should not be any surplus women left, or at any rate none that were worth marrying.

After a few weeks had passed, however, even the most enthusiastic supporter of the measure could not ignore what everyone knew, that many of the women dragged before a marriage official had not been willing. They had been terrified, or had been told — against the explicit wording of the Edict — that they had no choice. There were stories of young women being taken literally at swordpoint from their families, of wives who were only children weeping all day and all night for their homes, of bands of men lying in wait for a woman as she went on some errand and rushing her off to the marriage office to be contracted to one of them. There were tales without number of new, young wives cruelly treated by existing wives, and other tales of wives more evenly matched who quarrelled until the household fell apart in chaos or came to blows. A new prison had to be opened in one of the towers just to accommodate marital offenders.

"We must permit divorce," Jan announced.

The Elders muttered unhappily. Rothmann, who had fought plural marriage tooth and nail, now—foolishly, Dolling thought—began to protest against any diminution of it.

"Changing the meaning of marriage is not the answer," Rothmann said.

Jan looked annoyed. Everyone could see that he was getting very tired of Rothmann.

Someone said, "We've already changed the meaning of it.""

"No, we haven't," said Jan. "We've returned to its first meaning, which is the begetting of children."

"It's a knot that may not be untied," persisted Rothmann.

"Well, it will have to be, if we aren't to legalise abduction and rape," said Jan. "These excesses have brought discredit on us."

"What does that matter?" protested Krechting (who had four wives and was reported to be looking for a fifth.) "The rest of the world thinks we're damned already."

"I'm not talking about our enemies," said Jan, "I'm talking about our friends."

He was quite right, realised Dolling. Without the aid of the Anabaptist communities in the Low Countries, they could not sit out the siege for any length of time. How Münster conducted itself was vital.

"Our brother is right. We must have divorce," he said.

The mood of the meeting had already begun to shift. Jan always got his way in the end, and it looked as if this time the Elders had decided to spare him, and themselves, a protracted battle. The Dutch of course were always with Jan in any case. Rothmann gave Dolling a wry look. It was a pity, Dolling thought, what had happened between himself and Rothmann, but probably it could not have been avoided.

Jan said, "The law must be re-framed. If the marriage official suspects that the woman is being forced into marriage, he must refuse to perform the ceremony."

In the distance, one of the Bishop's cannon discharged itself against the ramparts, and the wind carried to Dolling's ears the jeer of the defenders. Summer, he thought, it is summer already, and we have held them off for a quarter of a year.

"And we must put right mistakes that have been made. Women who have been forced into marriage must have the right to petition for divorce before a magistrate."

It took a moment to penetrate. Then: "The wife may divorce the husband?" yelped Krechting, his little eyes popping.

"Well, of course," said Jan mildly. "How else can it be done?"

All round the room, Elders burst into excited speech.

Jan raised his hands. "Brothers, keep calm. They will still have to have a husband!"

Marriage had become like buying a pair of shoes and taking them back if they didn't fit, Rothmann thought. At least Mollenbecke had been spared that.

When Dolling had told Sara that he intended to marry again, she was preparing a piece of meat in the kitchen. She turned on him with the knife in her hand and such a blaze in her eye that he stepped back.

"I am required to take a second wife," he said. "I have to set an example."

"You are required," she said, mimicking him with biting scorn. "And do you have someone in mind? Yes, I see you do. When are you bringing her home?"

"Tomorrow."

All the colour drained from her face. She put the knife down. He had time to reflect that women were strange creatures: if she'd been a man, that would have been the moment at which she used it. She held herself rigidly upright, one hand clenched on the table where the meat was sitting in a puddle of blood, and asked, "What is her name?"

"Marianne."

"And how old is she?"

"Fourteen."

"I see."

Dolling feared the worst when, the next day, he brought his new bride to the house on Highmarket, but to his surprise Sara was ostentatiously kind to her. She showed Marianne the room that had been prepared for her, hung with pictures and decorated with flowers—Dolling did not know anything about these preparations—and asked her what she liked to eat "at home." This annoyed him and caused Marianne to burst into tears, at which Sara put her arms round the girl and comforted her, favouring Dolling meanwhile with a look he could not interpret. Thereafter she looked after Marianne as if she were a daughter, and indeed addressed her as "daughter" instead of the "sister" she was supposed to use.

Marianne, naturally enough, responded to this affection—if affection was what it was — gratefully. Dolling observed, with some dismay, a bond growing between them. The tighter it grew, the greater grew the distance between both of them and him. He had long given up hope of his relations with Sara, but with Marianne he had intended to start again. She was a young virgin, on the threshold of life and ready to be moulded. He intended to love and cherish her, and hoped that she would love and honour him. But he found little joy in their intimacies after the first delicious night. Her body might be his, but the rest of her lay beyond his reach. And if she was dutiful, what use was duty to a man who wanted love?

The other member of the household whose behaviour had concerned him was of course his daughter. For the first few days after Marianne's arrival, Lisabeta locked herself in her room and would not come out. She would not speak to Dolling at all, even through the closed door. Sara took food up to her, against his wishes. After a few days Lisabeta tired of this behaviour and rejoined the household. At the first meal they all shared, Dolling looked for signs of strain between her and Marianne, but saw none.

They seemed to have made some kind of pact. After that, he often heard them chattering in each other's rooms.

And in the end all three of these women seemed to be on their own island, their own little female island, separated by an ever-widening stretch of water from the island on which he stood, holding out a hand to them which they did not appear to see.

It was not what he had expected.

When Gustav, the neighbourhood leader, came to tell Martin that he had to take another wife, Martin was fitting the baseboards of the baby's cradle to the curved head and footboards.

Gustav the ratcatcher was a small and sharp-eyed man for whom Martin had always felt distaste, partly on account of his calling and partly because he gave himself such an air of importance. Gustav was one of the few people in Münster whose daily life had been virtually unaffected by the changes they were living through. He went on catching rats. The New Jerusalem had not succeeded in abolishing them.

Gustav seated himself on the bench in Martin's and Susannah's kitchen, spent a few moments in benign observation of Susi going about her business, rather slowly these days on account of her size, and Martin positioning the nail above the board with his left hand while readying the hammer with his right, and then said, "You know, brother, that there must now be two wives or more to each household, where the man is capable of fathering?"

Martin hit the nail off-centre and struck his thumb. Blood oozed from the wound and dripped on to the wood, staining it. Martin placed his thumb in his mouth and, with the hammer swinging lightly in his other hand, looked at Gustav with murder in his eye.

Gustav backed along the bench. "It is the law, brother." He darted a look at Susi, standing motionless by the table.

"Leave this house," said Martin thickly.

Gustav got to his feet. "I must warn you, brother, that the matter is serious. You have a week in which to take a second wife."

"And if I don't?"

Gustav lifted his little chin, and his small beard wagged. "It's not for me to say. But if the Elders choose to make an example of you..." He let the words hang there, and grow like fruit. "The best way to protect your family is to observe the law."

"It's an ungodly law," burst out Susannah.

Gustav turned his head to look at her. He said, "Perhaps the presence of a second wife would curb the spirit of the first." He walked to the door and opened it. "Good night, brother. Take thought."

Susannah did not cry. She carried on with her work in the kitchen, her head held high, and when Martin spoke to her she replied calmly. In a strange but intimate quietness they went on with what they had been doing before the ratcatcher came. Martin measured, fitted and nailed strips of wood with great care. He tapped each nail in as gently as if the unborn child were watching him. As if by gentleness he would vanquish Gustav.

When it was late, they went to bed. Martin blew out the candle and lay down heavily beside his wife. He felt exhausted. He lay looking at the ceiling, where a pale reflection flickered: a lantern somewhere. Then he heard voices in the street. Men returning from the first night watch. The life of the city went on, whatever the private griefs of its people. The voices made him feel alone, as if he was floating by himself in a vast sea.

He turned on his side and put an arm over Susannah, crooking his elbow below the great curve of the belly. She put her hand on his and turned her head towards him.

He kissed her long and tenderly. She sighed, at last, and pushed his face away with a light pressure of her fingertips. He let his mouth graze along her hairline, with its always mysterious smells of wax, violets and apples.

Then she laid a hand on him, between his thighs, and at once his organ, half-aroused already, sprang to life. He turned his face into the straw pillow, groaning. Desire, grief, anger, love and fear, all in one huge lump he had to swallow, made him want to weep.

She began to stroke him upwards with her fingertips. It was forbidden, what they were doing, doubly forbidden. But the fingers were like silk, they were a silk net that with every stroke grew subtly stronger. Her mouth returned to his and hung barely touching it, teasing and tickling, while her tongue darted between and across his lips. All the time her fingers went on stroking, and the net tightened, and he was at the same time flying and drowning, banqueting on delicacies and rushing to Hell. How she must love him, he thought, to do this when she was tired and with child and profoundly distressed; and then, unforgivably, the thought intruded of another woman's hand doing what hers was doing, at which the urgency of his onward-rushing flight became uncontrollable and then it was too late, too late, too late.

He lay there, cradled in her arms like a second baby, feeling the pool of wetness against his thigh. With the hand that had stroked his manhood, she stroked his hair. They fell asleep.

In the morning Susannah rose early and, when he awoke, summoned him to a breakfast of freshly made sweet pies. He sat across the table from her, noticing that she had tidied herself and put a clean apron on, and that there was beer on the table as well as milk. His heart ached. None of this would help, but how could he blame her for thinking that it might?

As he raised his eyes from the food to her face, she met his gaze with a strength and directness which astonished him. He had expected supplication.

"Martin, you must do what they say," she told him. "Otherwise they will punish you. You must find a woman and marry her. For my sake, if not yours."

One morning in high summer, the Bishop's heaviest cannon broke their silence with a dawn barrage. A lookout on duty on the outer wall was trapped by falling stone as the wall gave way under him. He was the first casualty of what was later known simply as the Battle.

The bombardment continued without respite until nightfall. As one gun fell silent, another took up the task. Under this titanic hammering the stone of the defences split and clove, or was knocked clean out of place, leaving a rent in the fabric through which the grass of no-man's-land could be seen.

The Münster guns replied. By nightfall, when the firing ceased, a pall of choking dust hung over the ramparts. In the unreal quietness, hundreds of women, walking in line and carrying stone and masons' tools, went up to the walls and began to repair the damage. Working by shrouded lantern-light, they pulled away the heaps of rubble and rebuilt the stonework so that it was again solid.

They worked all through the night. As they worked, they listened to the singing in the Bishop's camp. His soldiers were celebrating early.

The bombardment went on for three days. On the fourth the assault came. The sentries, peering at dawn through the veils of mist that hung over the meadow, saw what seemed to be a phantom army moving towards them.

At once, every gun on the ramparts spoke. Gunfire cracked in reply from the advancing, shadowy line, the powder-flashes luridly illuminating the haze, and several defenders on the outer ramparts fell. The ghostly shapes emerged from the mist, became abruptly flesh and blood, flung down bridges across the moat and streamed over them to climb the embankment on which rose the outer wall.

That wall was now thronged with men armed for close combat. They had flails, axes, swords, pikes, javelins, stones and slings. The flails were the most vicious. Jan, seeing the need for an effective weapon which could be handled by an untrained man, had ordered the smithies to turn out hundreds of them. They had the reach of a pike, and from the shaft of each hung, by a chain, an iron ball set with long, angled metal spikes. They could pierce armour, break a man's legs, remove his face or disembowel a horse with equal ease.

The first wave of the attack was borne by the Bishop's mercenaries, who rushed the defences with arrogant confidence. Looking down, Martin saw how the enemy line lapped all along the battlements, flinging up missiles and ladders, rearing up like a vast scaly serpent. As fast as a ladder was thrown down, another was raised somewhere else. Up the ladders, as soon as they touched the wall, swarmed the hired soldiers with loot, rape and murder in their faces.

Martin threw himself into the fray. A trooper was coming towards him like a figure in a nightmare, but he was blundering, blinded by gunsmoke. Martin lunged forward with his sword, and the man fell with his throat laid open. Martin pushed him off the wall, and saw him land on top of another soldier who had just set his foot on the ladder. The other man fell, and lay motionless. Martin dropped a stone on another helmeted head and turned to help Rudolf, beside him.

On another part of the walls, Jan fought his way through the smoke and confusion, slithering in the blood that already covered the parapet, to the most vulnerable part of the sector, St Maurice's Gate. There he found Dolling in the thick of the fighting with a cut on his forehead.

"Are you hurt?"

"It's nothing. We need more men on this gate."

"They can't be spared."

"They'll have to be."

Jan made his way back, with difficulty, to the south-east sector, where he took fifty men off the inner wall and sent them to Dolling. He filled the gap with a thin spacing of crossbowmen and arquebusiers from the round towers. Then he went to the place where the pipes had been laid.

A fire had been lit under a brick stove, and on it water seethed in iron cauldrons. Beside the stove was a lead-lined tank, from which ran the pipes. They would direct the water to the walls. Men in leather jerkins, and wearing thick leather gloves, stood by for his order. He told them to cover their faces against the steam with the cloths they had ready, and to pour the water from the cauldrons into the tank. The steam rose in a dense, lethal cloud. Jan flung his arm across his face: he had not thought of a cloth himself. Half-choking, his skin burning, he waited until the emptying was finished and then pulled the lever that operated the sluice.

There was a roar, a hissing like ten thousand snakes and a series of what sounded like small explosions as the boiling water ran through the labyrinth of metal, leaving behind it a white mist like gauze. He heard the second, more diffused roar as it erupted from the outlets built into the walls in a scalding torrent. A moment later, the screams reached him of men boiling like crabs in their armour. He ordered the cauldrons to be refilled and put back on the fire.

After that, he hardly knew what he did. He was touching off a cannon because the gunner had fallen. He was running a man through with a lance. The blood gushed from the man's mouth in exactly the same way as he'd seen water gush from a fountain in Antwerp. He was grappling with a trooper as big as Samson, who would certainly have killed him, but a Münster man came up behind and demolished the trooper's head with an axe. Mostly, he was running, clambering and shouting. Orders, encouragement, urging his men on, hoping when his voice was almost gone that under the grime, blood and soot they recognised him.

By the middle of the afternoon it was clear that the assault was weakening. By this time, the ground beneath the walls was a grim sight. Men lay with their brains beside them on the grass, with their skin separated from the flesh by blisters as large as plates, with their limbs hacked off. The small dips and hollows in the ground where normally dew collected and birds might make a nest now brimmed ankle-deep with gore. Over fallen bodies ladders lay tumbled, and on top of the ladders yet more bodies, flung from the ramparts or beheaded by cannon or pierced by a crossbow bolt or crushed by stone or scalded by the merciless water.

The defenders, seeing victory in their grasp, fought on for two more gruelling hours. But before dusk fell the retreat had been sounded, and the Bishop's men came out under flags of truce to pick up their dead.

The Münster wounded were taken to the infirmary, and the dead to the churchyards. The captains began a last round of the stained and pitted walls.

At those walls there later gathered the people of Münster. They held torches, so that the light of the city would be seen for miles over the plain. They sang, for the world to hear, a psalm of praise to God who had preserved His Jerusalem.

As the singing rose from the walls, a man called Dusentschur, who had once been a goldsmith, was taken up to Heaven and entrusted with a task.

9 Behold, I Make All Things New

In the days after the victory, the breaches in the walls were repaired, the blood was washed from the parapets and the dead were buried in the knowledge that they would soon rise again. The city rested. A watch continued, but it was clear there would be no further assault. Viewed from the ramparts, the camp seemed almost deserted.

Two days after the battle Dolling went to find Jan, whom he had not seen since the singing at the walls on the night of victory. Jan now had a household of several wives, and had moved into one of the mansions on Highmarket. Dolling was told by one of the junior wives that Jan was not seeing anyone at all at present. No, he was not ill, she said, in reply to Dolling's anxious enquiry: he was at prayer.

Dolling went on with what he had intended to do. He collected ten good men and set out on horseback to look at the camp.

They kept close to the wall at first, riding in tight formation and keeping the horses at a fast trot. But it was soon apparent that there was no danger. The camp was like a cornfield through which a storm has raged. Great gaps interrupted the ring of tents, and some had been pulled down and left lying in the grass like huge empty wineskins. The flaps of others were tied back, allowing a glimpse of tumbled belongings abandoned in haste. The Bishop's own tent, a splendid crimson creation which had arrived to dignify the camp when the weather improved, was not to be seen.

A few cooking fires were burning, and near them crouched surly-faced troopers. They watched with indifference as Dolling's little company rode by. Here and there men were cleaning equipment, grooming horses or carrying out other tasks, but with a lassitude that could be felt even at a hundred yards. No-one sent a shot after them. No-one even raised a jeer.

The only response, in fact, came from the dogs, a yelping pack of which pursued them as far as St Maurice's Gate. Facing the gate was a culverin which had given the walls a lot of punishment. Now it stood alone and untended on its wooden carriage, around which the ground was churned to glistening blackness. The land was marshy there: the troops had tried to move the thing but it had stuck fast.

A team of horses and some stout ropes would do it, Dolling thought. The important thing was to know the ground. A Münster man would not have put the culverin there in the first place. He was certain they could get it back inside the city. He led his men the remaining circuit of the walls without incident, and back through Ludiger's Gate.

At home, he removed his armour and went again to speak to Jan. He knocked on the outer door and, getting no reply, pushed it open and went in. For a moment he stood inside the threshold, listening. What he heard reassured him. Jan was talking to someone in an upstairs room.

Dolling walked down the passageway and went upstairs. The kitchen door opened behind him as he went up and a woman's face glanced out, and was immediately withdrawn. As he reached the top step the voices in the room ceased.

The door to the living room stood ajar. Framed against the window were Jan, holding a sheet of paper and tapping it with his finger, and a short, thickset, bald man whom Dolling did not know. Both turned to look at him as he approached.

"Good afternoon, Bernard," said Jan coolly. He did not introduce the other man.

"I'm sorry to interrupt," said Dolling. "I wonder if I could speak to you alone?"

"No, you may not," said Jan. "You can say whatever you have to say in front of brother Johann."

On brother Johann's face was something Dolling interpreted as a smirk. He said, "I'll come back when you have time to see me."

"No, you won't," said Jan. His face was pale and his manner was both abrupt and excitable. "You pushed your way in here, although you were told I was seeing no-one. You'd better tell me what you want."

Dolling's throat had gone dry. "I've been to look at the camp," he said.

"Oh, the camp." Jan gave a sneering laugh. "Is it still there?"

"There is still an enemy camp."

"Well?"

"They've abandoned the culverin facing St Maurice's. We could capture it."

"Is that all?"

Dolling pressed on. "I think we could send the whole lot of them packing. There are only a few men left, and they're demoralised."

"There's nothing there," said Jan. "You're dreaming. Just a lot of empty tents."

Dolling was speechless. The little fellow—how ugly he was, he looked like an ape—was now grinning openly. He put Dolling in mind of those small dogs which bark at people from behind their masters' legs.

"It's time to move on to new things," said Jan. "Anyone who doesn't understand that, or can't move on when moving on is necessary, has no place here."

"Move on to what things?"

"We have to thank brother Johann for a great revelation. Tomorrow he will speak outside the Cathedral, and everything will be made plain."

Perfection

By evening Dolling knew that brother Johann's name was Johann Dusentschur, that he came from Osnabrück, that he was subject to visions and that he lived in a small house in Fishmarket with two wives and three children. None of this was helpful.

Dolling had no wish to go to the Cathedral square the next morning and take his place among the multitude who were to be enlightened by brother Johann. However, there was no other way of finding out what was going on. He left the house with his wives and daughter as late as he could, hoping the square would be crowded and he would have an excuse for standing at the back. Unfortunately, as soon as people saw him they began making way for him, and he was obliged to go to the front.

At the front were Rothmann and his wives. He had married sisters, perhaps to save himself the trouble of choosing twice. Rothmann had always protested that he had trained himself to celibacy and did not know the difference between a pretty woman and an ugly one. However, the wives were not more than twenty and were very pleasant on the eye. Dolling decided that Rothmann was a hypocrite. He didn't know why he had never thought of this before. He smiled and nodded at Rothmann, who smiled and nodded back.

The apelike brother Johann had appeared, carrying a leather bag, and was climbing up to the platform that had been erected. Behind him came Jan. Behind Jan, at a discreet distance, came twenty-four Dutch guards marching in formation. Jan took his place next to Dusentschur on the rostrum, and the Dutchmen took up position on either side.

The little bald man began to speak. Dolling listened with growing scorn. A high-pitched, flat, nasal voice, which went oddly with the man's squat frame...saying what? Giving them his credentials for being up there, that was all. His virtuous life, his three children, his visions. The first vision had shown him where the true faith lay, the second had told him to leave Osnabrück. The third had revealed Münster to him (before Matthys had announced it) as the Holy City. The fourth had told him that after the death of Matthys a Saviour would arise for the people. The fifth...

Now he came to it. It was the fifth revelation they were gathered here to listen to. He launched into a long description of the circumstances — it had been after the great battle, he was in his room giving thanks — and of how afraid he had been of the message he was entrusted with, but an angel had reassured him...

Dolling could listen to no more of this. He turned his mind to a question which had recently preoccupied him: whether the arrow-slits in some of the defence towers should be widened to permit the use of artillery. Against the obvious advantages had to be weighed the drawback of weakening the structure; nor would it be a simple matter to get the guns into position. All the same it might be worth trying with a single tower, perhaps the one on the north-eastern sector where the wall curved to make almost a right-angle...

"This is the man whom God has chosen to be your king," said Dusentschur clearly.

There was no response for a moment or two. The word was impossible and could not have been uttered. Then a ripple of shock began to spread through the crowd, and at the same time Jan, with clasped hands, knelt. From his knees he then bowed himself forward until he lay prostrate on the platform.

"Praise God!" shrilled Dusentschur, "for this is the fulfilment of the prophecies. He has given us a King who shall reign over us until the throne is taken by Our Lord Himself!"

"Praise God!" suddenly cried the preachers, who must have been prepared beforehand.

There was a silence.

A few paces from Dolling, Rothmann cleared his throat. "Praise God!" he murmured.

"Praise God!" said Dolling, his wives and daughter.

"Praise God!" came from various parts of the crowd.

After another uncomfortable interval, Jan allowed himself to be lifted to his feet by Dusentschur. He closed his eyes in silent prayer, then, raising his face to Heaven, he cried, "Father, make me worthy of Your throne!"

"Amen," said Dusentschur devoutly.

"Amen," echoed the preachers.

Dusentschur now produced from his bag a shiny, circlet-shaped object which he held up with both hands for everyone to see and then placed carefully on Jan's head (now lowered, because otherwise he would not have been able to reach it).

Even the people (and there were quite a few of them) who had had difficulty understanding what was happening could see what this meant. After all, as Dusentschur was later to explain, it was only a model, hastily made from tin and coloured glass to give an idea of the real one on which work would commence the following day in the re-opened workshops, but still no-one could be in any doubt that it was a crown.

He had simply never thought about it. He had not thought about what he was engaged on, he had not thought about the prophecies he quoted for their usefulness. He had not believed in any of it.

That memory now made him shudder. How had he imagined he would fare on Judgement Day, squirming and worming under the enormous eye of God? But he had managed not to believe in that, either.

From time to time he was overcome by feelings of terror, and fell to his knees. He prayed fervently that his past might be blotted out. There were still moments when he felt in imminent danger of the fires of Hell, he seemed to see himself standing on the edge of a vast precipice with those fires burning like malign rubies far below him. He had deserved those fires, he deserved them still. It was only by an unlooked-for outpouring of grace that he was spared.

"Praise God," he murmured, "for He has redeemed His servant."

And in how strange a way!

The man had been frightened, and trying to hide something under his coat. When Jan asked him what he wanted, he could only stammer at first.

"If you have nothing to say, go," Jan had said.

The fellow began talking about a vision. Jan stifled a yawn. He had business to see to, including a new, young Frisian wife. He started to wander round the room as a way of making his visitor feel unwelcome. When he turned round, he saw with horror that the man was on his knees.

"Get up! What are you doing?"

"God commands me to kneel," said the wretch humbly. In an almost inaudible voice he added, "Your Majesty." He was shaking like a leaf. Still shaking, he produced that object from beneath his coat. That ludicrous, terrifying crown.

"Matthys would have had you executed," Jan told him.

But after he'd thrown the fool out, he could think of nothing else. He set the crown on a shelf above the fireplace. He had kept it because something about it obscurely pleased him. After Dusentschur left he realised what it was. Light of weight, deceptive, gaudy—it was a player's crown. He had worn one like it when he played Herod.

The memory of his acting days, instead of amusing him, plunged him into a strange melancholy. It seemed to him that he had been freer then than he was now, when he had a house and wives and a city did his bidding, and the eyes of that city were constantly on him. A sudden terror seized him that he would have to give this up, too—though how he could he did not know — turn his back on it as he had eventually turned his back on everything, not because it was itself insufficient but just because that was the way he was. He perceived that he was trapped as anyone else, but that while they were trapped by circumstances he was trapped by his nature. He had thought Matthys would rescue him from this. For a time it had worked. But in the end no-one could rescue him.

He sat and looked at the crown. It was as insubstantial as he was. As meretricious. As stupid. He could crush it with his foot, and for a while was on the point of doing so, but he could not summon the will to get up. He went on sitting there, and the longer he sat the more impossible it was to move. It was as if a huge hand was pushing him down into the fabric of the chair, stilling his breath, turning his blood cold and sluggish. In the end it would freeze and he would still be sitting there, a block of stone.

Time passed. Dusk began to fall outside the windows. He despaired.

"Open the Book," said someone in the room.

He knew he had heard it because the room had changed. There was something there that had not been there before. A sort of clarity, as if all the objects in the room had become more sharply themselves.

His heart was pounding like a hammer. Strength flooded into him through his feet, as if coming from the floorboards, and he stood up quickly. He walked to the small table on which Matthys's Bible rested. It had lain unopened for weeks. It seemed to him he had never seen it before. Its great bulk. Its mystery. Closed up inside, its myriad armed and glowing letters.

"Open the Book," he heard again.

He dared not touch it.

But as the moments passed and the presence in the room grew ever clearer and more commanding, he dared not disobey.

He put out a hand and parted the leaves, halving the book roughly. He allowed his gaze to drop to the thicket of print, but before it had alighted a sentence sprang out of that thicket and swooped into his eyes.

"The blessed man is come, having his sceptre in his hands."

His knees began to shake.

"Open it again," commanded the Voice.

His hands, less roughly now, closed the great volume and then, after a fearful interval, opened it a second time.

"The days are now coming, saith the Lord, when I shall make a righteous branch spring from David's line, a king"—the word smote him—"who shall rule wisely, maintaining law and justice in the land."

"Again," said the Voice. The room was full of light and he was nearly fainting.

"Behold, my servant shall prosper, he shall be lifted up, exalted to the heights."

He closed the Bible and turned wildly away. He said aloud, "Who is the servant?"

There was no reply.

He cried out, "Am I to be king?"

A door somewhere in the house slammed in a gust of air and the tin crown fell from its perch above the fireplace. He watched, rigid with fear, as it dropped on its rim and rolled towards him.

He realised then that he had no choice, and had never had any. He was the helpless instrument of the Power he had mocked. He began to weep. The tears came from some place beyond him and coursed through his body like an autumn torrent. He knelt, racked by sobs, on the floor with the tin crown in his hand. Jehovah came to him and flung him into the whirlwind. He prayed to be released, but there was no release for him that long night.

Dawn found him drained of all strength, but at peace. He knew what he was, and what he had to do. It was a task that would have made even Matthys quail.

The New Jerusalem was a kingdom!

That was the message the preachers now delivered from morning until night. This was the beginning of the golden reign at the end of time which had been foretold in Scripture. They were living in the nearest thing earth would ever see to Heaven.

"Praise God!" ordered the preachers.

"Praise God!" murmured the people, before dispersing to go about their business. It was a blustery autumn; a boisterous wind tore leaves from trees before they were ready and sent them swirling over rooftops. You could not stand listening to a preacher in this wind. They went away as if infected by the wind's impatience. They could not understand what a king had to do with them. They had received no visions telling them they must have a king. They were bewildered, and waited to see what this new state of affairs would bring.

The king appeared one day on horseback, riding slowly through the streets. He was dressed in silk and brocade. A green velvet cap embroidered in gold covered his head, and round his neck hung a heavy gold chain with a jewelled pendant. Jewels sparkled on his fingers, and golden spurs twinkled on his heels.

A pace behind him rode the chief queen, Devera. Behind, on white ponies, came the five junior queens. All were dressed in a manner which had not been seen in that austere city for many months. Behind the queens, on foot, came the body of men who until recently had been the Congregation of Elders but were now the Council of Ministers. Among them was the new prophet, Dusentschur. At the back, looking as if he would rather be elsewhere, walked Rothmann. Six paces ahead of the procession marched a detachment of the bodyguard carrying pikes, and another detachment brought up the rear.

The procession emerged from the lower end of Highmarket, turned west and, keeping the Cathedral on its right, entered Horse Lane, passed the Church-by-the-water, crossed and re-crossed the river and went on in an easterly direction until it had come in a full circle with the Cathedral at its centre. Then it set off along Fishmarket towards the walls, where it wheeled south, passing three of the city gates, including the one Matthys had ridden out of, before turning up Salt Street and returning to the royal apartments.

This event was witnessed by comparatively few people, and those who saw it were not sure how to react. There were no preachers in attendance to tell them what it meant. Accordingly, they could only use their eyes, and their eyes told them that the gold was gold and the silk was silk, and the king's horse was a very fine stallion.

Then a throne covered in gold leaf was erected on a platform in the marketplace. It was explained that the king would sometimes come here to judge lawsuits, because he took very seriously the administration of justice. The people of Münster began to realise that their role in the new kingdom was to be subjects; but that, more than that, they were spectators.

Jan had been all affability when Dolling went to see him a second time.

"Bernard!" he cried, as Dolling was awkwardly bending his knee. Dolling had no idea how to behave in the new situation. He glanced around for brother Johann, but could not see him.

Jan placed an arm round his shoulders. "I have a lot to talk to you about. We must sit down straight away and make a start. So much to do!" He laughed, and steered Dolling towards a map which was lying on a table. After a moment or two Dolling recognised it as the map he had drawn for Jan nine months ago, on the eve of the uprising. Many details had been added since, and more streets had been marked in.

Jan leaned over the map and pointed to a street with his finger. It was the curving street called Breul which followed the north wall. "Street of the Watchman," he said. He pointed to what Dolling had always known as Salt Street. "Tabernacle Way."

He moved to Fishmarket. "Street of the Loaves and Fishes." The finger rested on the Cathedral square. "Mount Zion." He looked at Dolling. "What do you think?"

Dolling returned his look blankly.

"We are going to rename the streets! The districts and the city gates, too. Everything."

"Why?"

Jan laughed gaily. "Because everything has changed. The city of God has become the Kingdom of God. How can we go on using the same street names?"

"Oh, I see."

"Renewal! Away with the old! That's what we're called to do!"

His laugh was new, too.

"I think," said Dolling carefully, "that people will find it confusing."

"What does that matter?" Jan studied the map a moment longer, then asked, "What do you think of Dusentschur?"

Dolling's tongue stuck fast in his mouth.

"You aren't very talkative today, Bernard. You don't like him, do you?"

Dolling pursed his lips and bent his head towards the floor. It was not exactly a refusal to reply.

"We need Dusentschur," said Jan. "God has chosen to guide us through him." He fixed Dolling with a serious gaze. "The revelation didn't come to me, you know. I was given my own revelation, and I shall never forget it, but it was Dusentschur who had the vision itself."

Whatever had happened to him, Dolling thought, something had happened. "Dusentschur must have a place at my right hand." Jan paused, considering. "As must you, of course. I need both of you."

Dolling inclined his head. Jan smiled brightly. It was the smile that went with the new laugh. "You must be Chief Minister," he said.

This time Dolling bowed. The king seemed to like that.

"We must have a court."

"A court?"

"Well, naturally. This is a kingdom, so it must have a court. We must do everything properly. Court procedures, manners of address, liveries." He shot Dolling a humorous, inquisitive look. "Do you know about that sort of thing?"

"No," said Dolling with a heavy heart.

"It's very important that we do it right. There isn't much time. We have to make a kingdom out of nothing. Well, nearly nothing. And it has to be perfect. Nothing short of perfection will do. Do you see that?"

Dolling swallowed to ease a constriction in his throat.

"Dusentschur will help, I suppose. He's very talented. He used to be a goldsmith."

"So I hear."

"We shall have to find something for Rothmann to do. Where is Rothmann, by the way? I haven't seen him for weeks."

"He's writing a book."

"That's no excuse. Do you think he had anything to do with that Mollenbecke business?"

"I'm sure he didn't," said Dolling, who was not sure.

"I hope you're right. I don't want to have to execute him."

As Dolling was taking his leave, Jan said, "Bernard, I hope you don't think I wanted this. It was as great a shock to me as it is to you."

Sister Agnes was very happy with her husbands. She had no preference between them, and thought of them, in a way, as being one person. Nevertheless there were obvious differences between them. Georg had a big chest and a beer stomach; he had thick black hair and a beard which he trimmed short and square, and he was short and square himself. Karl was thinner and a hand taller; his hair was brown and wavy and he wore it long to his shoulders, and he took more care generally of how he looked than Georg, who spent all his patience on trimming his beard and had none left over for anything else. Karl said less, and thought more about what he did say, while Georg usually said the first thing that came into his head, but very often they were really saying the same thing even when they thought they were arguing.

Neither of them had ever had a wife. They seemed to have lived together in the cottage for years, working on the river and growing a few vegetables in the garden. (They had some planted now: onions, a few cabbages, some white turnips.) She wasn't curious about what they'd done before she met them: she didn't think it was any of her business. As for what she had done, there wasn't much to tell, apart from Brother Ignatius, but she told them about that and they laughed fit to shake the roof off.

Their life together had a regular course. She would get up first in the morning, and go to the kitchen to do the chores. When they had had breakfast, Georg and Karl would go up to the walls for their turn of duty. They looked handsome in their leather jerkins with their swords buckled on. She would kiss them both goodbye and ask the Lamb to look after them (which they didn't know about). Then she cleaned the house and made bread if it was needed, and she'd make a tasty stew for supper. It was beans more often than not, but there was nothing wrong with beans. If she had time she would do a little gardening, weeding the turnips and onions and picking a few herbs to dry. She had learnt these things in the convent, and now she was glad of them.

When she'd done all this she would have to go out, because it was time to collect firewood. Normally she would have gone out to do her stone-carrying duty at this time of day, but Georg and Karl didn't want her to because they said the other women would ask her questions about where she was living and who her husband was, and it was better not to get into a conversation like that. The walls didn't need repairing in any case, they said, which was clearly true. She hadn't heard a gun fired since the day of the Battle.

Jan constantly reminded himself that he was nothing, a leaf blown by the wind. His being king had nothing to do with his merits. It could have happened to anyone: God's election, being outside reason, could have fallen on any man walking out there in the street, whose deserts would have been equally irrelevant. But it had happened to him.

He knew he must cling to this idea or the fact would unhinge him. He could only keep his feet by remembering that he was not of his own nature the King of the Last Days, but as it were the player cast in the part.

He was aware of the great mercy in this. It preserved him. He would be consumed otherwise, a walking flame.

But he believed that this preservation was conditional on his remembering the gulf that existed between him and the figure he impersonated. If he forgot it, he was damned immediately and without reprieve. Anything, therefore, that kept this gulf present in his mind was good.

But also—and here was another great mercy—he had recently begun to realise that, just as there was no connection between his past actions and the role he played, there was no connection between that role and his present actions, either. How could there be? Everything he was and did, and might do, fell into that infinite gulf and was lost. It did not matter.

He began to see there was a path he must tread, although it presented itself to him differently at different times. Sometimes it seemed to him that, since his soul was unworthy of its great companion, he must mortify his soul. At other times he thought he must light up the gulf between them, as if by throwing fire into it. At yet other times he was transfixed by the idea that, precisely because it did not matter what he did, it was his duty to explore every forbidden thought and action as if mapping a new continent, and that for this reason and this alone had the kingship been given to a man so steeped in wickedness.

Amid all this, there shone the simple truth to which from the beginning he had devoted himself. His task was to bring a kingdom to birth. He had been given the place, the people and a small stretch of time. All his strength and that of the community would have to be poured into the transformation. God would not wait while he dawdled.

Before the renaming of the streets was finished, it was announced that the days of the week must also be renamed, since they were pagan. After that, it was obvious that new names must be chosen for the months, too, and perhaps also the seasons. Dusentschur suggested that they should rename, or rather renumber, the year, but Jan told him curtly that numbers were ordained by God, which put an end to innovations for the time being.

Meanwhile other signs of the new order were everywhere to be seen. Dusentschur had designed an emblem for the kingdom: it showed a globe pierced by two swords (signifying the king's dual power, both earthly and spiritual, the preachers explained), the whole surmounted by a crown. This design now appeared worked in gold thread on court liveries, emblazoned on the flag that flew over the royal barracks, stamped at the bottom of the numerous proclamations that were nailed up giving out the new names of the streets, and engraved on the windows of the royal palace which, with the creation of a court and the steady increase in the number of the king's wives, now occupied several adjoining houses in Highmarket. And it was embroidered on the gold cloth which covered the throne where the king sat to judge lawsuits in the marketplace.

He would arrive on horseback, dazzling the eye. The treasury had been ransacked for the jewels in his crown, on his fingers, on his breast. The Cathedral vestments that had escaped the flames now yielded the cloth for his robes. The townsfolk were silent as they watched, unless stirred into cheering by the preachers. Many were still bewildered by the advent of the Kingdom. Some meekly accepted everything that happened as God's will, but others were silent because they did not dare to say what they thought.

Houses were being visited again by the deacons, who were carrying out further requisitioning. Goods were still unevenly distributed, the deacons said, there were still immigrants in need of clothing. Perhaps there were, muttered householders who saw a necessary shirt or pair of shoes disappearing into a deacon's bag, but you only had to turn your eyes in the direction of the court to see a lot of immigrants who were not in need of anything at all.

It was at this point that the new prophet, Dusentschur, had another and very unpopular revelation. God announced that there was still some extravagance of dress among the ordinary people and that this was abhorrent to Him. So here came the deacons yet again, sniffing about for a bit of forbidden lace or a jacket sinfully slashed to show off the lining. Not that anyone had worn such things for almost a year. So the deacons seized anything, since they had been told they must seize something, and took it off to the Town Hall, which was now the Hall of the Covenant.

The general feeling was that it was time Dusentschur had a revelation telling him to go back to Osnabrück. He did not, however.

Dolling hated the court. It wasn't so much the meaningless protocol the King and Dusentschur had invented, although he was impatient with that. It wasn't the fancy costumes, although he was embarrassed by his and would gladly have traded it for the sober black cloth, trimmed with sable, he had worn a year ago. No, it was that the court had spawned a race of people who apparently had nothing to do. Every time he went to the palace he had to elbow his way through roomfuls of gossiping Dutch courtiers. The knowledge that some of them were gossiping about him did not improve his temper.

It was the waste of time that infuriated him. He did not think time was any less precious now than it had been when they were struggling to organise themselves in the first days of the siege, since the siege was not over, although everyone behaved as though it were and Jan refused to discuss it. "We must continue with the watch," Dolling had said, "we need to replenish the cannon shot, we ought to…" "Then see to it," said Jan, "but don't bother me with it." He had been studying keenly, as he spoke, a design of Dusentschur's for some fiddle-faddle or other. What had it been? A coin! They were to have coinage again! But it would be purely ornamental. The King's head on one side, and no doubt that wretched globe on the other. Dusentschur's initials, "J.D.," in a modest corner.

More tents had sprung up in the past week. The camp had an air of activity which Dolling did not like. He liked still less a report which had reached him from Koblenz. Franz von Waldeck was there, and having meetings with the Duke and the heads of other German states. He was trying to put together a new alliance. He had been trying, admittedly, for nine months. What disturbed Dolling were the names on the list. Jülich-Cleves, Cologne, Essen…Even Philip of Hesse had sent a representative. These were not men who, having made up their minds, would weaken or run out of money.

Dolling elbowed his way through the throng in the royal apartments and enquired where the king was to be found. Consulting with the prophet Dusentschur and not to be disturbed, he was told by some smirking flunkey.

Dolling said, "I imagine he will see his Chief Minister."

Dusentschur was speaking as he entered the room, and the king, seated with various preachers, was listening respectfully. As

Dolling closed the door behind him, Jan raised his head and fixed him with a curious look.

Dusentschur stopped speaking, and for a moment nothing broke the silence. Then, "What have you come to tell us, Bernard?" asked the king.

Dolling said he had received a report that the Bishop had been holding meetings with other princes in Koblenz.

The king's brow puckered. "Of what interest is that?"

"Your Majesty, he is putting together a new alliance."

"What of it?"

"It will be a formidable one."

"We are preparing for the Second Coming of Our Lord Jesus Christ," said Jan. "In readiness for that sublime Event, everything in our city has been transformed. Even the streets have been given new names. Brother Johann has now made a valuable suggestion about the celebration of the Sabbath. He has reminded us that there is no Biblical warrant for holding it on Sunday. We are considering what we are called to do about this. That is what you have come blundering into with your bits of paper."

Dolling had in his hand the letter which a man had risked his life to bring through the Bishop's lines. He folded the creased and stained paper carefully, and put it in his pocket. Keeping his voice level, he said, "My Lord, if the Bishop can forge this alliance we shall be faced with the most serious danger we have yet seen. Furthermore, other princes, seeing the alliance, may also decide to join it, since it will promise to be successful. There are many distant rulers who look on us as a threat. They did not expect us to survive so long, and our survival is an encouragement to Anabaptist communities in their own lands."

There was a shocked silence when he finished speaking. Eventually Dusentschur said, "These victories were granted us by God. How can you speak of them in such a manner?"

"Exactly," said Jan. "Brother Johann has put his finger on it, as usual."

Averting his eyes, because he knew the creature was smirking, Dolling said, "I am in charge of the defence and it is my business to think about these things. If I give offence in the way I refer to them, I apologise."

Jan smiled thinly. "That's an apology, is it? Well, the fact is that you're wrong, Bernard. The Bishop has never been able to raise an army worthy of the name, and there is no reason why he should now. The Emperor won't support him because the war against the Turks is more important, and without an order from the Emperor none of the Catholic princes will give him more than two gröschen-worth. And the Lutherans don't want to get their hands dirty."

"They gave us a bad shaking when they came in the summer."

"Nothing to the shaking we gave them."

"But they will come back," insisted Dolling, "and this time they won't make the mistake of expecting an easy victory."

"You're determined to have your battle, aren't you, Bernard? It will come when God decrees it, and its outcome will be what God decrees."

Dolling had heard all this before. Matthys had said it. However, Matthys had not been sitting in a velvet-upholstered chair embroidered with a gold crown and playing with a jewelled bauble when he said it. Repugnance and despair spread through Dolling together.

"Don't you know, brother," bleated Dusentschur, "that the whole earth is promised to us?"

"The earth? If we don't have reinforcements, we won't even hold the city."

Jan said, "You are the only person inside these walls who doesn't understand that the time for such considerations is over. You're like a boy who can't stop playing soldiers."

Dolling excused himself and left the room.

"Restoration" was written, and the proofs lay before him.

Rothmann picked up his pen, dipped it in the ink and laid it down again. He had been unable to concentrate all morning.

With resolution he picked up the pen once more and read a page. As luck would have it, it was the part about the abolishing of rank and title. As he read his own high-minded words, bitterness collected in his mouth.

He gazed at the perfect page of type — not one mistake, the printer had done his finest work — and found tears clouding his eyes. He wiped them away with the heel of his hand. No point in giving in to weakness. Every man had his cross to bear, and this was his. He read on, his hand hovering at the edge of the paper.

His mind rebelled. This cross was a monstrosity, and no-one could carry it. It wasn't God who had placed it on his shoulders, it was the Devil.

He leafed back through the printed sheets. Here he had written of human history as a series of falls and restorations. The fall of Adam from Paradise, the restoration through Christ. The fall of true religion in the century after Christ, and its eventual restoration in their own times...

He should have started with the fall of Lucifer, he thought. For he, Rothmann, had also been blinded by pride. He had believed he was shepherding the people towards the truth, and that no-one else could take his place. He had been shown how wrong he was when Matthys arrived. The state of affairs he had worked steadily towards was suddenly achieved overnight. From that moment on, he was mercilessly punished for his presumption. Every word was taken out of his mouth before he said it. The new Dutch leaders didn't trust him, and the preachers undermined him. It was impossible to explore what God's will might be with the men who now ruled the city, because they were convinced that they and no-one else knew what God's will was and all debate sounded to them like treason.

He supposed he was a coward, and that was the miserable truth of it.

He put his head in his hands. Rothmann, that lion among preachers! Rothmann, fearless champion of the oppressed! Mollenbecke had come to him for help, but he had refused it. Afraid to help a brave man take up arms against tyranny. He had seen Mollenbecke's tortured face in his dreams for weeks.

But Mollenbecke had intended to hand the city over to the Bishop. Rothmann could not have accepted that.

But then again, Mollenbecke had to hand the city over to the Bishop because he could not govern it himself. He was not a leader of men, and he had no vision of where the community should go, only a clear idea of where it should not be going. If Rothmann had joined him, Rothmann who had once been a lion among preachers...

He groaned. Yet even now he knew he could have done nothing else, taken no course but his shameful inaction, because if he had had the will to seize events then he would have done it before Jan arrived.

Jan.

Worse than Matthys, far worse, a snake of so many skin-sheddings you could not keep up with his transformations. Now they had the most abominable of all. A king! Robed and crowned. In a city where rank and title had been abolished. Which triumphant renunciation was celebrated in the book he was about to publish.

He could not see the print for tears.

By the time Dolling reached his house, he was boiling with anger. Not even Matthys had so humiliated him in front of his peers. Nor had Matthys ever acted with such coldness and calculation.

It was Dusentschur's doing. What else could it be? It was only with the little ape's appearance that Jan's behaviour had changed.

At first, Dusentschur was all Dolling could think about. He schemed the upstart's death in a dozen ways. Sword, noose, throwing from the battlements, poison, an accident with a firearm. None difficult to encompass, if he could be detached from Jan's protection. But there was the problem. Moreover, if Jan persisted in his regard for the horrible creature, it would profit Dolling nothing to do away with him unless the blame for the deed could be cast on someone else. In fact he was so angry and filled with hate, while nursing in a corner of himself the knife-thrust of Jan's coldness, that he did not care what happened to him as long as he could have his revenge.

But as he was contemplating with pleasure the image of Dusentschur swinging purple-faced from the gibbet in what was now called Penitence Place, it came to him what a stupid error he was making in mistaking the monkey for the piper. Jan was not a man whose mind could be swayed in this or that direction by every new voice that spoke in his ear. Dolling had never known him to be swayed by anyone at all, in fact: he had preserved his distance even from Matthys. If he was listening to Dusentschur, it was because for some reason it suited him to do so. What that reason could be Dolling was unable to imagine: he had never been able to see far into Jan's mind, it was a place of mazes, mirrors, precipices and bottomless lakes. But if he looked squarely at what had happened in the past weeks he was forced to admit that only one person could bear the responsibility for it.

It was hard for him to admit this, because he cared for Jan. He had never felt so close to any man — not to any other human being, except his daughter. It wrenched his heart that Jan should throw him aside. He had been deceived in the man. And he had been made a fool of.

He thought bitterly of intimate conversations in which he had entrusted Jan with confidences he would never have poured into the ear of anyone else. His domestic troubles, his hopes for his daughter, his fears that his past as a capitalist might have damned his soul, his doubts in certain matters of belief. Jan had listened with such understanding—or Dolling had thought he did. Perhaps he had not been listening at all, but amusing himself with some private sport at Dolling's expense, or perhaps thinking about something else altogether. Then, the confidences Jan had shared with Dolling!—or so Dolling had thought. But what could they have been but empty wind, mockeries? As he recalled conversations held as the two of them walked the length of the walls, or inspected the weapons in the armoury, or sat over a glass of wine and a dwindling candle in Dolling's house (Jan's own lodgings in those days being cramped and uncomfortable), it seemed to Dolling that Jan had always given the impression of imparting something from the depths of himself, precious childhood memories or a young man's peccadilloes or—mirroring Dolling's own confessions—a discreet reservation about something Matthys enunciated as an article of faith, but that, examined, these offerings were tawdry and shallow, and had an air of having been fabricated for the purpose.

Well, they had been fabricated for the purpose. Jan had invented them because he needed confidences to exchange for Dolling's, and he needed Dolling's because they gave him power over Dolling. He knows me inside out, Dolling thought with a chill. There was nothing in Dolling's heart he hadn't swept with that curiously cool, bright gaze. Dolling touched his own flesh protectively, as if to keep it from Jan. As if what he feared was some kind of demonic possession. And perhaps in truth he was possessed by Jan, or stood in imminent peril of it, because there was something insubstantial and much too quick about the Dutchman; it seemed indisputable that his flesh was somehow less fleshly than Dolling's.

And as he had invented his confidences, he had invented himself, was that it? Could a human being do such a thing? But then, what Dolling was on the verge of believing was that Jan was not a human being, but some kind of spirit which had taken human form. Dolling shuddered. His mind had run away with him. He could see madness lying in wait. He poured himself a measure of wine, mixed it with water and drank it down.

Invention. Yes, it was all invention. This man who had turned himself into a king was pure sham, pure mockery,. He had not meant a word he uttered, or believed anything he professed to believe. All of it had been vanity, pretence and the stealing away of people's souls. That was what Jan had done. He had stolen people's souls. He had stolen Dolling's.

Dolling was so shocked by this that he could not move a muscle for quite a long time. Then he clutched the wine jug and poured himself another measure, and raised it with a trembling hand to his lips. Perhaps it was not as terrible as that. He cast around for some hope. He found it in the memory of the great battle, when they had beaten off a fierce assault by professional troops. That victory they owed in large measure to Jan's leadership, his inspiration.

No, they did not. They owed it to him, Bernard Dolling, to his unstinting work, painstaking eye, resourcefulness and knowledge. They owed it to his lists.

He had made Jan.

That was what Jan had needed him for.

He drew his knuckles across his teeth, and bit them to feel a real pain and not the one in his mind. He bit them until blood filled the teeth-marks and overflowed on to his silk stockings. He sat watching the blood soak into the fabric. He had another pair in the chest. He had several pairs. He had slashed doublets and a fur cape. He had a different shirt for every day of the week, re-named or not, and shoes in what was conceived to be the latest fashion. He had a dagger with a gold-encrusted pommel and a ceremonial executioner's sword. He had to have all these: he was Chief Minister. He had made Jan, and in return Jan had told him what he was.

I am Bernard Dolling, he thought. I am not anybody's minister. A breath of freedom came to him from a seemingly very distant past: he felt the north wind on his face, and on his head the Flemish felt hat he had worn for years on his morning walk to the warehouse, and he felt the cobbles of a free, proud merchant city under his feet. He smelt herring on the wind, and the charcoal fires that drove the smelting works, and a drift of stench from the tannery. An unbearable nostalgia welled up in him for what had been lost, for what Jan and his Dutch vagabonds had stolen away.

Evening began to settle down over the city.

Hooves clopped.

Dolling felt the ends of the carved armrests with his fingertips. Good workmanship, even if done in a hurry. The King could not wait for anything. He would live to regret it, though. The wood was unseasoned.

Since the wood was unseasoned, it would shrink and the gilding would craze. The gilt would start to flake off. When the King got up from his seat, little specks of it would stick to his robe. They would gradually detach themselves as he rode back to his palace, floating down to the cobblestones to be stared at in wonder by the populace, convinced at last that the prophecies were true and the New Jerusalem was built of gold and gemstones.

Nearer, the hooves. The bodyguard was mounted, these days. He'd requisitioned every horse in the city.

People stood around the marketplace, pointing and gaping. At him. Then a faint cheer went up (the King liked to hear cheering, so the preachers were there to encourage it) from Salt Street, which was not Salt Street any longer. A pity: Dolling had always liked that name. As a boy he'd looked for the salt as he walked down it, fancying he saw it whitening the cracks between the stones.

All gone now.

A gust of wind drummed the canopy above his head, making a sound like gunfire. Then the King was in the square. Preceded by pikemen, flanked by mounted guards, but nevertheless with the air of a man alone.

He spurred his horse forward, and stopped only a pace away. Although the throne was on a dais, Dolling still had to look up at him as he sat his mount, and found the autumn sun at that angle shining directly into his eyes.

The horse lifted its feet and snorted. Dolling felt suffocated by Jan's nearness and by the heat of the horse and its sweet, rank smell. The King said nothing, and his silence pressed on Dolling like a ton of stone. His stare contained not even anger, but was like a stare from the depths of the sea.

At last he spoke. "By what right do you sit on my throne?"

Dolling heard his own voice from far away. "By what right do you sit on it?"

He felt the crowd sigh, and recognised that sigh. It was the sigh as the man condemned to death appeared before them.

"I sit on it by divine command," said the King.

"You sit on it at Dusentschur's prompting," said Dolling. A lightness had taken his head, as if it was already parted from his shoulders, and his tongue was loosened like a drunkard's. "An out-of-work goldsmith who wanted to make a crown. A prophet nobody listened to, until he thought of something that would make them listen."

"Hold your tongue."

Dolling's voice appealed to the crowd. "People of Münster, who is this man who calls himself your king? He came to this town a penniless Dutchman, the disciple of another penniless Dutchman. Now he sits on a gilded throne and calls himself the new King David. If he can be a king, I can be a king!"

"Can you?" said the King.

"Why not? I have as much right. I have more right. I have served this city for many years. I have watched over it, I have defended it with my sweat, blood and brains. His title was earned by my labours. I made him king!"

"God made me king," said Jan icily.

"Why do you believe him?" babbled Dolling. Still there was not a sound from the crowd, only an open-mouthed watching. "He can say what he likes, and no-one dares contradict. Just look at him! Look at his clothes, his jewels, his horses!"

"Do you want them?" said Jan. "You may have them." He took off the ruby ring that sat on the thumb of his left hand, and tossed it at Dolling. It struck Dolling's shoulder and fell into his lap, resting between his thighs. He took off his heavy chain with the pendant Dusentschur had made, and threw that at Dolling, too. Dolling caught it with a vague idea that it should not be damaged. Then he unbuckled his sword with the jewelled scabbard, and dropped it on to the cobbles. The horse whinnied uneasily.

"There you are," said Jan. "They're baubles. Their whole purpose is symbolic. You are the only person who doesn't understand that. They don't belong either to you or me, they belong to God."

He sat his horse, and watched Dolling. It was always the same. He was not one move ahead of Dolling, but several. He saw the whole game.

Dolling's lightheadedness was deflating, he felt himself spinning earthward. He thought, at least I know something they do not, and I will tell them it.

"It's a game," he said to the crowd. "That's all it is. Anyone could play it if they knew how."

Jan laughed. It was a harsh laugh with more satisfaction than amusement in it. Dolling thought he had heard that laugh before, in the days of his youth when he visited drinking-houses. It was the reckless laugh of a gambler who sees the stakes raised as high as they can go. He knows, Dolling thought. He knows that I know what he is, and I am dead for certain.

"Do you know how?" Jan asked.

"Oh, I can play the king," said Dolling. He pretended to bless the crowd. He had entirely lost his wits by this time. "God will come to you in the person of Bernard Dolling, and his kingdom will have no end."

"You are trying my patience," said Jan. He turned to the guards. "Take him away."

10 The Third Blast of the Trumpet

November came, and with it the return of the encircling tents. The men watching from the ramparts saw the gaps in the ring slowly filled up, the ring thicken and become several tents deep until the camp was like an endless street of canvas curling back on itself, a town without a centre. They saw cannon brought over the marshy ground by straining teams of horses, and saw more horses, fine cavalry animals, exercising in the meadows. They heard music, drums and laughter. They saw the fires burning at night. They began to think about what was being cooked on those fires.

Their diet was monotonous. In the summer it had been varied by fresh vegetables, but now it had gone back to beans and rye bread supplemented by the occasional cabbage, and with winter ahead it was unlikely to improve. There were rumours of feasting at the court.

The king told them the present state of things would not last much longer. These were the Last Days. Soon, all of them would be kings and queens. They would eat off gold plate and think nothing of it, he said. Rubies would be as commonplace to them as hazelnuts. The birds would drop pearls before them. When these things happened, they would understand how completely unimportant gold and jewels were.

Life was drab and cold in the New Jerusalem these days, and many people found it comforting to believe him.

Just before winter got its grip on the land, the King announced the fulfilment of another divine command. Apostles were to be sent out from the city, carrying the faith to distant parts. Twenty-four had been chosen, and they would travel in pairs, taking nothing with them except a day's food and a wonderful book which had been written by Rothmann. This book explained how everything that had happened in their city was vindicated by Scripture, and that Münster was the New Jerusalem.

The apostles were presented to the people in a ceremony in the Cathedral square, and God's protection on them was invoked.

Dolling had been put in the smallest, darkest cell of the prison. It was below ground, and to reach it you had to go through the adjoining cell, which was empty. They did not want him to have neighbours.

His cell had no opening to the light. Towards what he imagined to be the middle of the day a strip of paleness appeared on the ground at the foot of the door, and the darkness in the tiny, fetid space was slightly thinned. This blessing, the filtered residue of the dim light which reached the adjoining cell from a grating in its ceiling, lasted only a short time before it was withdrawn again and his cell returned to complete blackness.

Just about the time when the strip of light started to appear, the jailer brought him food. The door was opened a little way and a bowl of bread and slops was put on the floor. Every time the jailer did this, the cell was flooded for an instant with thin yellowish light. Every time the door, having been opened, was shut again, Dolling thought he should have used the chance to try to escape. He could have seized the door and pulled it open, hauled the jailer inside and disarmed him... But each time the door opened he was transfixed by the light, and then he had to dive for the bowl while he could still see where it was and before the rats got it.

The idea of escape was a fantasy. He knew this. It was just something his mind played with, and he allowed himself to play with it because to think about doing anything was a way of keeping the darkness at bay. If he did not keep his mind working, the darkness would swallow him.

He was afraid of losing his sight, although at the same time he believed he would not be there long enough to go blind. Didn't it take months? This fear was partly why he stared so hard at the light when it appeared.

He was afraid of losing the use of his limbs as well, and thanked God they hadn't chained him, so that at least he could walk the few feet of space the cell afforded him and flex his arms and hands.

There was a slab of stone, on which he sat and where he stretched out to sleep; it protected him from the vileness of the floor. There was a bucket, which he found by knocking it over. It had not been emptied after the previous occupant used it. There was nothing else, except the rats.

The cell was alive with them. As soon as the door clanged shut for the first time he had heard their squeaks as they bumped into each other in their hurry to investigate his boots. He had kicked them away, cursing. But they came back, however often he lashed out at them. He prayed that if they ate the leather they would not start on his feet. This dread kept him awake at first, but after a while he ceased to worry about it. He learnt to sleep, and disciplined himself to eat every scrap of the disgusting food that was given to him and to keep walking, until he was dizzy, the tiny space of his cell.

It surprised him that he wanted to live. He had thought the opposite when he was brought here. He certainly had not expected to live: he had thought he would be taken out and executed at any moment. Or perhaps that a man would come to stab him as he slept. If they took him out to die, he hoped they would not torture him first. He was afraid of that. But he was not afraid of dying. What was there to live for? He had left himself no chances of a life.

That was why escape was a fantasy. It was pointless. Where could he go? The whole city was in the pocket of the man who had put him in this cell.

He did not think about Jan, or about his own act of rebellion, which now seemed more fantastic than the wildest dream. He did not think about the court, the siege, Dusentschur or any of the things which had occupied his mind for months. He thought about being in a cell that had a window. About being in a cell that was not running with underground water and in which he did not see the lurid eyes of rats. Sometimes he thought about his childhood and the places he had travelled to when he was learning the business. He thought, in this connection, about his father, an old-fashioned man whose methods he had quickly discarded but whose morality he now surveyed with increasing respect for its gravity and justice. He thought about his daughter, Lisabeta, and as time passed he forgot the estrangement that had come between them and remembered only the happiness, the loving tie that had bound them for twelve years. It was Lisabeta he would live for. He would live for the sight of her, the sound of her voice.

If he was allowed to live. But as the days, if they were days, went by, a new dread began to take shape in his mind. It was quite possible that Jan had forgotten he was there.

A trumpet blast shattered the comparative quiet of the streets one morning. The inhabitants stared about them in fright, and then looked up. However, there was nothing unusual to be seen in the sky, which was grey and threatened rain.

They waited for something extraordinary to happen, but nothing happened at all. After a short interval, they went on with whatever they were doing. The more devout took it to be a sign the meaning of which would later be made clear to them. The rest assumed it had something to do with the guards' barracks near the Cathedral.

In fact the trumpet blast came from the watchtower of St Lambert's and the trumpet had been blown by Dusentschur, who, not having learned to play the instrument, was obliged to limit himself to a single note. He regretted this: he would have liked to play a fanfare, although the vision had told him only that "the trumpet shall sound three times." After waiting for it to sound for some days, he had received an illumination that he was meant to blow it himself.

It was the trumpet of the Lord all the same, whoever blew it. He felt, however, that not everyone would appreciate this, and that it might be better if he did not reveal that he was blowing it. For this reason he stayed inside the tower, and blew the trumpet at one of the window slits. The sound was slightly muffled. He did not think that mattered.

Jan, in his palace a short distance away, sighed with irritation. Almost everything had irritated him in the past week: Dusentschur, whose voice was detestable; his own wives, whose names he forgot and who competed for his attention; Rothmann, who was never to be seen and devised elaborate reasons for his absence; the court itself, which he had invented and set up for the glory of God, and which now seemed to him full of idiotic men and women wearing idiotic expressions and doing idiotic things.

He had known that the kingship would sometimes be a great mental burden, but he had not been prepared for the form in which the burden manifested itself. This was an irritation amounting to disgust with everything around him. Also with himself. He disgusted himself. That was the hardest to bear. Sometimes he looked in a glass and wondered who this ridiculous creature was.

The sundering from himself that he was forced to endure, the haunting by an overwhelming double, were at times nearly intolerable. He hated the splendid figure he was made to be, because he was not It; and that in him which was It hated the unregenerate part which dragged him down from the glory. Thus torn, tormented, sunk in self-loathing and terrified, at moments, that after all he had misunderstood God's will, he would spend hours or sometimes entire days in a dark introspection from which he longed to be delivered but from which he forbade anyone (because it was his destiny) to distract him.

Fortunately he had found a means of relief. He used it only when his blackness of mind was more than he could bear, because he was afraid of wearing out its efficacy.

He would go, with a small bodyguard, to one of the prisons. There were all manner of people there, who had committed all manner of crimes. Leaving his guard at the gates, he would visit the cells with only the jailer for company. He would talk to the prisoners and find out why they were there. He would select one, and then ask this prisoner to be brought to him in a private room. So far it had always been a man, although there were quite a number of women in prison, so he was told. Alone in the room with this condemned human being — they were all condemned, there was no hope for any of them — he would talk, and invite the prisoner to talk. In the end, they did. It was surprising perhaps, you might expect terror to paralyse their tongues, but in the end all of them took this last chance to bare their souls before a fellow-creature and make some kind of confession before they went to meet God.

He was astonished at the sort of thing they said. Astonished at the depth of, perhaps, their self-understanding, perhaps their despair. No conversations he had ever had had excited and moved him so much. Nothing held back, a pure and burning communication. And, in it (this was part of the excitement) he, too, laid bare his soul. He must, or they would quickly reach a point where they would go no further, unless he kept them company. Later he found he was cleansed and lightened by what he had said.

Thus exalted and moved, he would leave the cell. He would summon the jailer, and the prisoner would be taken into the courtyard and executed in his presence. This remedy never failed to calm him. He would be free of oppressive thoughts for several days afterwards.

So here now was Dusentschur blowing a trumpet on St Lambert's. The man did not know his place. Jan did not believe in this latest vision, if only because, now that he combined the supreme temporal and spiritual authorities in his own person, it was not to be expected that important revelations would be granted to anyone else. But in any case, he did not like the vision.

According to Dusentschur, the trumpet of the Lord would sound on three separate occasions and at the third blast the Elect would muster and issue from the city. They would overcome their enemies in battle, and God would lead them to the Promised Land.

But this was the Promised Land! This was Jerusalem. To make the fact clear beyond any possible doubt, he had recently renamed the River Aa the River Jordan. How could they travel to a place they were in already?

He could see Dusentschur leading the procession. With that pious smirk of his.

No, he could not see Dusentschur leading the procession. He could not see it happening at all. It was a deranged idea, and the last person who had it was Matthys. There would be no mustering and issuing from the city. The people of the New Jerusalem would stay where they were and wait for the Lord.

However, he did not want to contradict his prophet openly, and in any case there was an undeniable usefulness to this fancy of Dusentschur's. The minds of the people had to be kept occupied. Winter lay ahead, and the hardest time they had yet faced. Shortly brother Johann would expound his vision and the meaning of the trumpet to the populace. That would give them something to think about.

Martin heard the trumpet as he walked to the ramparts. He could not imagine what it meant, but it raised his spirits. It was a martial sound, and these days the only thing he understood was the war.

He lived in an uneasy peace with himself. He now had two wives and a baby son. The boy was called Zacharias, not a name Martin would have chosen. All newborn babies were now named by the king.

He had married a woman from the next street. She was one of the "declared-to-be-single" women married to an unbeliever. It had presented itself to him one day as a clever solution. The woman did not want to marry again but was compelled to; he did not want to marry again but was compelled to. They could come to an agreement.

It was swiftly concluded. Both of them, by that time, had seen how people disappeared into the prisons for disobeying the marriage edict and, having disappeared, did not come out again. They married at the local office, and she came to live at his house. Her name was Sibylla.

He felt so awkward at first, so clumsy, embarrassed, so angry at himself and at Sibylla for being there and Susi for telling him to marry, and at the law and the king and everything that had happened to them since Matthys went, that he could hardly speak a word to either of the two women who now inhabited his house or even look at them. He spent hours in the evening bending over the baby's cot or staring into the fire. He pulled himself out of this state eventually, realising that he had a duty to be civil, and discovered that while he had been absorbed in himself his wives had been getting to know each other and coming to their own arrangement about the house and its tasks.

Sibylla was to sleep in the small room under the roof which had been Jakob's. It was very small, like a monk's cell: the roof sloped down to within a couple of feet of the floor at the eaves. It had a tiny window, from which you could see the trees in the Cathedral square. They were leafless now, but she would enjoy watching them green in the spring, he said.

She was taller than Susi, five years older, and healthy-looking rather than attractive. She said sadly that she had once been a good cook, in the days when there had been something to cook with. She was good with Zacharias, and seemed fond of him. Martin was surprised that she had no children of her own, having been married for six years; perhaps she could not have children. If so, it would protect them from the asking of awkward questions when she failed to have a child by him.

He had pledged Sibylla that there would be no marital relations between them. They would live, in the eyes of the world, as man and wife, but they would not be. This was the condition of their agreement. He had promised Susi also that he would not make Sibylla his wife in more than name, although she had never asked him for such a promise. Having embarked on this enterprise in desperation, there being nothing else that would answer, he was humbly grateful, weeks later, to find that it had worked. There was amity between the women, there was peace in the house. Gustav the ratcatcher called, and Martin thought he was crestfallen, finding all three of them at their meagre but cheerful supper, to see that the law had been complied with and no-one was miserable as a result of it.

He had much to thank these women for, Martin realised: both of them. He said as much to Susi that night as they lay in their warm bed. (It was the only place that was warm. Firewood was becoming unobtainable.) She pressed his hand in the darkness. "We all have to be friends," she said, "because it's the only way we shall come through this." He thought how wise she was. Then she looked up at the ceiling, which had just creaked as Sibylla turned over in her bed. "I think she's lonely," she said.

This remark, no doubt casual, had an extraordinary effect on him. His heart was torn with pity. A different aspect of the situation, never before considered, presented itself to him: that he was simply making use of Sibylla for his own purposes. Certainly he had never thought about whether or not she might be happy in a household where she knew she wasn't wanted, living with a couple whose intimacy must remind her constantly of the marriage she no longer had.

"What's the matter?" asked Susi.

"Nothing." He raised her nightgown. He found he was very aroused.

He could not look at Sibylla in the same way the following morning. Nor the next day, nor the day after that. Something had happened which he could not undo. He wished bitterly it had not. At the same time there was a heady pleasure in this new way of looking.

Susi noticed. That did not surprise him. What she said surprised him: "I don't mind, you know."

At first he didn't believe her. Then, when he began to believe her (because why should she have said it if she didn't mean it?), he was so confused, excited, guilty and angry that he did not know what to do. He was angry because of an obscure sense that he had been tricked. By whom, he had no idea.

The third blast of the trumpet rang out on a grey December morning.

As the sound died away it was succeeded by a very curious hush. It was as if the population was waiting for the blast to be rescinded. For the clouds to part and tell them that the expedition had been postponed. There was by this time no-one who wanted to march out of the gates and proceed to the Promised Land in the teeth of the Bishop's cannon. And there was not one of them who had not made the short journey to the ramparts and seen how the camp had grown, a circle of Devil's mushrooms inexorably pressing closer.

They began to get ready for their last journey on earth. The men, as instructed, put on armour and picked up their weapons. The women dressed the children and debated whether to take a bit of food concealed in a scarf, deciding in most cases not to because they had been told that God would feed them and they feared the consequences of appearing to disbelieve. They put on their bonnets, damped down the fire if they had one and left the house with husband and children, careful to close the door behind them so that when the Lord, or the Bishop, came the doors would not be found blowing untidily in the wind.

They walked along the streets, so familiar underneath their new names which no-one could remember. They came to the Cathedral square, which was now Mount Zion, and there sat the king on his horse, and beside him on a pony Dusentschur. The king was in full armour. Well, that was something. Matthys had only worn a breastplate.

They had been told to muster by district, under their leaders. This took a long time to achieve, because although many people went straight away to the right place and remained there, hundreds didn't, because they couldn't find the right place and went on, in the crush and with the children crying, being unable to find it, or because they had just met in the crowd their brothers or sisters or the person they had been secretly in love with for half a lifetime and did not intend to be wrenched away from now when the world was about to end...or because finding the right place was simply too exhausting, and moreover it had started to rain. The district leaders, seeing all this confusion and flouting of the rules, were frightened and tried to make the people who were in the wrong place go to the right place, because who knew what might happen if they did not? So the confusion persisted, and worsened as the children grew tired and hungry and wanted to go home, and the rain came down harder and the king went on sitting there in his armour, which at this rate would have rusted by the time they set off.

Then preachers came round with more instructions. Each group must choose officers. The election for these took up another very long time.

Eventually each district had its officers. They were summoned to the king, who gave them a blessing.

Surely everything was now ready? The sun was getting low in the sky. If they didn't leave soon the expedition would have to be postponed until the next day, and Dusentschur would have to blow his trumpet again. (They all knew it was Dusentschur. A boy had seen him going up to the tower with the instrument peeping out of his coat.) Even those who were most afraid began to want the business to be over and done with, because the waiting was intolerable. They were cold, too, and sinking steadily into a misery in which it was all the same whatever happened.

No, everything was not yet ready. Dusentschur was going to make a speech. He rose in his stirrups and addressed them with evident passion and many eloquent gestures. Unfortunately, hardly anyone heard what he said. But then he raised his right arm high in the air and with a shout of the war-cry "Jerusalem!" he turned his pony in the direction of Ludiger Street. This was the signal to move off.

People looked—with frankness, because it was for the last time—into the eyes of their neighbours in the crowd. Husbands, wives and children embraced hastily and then concentrated on not losing each other as they made their way out of the square. There was a clattering of weapons and the massed, damp tread of feet on fallen leaves. Over these sounds hung a heavy quietness, because no-one in the vast procession that was trying to form could find anything to say.

All this was abruptly shattered by a gunshot.

Only a handful of people had yet left the square. Fearful of some new disaster, the rest turned to look at where their king still sat his horse, unharmed, with a guard beside him holding a smoking arquebus whose muzzle pointed skyward.

And now the king raised his arm. And the gesture he made was as commanding as Dusentschur's but left no doubt that they were to stay where they were. They were to listen while he, too, made a speech.

It was very short and many more heard it than had heard the previous one. He thanked them, his people, from the bottom of his heart for their loyalty and courage. He said that God had devised this as a test for them. The next day, a service of thanksgiving would be held.

Those who bothered to look at Dusentschur saw that he had gone a quite sickly colour under his helmet.

When the guards came for him Dolling thought it was the middle of the night, and took this to mean that his last hour had come. But when he asked them what time it was, they told him it was about nine in the evening.

They took him up narrow, winding stone stairs. Living in almost unbroken darkness had confused his sense of everything, not just of time, and he did not know where he was. But as the guards pushed him through a doorway into the precious air he saw stone ramparts about him and realised he had been put in the dungeon of one of the towers that dotted the wall.

They tried to march him briskly down the street, but he stumbled and fell at their feet. They hauled him up, and supported him the rest of the way across the city to a house he didn't know in a street off Fishmarket.

The door was opened by one of the Dutch bodyguard. He was taken down a passageway and thrust into a room lit by one candle burning in a lantern on the wall. It illuminated Jan's face.

"Leave us," said Jan to the guards, and went on with what he was doing. He was picking with the tip of his sword at the mortar in the bare stone wall. After a while, without looking at Dolling, he said, "You stink."

"I expect I do," said Dolling. He blinked like an owl in the lanternlight.

"Why do you stink?"

"Because I was put into a stinking cell."

"And why were you put in it?" Jan lowered the sword and rested the tip against the side of his high-heeled boot. "We all get what we deserve," he mused. "Do you really want to be king?"

"No."

"Then what were you doing?"

"I don't know." This was the truth.

"Really?" Jan moved the sword up casually and held it so that it pointed at Dolling's throat. "I know what you were doing, so it's curious that you don't. However, let's leave that for the moment. What do you expect to happen to you?"

"I expect you to kill me."

"Well, at least you acknowledge the gravity of the offence." He gazed flintily at Dolling. "In the time you've been in this room I could have heard a lawsuit. In all that time, you haven't said you are sorry, or begged to be forgiven, or even bent the knee to me."

It was true. Dolling had been standing there like one of the carved figures on the Town Hall, kept upright and immobile by an obstinacy he did not know he possessed. Slowly and stiffly, he lowered himself to his knees. Jan watched every inch of the descent. When he was kneeling, Dolling said, "I ask your pardon for what I did."

"Do you repent?"

"I do."

Jan flicked a piece of fluff from his stocking with the tip of the sword. "I don't believe you," he said.

Dolling looked up and saw cruelty in his face.

"You are not sorry," Jan said. "You're a proud, stubborn, vain man, whose pride is vanity. There is nothing in you, you're completely empty, and yet you strut about the city and call yourself Master-at-Arms. You're less important than the woman who washes the steps of the Town Hall. You're nothing. You're nothing because you do not believe that this is the Holy City. Do you?"

Dolling began to shake.

"You don't believe, and yet you're our captain. You defend the walls, but you have no interest in what the walls defend. Hence your insistence on continuing to fight an enemy who's packed up his tents and departed. What a mockery! No wonder you have to distract everyone's attention from it by claiming that I am the one who's playing a part! I shouldn't suffer you to live another minute."

The shaking spread to all parts of Dolling's body. It was as if a tension which had held him together for many months had snapped.

"Empty, empty. And you have filled the emptiness with me."

Dolling prayed he would stop. He continued.

"You have made use of me. You were drifting without a rudder when I arrived. Rothmann had been your rudder, but now Rothmann was useless and so, therefore, were you. Then I came. Suddenly your life began again: you knew what to do. You didn't get along with Matthys, but Matthys, fortunately, was soon out of the way, and then you had me to yourself. You took everything I had to give. You demanded my friendship, my company, my approval, a place at my right hand. Oh yes, you did." (Dolling had protested feebly.) "You claimed it, by what right I don't know. Oh, you worked hard, you were a good lieutenant, but dozens of others could have done the same. They were never give a chance. You saw off all rivals. All except Dusentschur. Dusentschur was something you hadn't bargained for."

The sword tip tapped a few times on the toe of the boot.

"What a pity that it's come to this. That you are so childish, so jealous of your place in my esteem, that you throw down a public challenge to me. A tantrum in the marketplace! You behaved like a jilted girl. But you were not some silly girl, you were the Master-at-Arms, spouting blasphemy and rebellion for all the world to hear. If I don't make an example of you, I don't deserve my throne."

Somewhere in the depths of Dolling's soul, like a clear pool in a tangled forest, was gratitude. He was grateful that his confusions and pretences had been penetrated and he had been understood.

"What will you do?" he murmured.

Jan said thoughtfully, "You will be torn with tongs in the marketplace."

Dolling, on the floor, wept in an abasement of terror.

After some time, a sword pricked the back of his neck.

"Get up. You're ridiculous."

He dragged himself to his knees.

"Very well. Now listen. Dusentschur has gone."

Dusentschur? He was being told something. He tried to make sense of it. Slowly, it began to take on meaning. It was like seeing the sun rise through dense mists.

And now Jan was saying something else. "Whom am I supposed to rely on? Whom can I trust if I can't trust you? Do I have to carry this burden alone?"

Dolling heard this appeal with bewilderment. Then abruptly an obstacle shifted in his mind and he saw what had happened in a quite different light. His tears began to flow again., but this time they were generous, healing tears of repentance. Yes, it was true, he had betrayed Jan, who had been closer to him than any other man on earth. And it was true, of course it was true, that there was no-one else Jan could trust. And now he was being given another chance. A great confusion of emotions overwhelmed him.

He stammered something through his tears. Something about his grief, his guilt.

Jan waited while Dolling regained, at least outwardly, his composure. Then, "Stand up," he said, and tapped his boot lightly with the tip of the sword.

Dolling stood up.

"You will resume your duties tomorrow," said Jan.

Dolling bowed as deeply as he was able. He could not speak.

To cement our new relationship," said Jan, "I think I should marry your daughter. I know you'll be happy to give your consent."

It was still possible for a courier to slip through the lines. One arrived in early December and brought Jan news that, of the twenty-four apostles who had been sent out, nine had been caught and executed by the authorities.

Jan received this news in silence. The sending out of the apostles had served several ends. One of them had been a display of defiance. And although in his address to the people he had spoken of conversion, he had sent them to places where there was already a sympathetic brotherhood of Anabaptists. Their real purpose was to stir up trouble. He had not, frankly, expected them to live long. If they survived long enough to inspire the people they arrived among with the idea of an uprising in support of Münster, that was enough. And if nine had been captured, fifteen were still unaccounted for.

Copies of Rothmann's book were circulating, eagerly read, the messenger told him, even though possession of it was a death sentence in many places. Jan felt a twinge of jealousy. He should have written a book. He had not had time.

Sister Agnes was out when the deacon came. She was collecting firewood along the bank of the river. It was quite a good place, because no-one else seemed to have thought of it. Most people went to the hedgerows, coppices and orchards for their firewood, with the result that there was never any there. You could spend half the afternoon wandering around, and come back with a handful of twigs and a bird's nest.

But branches often fell into the river and were carried along, until the current lodged them in some hollow of the bank, and there Sister Agnes found them and hauled them up on to the grass. They were saturated with water, of course, which made them heavier than they would normally be and meant that her clothes got wet and muddy going home, but she didn't mind that. And the branches would take a long time to dry out, under the cover in the yard that Georg had put up. But that was all right, too, as long as you fetched some every day, because then there would always be some drying out and the wood you fetched a week ago would only need to stand by the fire a day and then it would be ready to burn.

"You don't have to do this," Georg said to her once. She did love him, with his paunch and his funny square beard. "We can fetch the wood."

"I like fetching it," she said. "I like going over the fields. I like the way the branch feels. I like the way it bounces behind me when I drag it along over the grass."

"You're all wet."

"I don't mind."

He arranged the branches neatly under the little roof of thatch he'd made for them, and when they were dry enough he cut them up with his saw.

They had good fires in those autumn evenings, as the dark came a little sooner each day and the bite in the air sharpened. Sister Agnes had dug the last turnip and picked the last pumpkin. The onions hung in a plaited string by the chimney. The carrots were under earth in the yard. She made soups and stews, and baked bread. Sometimes Georg or Karl caught a fish in the river. The three of them ate, wiped their bowls with the hearty bread, and often fell asleep by the fire.

"It would be nice to have some chickens," said Sister Agnes one day.

"It would," said Georg.

"You can't get chickens any more," said Karl.

"I reckon I know where I can get a couple," said Georg.

He brought them home a few days later. One white, one brown, one black. They clucked around the floor.

"All hens," noted Karl.

"We got enough cockerels here," said Georg.

Sister Agnes had gone out for firewood. Georg watched the hens with pleasure, and threw them crumbs of bread. He had exchanged his hunting knife for them. Her face would light up when she saw them.

There a knock at the door. A small man with a weaselly face stood there. He said he was a deacon and was authorised to inspect their clothes and bedding and take away any surplus.

"We've got no surplus," said Georg.

"All the same. May I come in?"

There was no way of keeping him out. He looked at the hens, he looked at the plait of onions hanging by the fire, he looked at the loaves of bread that had just come out of the oven and were cooling on the table, and he said, "You do pretty well here, don't you?"

Neither Georg nor Karl said anything. He looked at both of them then, carefully, one and then the other and back to the first again. He began to walk around.

He stooped over a muddle of clothes that were Georg's and Karl's mixed up together, shirts and jerkins and belts and what-have-you. "You don't need this many shirts," he said. "How many people live here?"

Karl moistened his lips. "Three."

Sister Agnes's spare apron was lying on a stool. Her bonnet sat in the windowsill. The deacon's eyes passed over them. He turned and looked at the bed.

"Where's the woman of the house?"

"Fetching firewood."

"Which of you is married to her?"

"I am," said Karl instantly. "This here's my brother."

The deacon surveyed them again. There was not the slightest resemblance between them.

Sister Agnes's step was heard in the yard. Also the sound of something heavy being dragged along the ground and dropped.

The latch lifted and Sister Agnes stood in the doorway. Her face was flushed with walking and her eyes sparkled. The deacon stood between her and the men. Georg sent up a silent prayer.

"Is this your home?" asked the deacon.

"Oh yes," said Sister Agnes happily.

"Which of these men is your husband?"

Sister Agnes had never told a lie in her life.

Dolling was called urgently to the king one morning, and found him alone with a man who was dressed in a wild assortment of clothing. He had on his wrists a pair of manacles of which the linking chain had been severed, so that his hands were free.

Jan introduced him as Wilhelm Greff, one of the apostles who had been sent out during the time "when you were not able to be with us, Bernard." He asked Greff to tell his story again, to Dolling.

It was a strange story. Wilhelm Greff had set out with a companion for the town of Warendorf. They had got through the Bishop's lines safely, aided by the confusion that reigned in the camp because new contingents of troops were arriving. However, because of all the troop movements on the roads, it had taken them four days to reach Warendorf, although it was only a short distance away. They had hidden in barns and cowsheds, and once slept in a windmill.

The man rubbed his hands together all the time, as if cold, while he was talking.

When they reached Warendorf they had begun at once to preach in the marketplace. A crowd soon gathered, and was very sympathetic to their message. They were made welcome in the homes of believers.

"We preached for several days, and weren't molested," said Greff. "There were always a few soldiers at the back of the crowd, but they did nothing to stop us. We were very encouraged by this: we took it to be a sign that God was already making His power felt in Warendorf. We planned to stay there another week, preaching and baptising, and then move on. But on the eighth day we were arrested."

Jan leaned forward, listening intently as though he had not heard this story before. He seemed entranced by his returned apostle. From time to time he would touch one of Greff's manacles.

"A squad of soldiers surrounded us in the marketplace and marched us off to the magistrate. When we told him where we had come from, and what we had been preaching, he despatched us to prison. We were put in separate cells. I have not seen Klaus, my companion, since."

He looked at his wrists. The chains dangled like strange ornaments. The cut metal was fresh; the raw ends glinted.

"I had it cut when he arrived," said Jan. "You should have seen the state he was in. Half-naked, no shoes. And his wrists manacled."

"I was in prison for forty-one days," said Greff.

Dolling wondered how he had kept count. He had given up, himself, after seventeen.

"Several times the man who brought me my food told me I was going to be killed. He described what they were going to do to me. But I put my trust in God."

He rubbed his hands. He had been doing it more and more vigorously as his tale proceeded. Perhaps he had got into the habit of doing it in prison, Dolling thought, to keep the blood flowing.

"And then..." prompted Jan eagerly, looking as though, if Greff did not get to the point soon, he would pluck the story out of him.

"And then," said Greff in a hushed voice, and his face took on a look of wonder. "Last night I was asleep in the corner where I normally sleep, and it seemed to me that the door opened without making any sound, and that a...an angel...stood there."

Dolling's eyes fixed on his face.

"The cell filled with light. I had to cover my eyes. I didn't know if I was dreaming...if it was a vision...or even if I was dead, because perhaps I had been killed while I slept. And then the angel beckoned to me, and I walked forward, out of the cell and down the passageway, following the angel, and at the prison gate I saw the guards lying unconscious on the floor. The gate stood open, and I walked out through it. There was a hard frost on the ground, and as my feet touched it the cold went into me like a knife, and I thought, I'm alive and this is not a dream. The next moment there was a great rushing like a wind, and then came another dazzling light, and I fainted." He stopped, staring again at his manacles. "I remember nothing else until I found myself just a little while ago outside St Ludiger's Gate. With the irons still on my wrists."

There was a reverent silence. Then: "Have you ever heard a story like it?" marvelled the King.

It sprang into Dolling's mind that he had, and that it concerned Saint Peter, but he did not think it wise to say so.

"A miracle," he replied, "no doubt about it."

"As soon as we've found a locksmith to take these irons off, we must present him to the people. It will raise their spirits wonderfully."

Dolling thought Greff was too clean for a man who had been in a prison cell for forty-one days. But perhaps contact with angels had a cleansing effect. "A miracle," he said again.

11 Feathers

Through December the ring around the city continued to close. Blockhouses and trenches started to appear, turning the city's own defences into a prison. At night, the lanterns on the walls formed an inner ring of tiny lights within the greater circle of the camp's watchfires.

There was no feasting at Christmas. Not in the homes of the ordinary citizens, at any rate. Meat had disappeared from their tables some time since. Bread there still was, and they thanked God for it every time they put a piece in their mouths, and there were turnips, and onions if you had had the sense to grow your own and hide them from the deacons. There was still a little oil in the warehouses although the weekly ration was now extremely meagre, and there was still salt, of which no-one knew how much was left and no-one talked about it. There was not much else. The skies were scanned for anything feathered that might go in a pot. Boys who could bring down a pigeon with a slingshot suddenly found themselves very popular in their neighbourhood. Shooting pigeons was illegal because it created private property, so it had to be done as quick as lightning and the feathers burnt or buried at once, and a watch kept for deacons who, it was presumed, could detect the smell of pigeon soup a mile away. The number of pigeons decreased rapidly through the first half of the winter and by the end of January there were none left at all. By that time, the people who had wondered whether a sparrow was worth eating had discovered that it was.

The arrival of hunger had naturally been foreseen by everyone, and diligent attempts had been made to prepare for it. Most of these attempts were thwarted by the deacons, but even those that appeared successful turned out to have limited usefulness. It was simply too dangerous, in a street of hungry people, to look as though you had enough to eat. It was dangerous to cook anything that smelt of more than turnips. Families who had hoarded food under their floor or in a wall cavity (and managed not to lose it to mice or mould) were driven to eating it uncooked, in the dark, as if not wanting to acknowledge even to themselves what they were doing. Some took an obvious but difficult step, and shared it clandestinely with the neighbours.

Perhaps the King could execute an entire neighbourhood? No one knew. But a boy of ten was hanged in the marketplace for stealing a cabbage.

Greff's dramatic return created a flurry of excitement, but it soon died down when no further wonders were forthcoming. In the palace, however, it was a different matter. The King wanted to hear the miracle constantly discussed. He debated with his advisers how to take the fullest advantage of it. At first he wanted to send Greff out again straight away to visit as many towns as possible and show his miraculously-rescued person and his manacles, but he was persuaded that it was too great a risk. You could not count on a second divine intervention, and if Greff were captured again and executed (and this time he would be executed), all the glory of the earlier miracle would be lost. Jan saw the sense of this. Greff must be kept in reserve until the proper use for him was found.

Meanwhile he kept Greff by him, spoilt him, referred to him in all matters and treated him as something between a pet and an oracle. He gave him a house in Salt Street and an allowance of food and firewood from the royal warehouse. He made Greff tell his story over and over again, to the court and to the people: he even exhibited him, on one occasion, on a specially-furnished stage designed to look like a prison cell. When he reluctantly recognised that everyone had heard enough of the story, he still kept Greff beside him at public appearances and asked him to preach. Greff was his vindication. Greff was the promise that the city would be saved.

One day a woman who had made her way through the camp disguised as a laundress brought a message which seemed to be the answer to all their prayers. An army of fellow-believers, led by a prophet, had mustered in Groningen and was on its way to relieve the city.

"I knew it," said Jan. "We shall be saved by Easter."

This was the result of his inspired sending-out of the apostles. The Groningen prophet would march southwards at the head of his army, and he, the beleaguered holy king, would sally forth from the battered citadel to meet him; and then the hosts of Satan would vanish like a puff of smoke.

When he thought about it, it was obvious. The Elect would gather, wherever they were scattered, and march to the New Jerusalem: this would fulfil the prophecies. One hundred and forty-four thousand, it was written in Revelation. That meant there were tens of thousands who still had to answer the call. (Would they all fit into the city? The walls would miraculously expand to make room for them.) Deliverance would come at the hand of God, when all were gathered together. It was that very gathering that would achieve it. He was amazed that Matthys could have thought he could set the vast machinery of the end of the world in motion with twenty men.

He called Dolling to him and told him the news. Dolling's response was, he thought, typical.

"How big an army is it?"

"A thousand men."

Dolling looked both pleased and thoughtful. "Wonderful news. Thank God. I could wish for more, that's all."

"Gideon had three hundred. David—"

"Oh yes. Quite."

"There will be more," Jan promised. "There will be uprisings in every country. Wherever people hear the voice of truth, they will throw off their shackles and come to join us."

"Pray God they do."

He would never change, Jan reflected. The spell in prison had not fundamentally affected his scepticism. There were some people who would never believe until the sky opened over their heads.

The following day, a proclamation was issued that the city would be saved by Easter.

The preachers announced it in all the districts, bells were rung from the churches and the population was commanded to praise God. It did, out of habit. But Easter was more than two months away, and most of the people who heard the proclamation did not know how they would manage for another two months, with the stocks of flour almost dwindled to nothing and the camp outside the walls growing like a fungus, ready to smother them.

But the preachers told them that Easter was almost within reach. Two months was nothing! After all, they had already held off the entire world for nearly a year! Surely they could manage another two months?

Dolling was getting through one day at a time. Without giving way on essential points (for, as the king's absorption in the end of the world deepened, his grasp of military realities weakened), without yielding an inch of his position to the court jackals who, having seen him humbled once, wanted to see it again, and without saying anything which would get him sent back to the place he had recently come from. It was like threading his way through a maze. He didn't know whether he was trying to get to the centre or whether he was trying to get out. All he could see were the walls, and the snakes that lived in their crevices.

He was aware of a feverishness that had infected life at court in his absence. You could see it in people's faces — the bright eyes, the fixed smile — and you could hear it in the too-rapid speech that filled the rooms of the palace. At the same time, court life, which had never had any substance to it, became ever more fantastical, more removed from meaning. He could not imagine where it would end. Perhaps Jan would just get tired of it all one day, and abolish the kingdom and all of them with it.

Meanwhile, the ordinary people were not withstanding the winter well. They looked underfed and ill-clad. If another attack came, he was not sure they would be able to repulse it. He knew that if he said this to Jan, who refused to listen to any conversation about food stocks, he would find himself back in the dungeon.

Admittedly, the army outside the walls was doing everything but prepare for an imminent attack. It was preparing for a future one. It was digging trenches, piling up earth ramparts and building fortifications, all with the intention of putting a third wall around Münster behind which its troops could safely mass. Whoever was in charge of the Bishop's army now — obviously no longer the Bishop — he knew what he was doing.

And time was on the side of the new commander. He need do nothing at all, and hunger would do his work for him.

Sister Agnes would not have chosen to be in prison, but after a few days she settled down to it comfortably enough.

The cell she was in was quite large, and almost circular. It was part of one of the round towers that stood in the city wall. It had an earth floor, bare stone walls and an iron grille through which you could see the sky. If you jumped (you had to jump because the grille was set high in the wall), you could see the top of a stone rampart and a bit of field. Sister Agnes was quite happy just to see the sky.

There were twelve other women in the cell. They were all there for breaking the marriage laws. Three women were married to men who had left Münster, and they had refused to accept that the marriage was null and marry again. There were five first wives who had refused to accept their husbands' later marriages and had made the house uninhabitable for the new wives. One woman, severely beaten by her husband, had turned on him one day with his own sword and cut off his ear. Another, a small, quiet creature called Lisa, who did not look as though she had a scrap of defiance in her, had denied her husband his rights in bed. Lastly, there were two girls who had denied nobody anything, but had been found by the disbelieving husband doing things with each other which neither should have been doing with anyone but him. There was much discussion of these crimes, and of which ranked as the most serious. Some women said the cutting off of the ear must be the worst, but others thought that the two girls, having committed a crime which hadn't even been thought of, would be the first to be executed.

Sister Agnes was asked what she had done. She said that as far as she could make out she was being punished for having two husbands. This created a sensation. After vigorous debate, it was decided that Sister Agnes would be the first to be executed, even before the two girls. Not that anyone had actually been executed for months. The king had forgotten about them, the women said.

For a few days, until the other women tired of the subject, Sister Agnes was an object of wonder. She took it calmly. Being in the cell was a bit like being in the convent. You accepted the way other people were, and with luck they accepted the way you were. At night she spoke to the Lamb. He was reassuring.

Then one evening the door creaked open at an hour at which it never normally opened. The little window had gone dark long ago and filled with stars. Some of the women were lying on their straw talking, but most were asleep. Then the door opened and two men stood there against the dense darkness of the passageway with a lantern between them. The stocky outline of the man holding up the lantern was as familiar to them as the stone walls they lived between: he was the jailer. The other, tall, wearing a white shirt on which something shining lay, with a small beard and eyes which seemed to pierce the gloom with unusual brightness...Surely he was the King!

They scrambled to cover themselves up, wake their neighbours on the straw and get to their feet. What did it mean?

"Don't alarm yourselves," the King said.

It was the first time they had heard his voice at such intimate range. Before this, they had only heard him speak to a crowd of thousands on the Cathedral square. It frightened them nearly out of their wits. But at the same time there was something in the voice to which they gave their deepest attention, because in some strange way there was security in it, and moreover none of them had spoken to a man for weeks or months, except the jailer, who didn't count.

And of course none of them had seen a man for that length of time, either; and now here was this man of whom they were all dreadfully afraid, and by whom they were nearly all terribly fascinated, walking slowly round the cell which had all of a sudden become small and smelly, and asking, as the jailer held the lantern to their faces, what they had done to be put there.

The first two women who were asked responded in faltering voices. Then he came to the quiet woman who had denied her husband what he married her for. As the king stopped in front of her, she lifted her chin. Without a tremor she said, "I'm here because I would not share the bed of the man who married me."

"Why not? Did he force you into marriage?" asked the king.

"No. He had no need to. You have forced us into marriage."

Every eye in the cell stared at her. The king stroked his beard.

"You have misunderstood, daughter."

She didn't lower her gaze even then.

"You had a duty of obedience," he said. "Marriage is ordained for the getting of children."

"I can't believe that God has given men rights over our bodies whether we are willing or not," she said.

These astonishing words were followed by a profound silence. After a few moments, the King turned on his heel and walked to the next prisoner.

"You, what are you here for?"

"I wouldn't renounce my husband."

"Is he an unbeliever?"

"I don't know what he believes. All I know is that he is my husband."

"You know the penalty for disobedience," said the King. He left her and came to Sister Agnes.

"And you?" he demanded.

Say nothing, said the Lamb. Just curtsey.

She lowered her eyes and curtsied.

"Why are you here?"

Say nothing.

Sister Agnes said nothing.

"This one's a bit simple, Your Majesty," said the jailer. "I don't think she knows what's going on half the time."

"But why is she here?"

"They say she had two husbands." He chuckled. "If you ask me, she wouldn't know what to do with one, let alone two."

"Did you have two husbands?"

Say nothing.

She curtsied.

The King shook his head impatiently, and passed on.

He came to the two girls who had done something that didn't even have a name. He asked them why they were there. Neither could answer from terror. He turned to the jailer, who told him in a hushed voice.

The King stepped back and looked at the two girls with curiosity. He seemed to be about to say something, but did not. The girls began to cry.

"These young women should not be here," said the King. "They're taking up space and eating good prison food. All that matters is that women should have children." He said that the girls should be returned to their husband and should each produce a child within a year. If they failed to do so, they would be hanged.

Then he and the jailer left the cell. Shortly afterwards, the jailer came back and took away the quiet woman. She was not seen again.

Jan realised that he must give thought to occupying the minds of his people. With the nights long, the weather bitter and the enemy at the gates, they needed to have their spirits kept up or they would not be able to play their part in the mighty drama that was being prepared.

Accordingly, he made a tour of the city on horseback with his retinue. Light snow was falling. He admired its purity. He observed its kindness, how it softened the severity of everything on which it fell: the long spine of the Cathedral roof, the stark branches, the crossbar of the gibbet. It subdued to a powdery crunch the noise of hooves behind him.

The party moved down Street of the Servant (formerly Highmarket), along Street of the Wise Virgins, down Epiphany and turned up towards Jacob's Ladder (formerly known as Our Lady's). Here it came to the river Jordan. The weather had been very cold and the river was frozen. The ice was a transparency so thickly feathered with white that all you could see at first was the whiteness, but as you looked longer you saw that under the white was a blueness, and under the blue lurked black.

Jan spoke over his shoulder. "Bernard, walk out and see if the ice will hold you."

Dolling's eyes looked into his. Dolling was a heavy man, and he was wearing half-armour because he had been on the ramparts. There was a short pause before he dismounted and stepped on to the ribbon of white. His boots crunched on the ice. He walked with slow and careful steps across to the opposite bank, watched in silence by the court.

A little ripple of applause broke out as he reached the other side.

"All right," said Jan, irritated. "He hasn't walked on water." He turned his horse and led the party up to the bridge, where they all crossed the Jordan quite safely and rode on following the curve of the wall.

As a result of this excursion, a public entertainment was decided on: a fair on the frozen river.

The winter fair opened in the middle of January. Everything had had to be done very quickly, but all the court agreed that it was a great success.

Booths were set up along the riverbank. In each was displayed a lanternlit tableau illustrating a scene from Biblical prophecies of the Last Days. The figures were richly costumed and stood against a painted backdrop showing a countryside like the one around Münster. It all looked very impressive, although some of the sharper-eyed visitors noticed a striking resemblance between the figures and the saints that had been in the churches.

The most popular attraction was not the tableaux but a figure of Antichrist set up in a booth of its own. There was always a line of eager spectators waiting their turn outside this booth. No pains had been spared to make Antichrist terrifying: he stood much taller than a normal person, had fearsome clawed feet, red baleful eyes and a scaly tail. To make him appear still more monstrous and unnatural, his chest and arms had been covered in chicken feathers.

Where did they get the feathers? the spectators wondered aloud. When chickens had not been seen for months.

After the first day, a guard was put in the booth. The explanation given was that some people might be so roused to fury by the representation of Antichrist that they would try to damage the figure. After this, public speculation over the chicken feathers ceased.

In addition to the booths, there were strolling minstrels to entertain the crowds. There were even jugglers, acrobats and tumblers. The King had gone to great lengths to recruit anyone who had any talent in these arts, and the results were mixed, but the effect was at any rate colourful.

The fair-goers were encouraged to skate on the ice. That was the point of holding the fair on the river. The preachers in fact circulated among the crowds telling people that if they loved their city it was their duty to skate on the ice. Bonfires were lit, music was played and jugglers who couldn't juggle threw objects in the air in order to persuade them to do it.

The thin and ill-clad citizens who wandered along the bank to the fair did not understand why they had to skate. Why it was so necessary that they should enjoy themselves. All most of them could think about, most of the time, was their hunger. The first question they asked themselves on seeing any object was whether it could be eaten. This was the real danger in which Antichrist stood, although the trooper guarding him did not know it.

They skated, being used by now to doing what they were told. They skated sombrely and clumsily, not having the strength for intricate manouevres. Some of them would not have minded too much if the ice had given way.

There was not a cat or dog left in the city.

It was Greff who opened the fair. Jan had turned him into a sort of performing animal, Rothmann thought, giving a rehearsed speech about the angel and holding up his wrist-irons for the public to marvel at.

It was an amazing story. Rothmann did not believe a word of it.

He was within a hair's breadth of losing his faith entirely. All around him he saw the ideals that were dearest to him mocked, and the mocker unpunished. He saw the equality he had fought for inverted into an inequality greater than existed anywhere, even at the court of the Emperor, where at least the Emperor was bound by law. And at least the Emperor, if his loyal subjects were starving, would attempt to do something about it. There was enough food in the royal warehouses to feed the king and court for months. Rothmann had seen it.

The mocker had turned justice upside down. He had made the thought equal to the deed when man's only glory was that he did not have to act on the promptings in his skull. The mocker had mocked everything there was: community (this was a city that spied on itself), marriage, propertylessness, voluntary poverty...

And God did nothing. He would not rescue His people from the clutches of this devil. Rothmann prayed to Him nightly to do so, and every day Jan rode abroad unharmed. His bodyguard drilled on what was insolently known as Mount Zion.

Rothmann would not have believed in Greff's miracle in any case, because it served the Devil.

He had sought out the returned apostle as soon as the story became known. Greff was living in a luxurious apartment. There were curtains and wall-hangings, a rug on the floor, a four-poster bed, a pile of wood in the grate.

Rothmann introduced himself (which Greff had the courtesy to tell him was unnecessary) and said, "I wonder if I might ask you a few questions about the angel."

"Ask whatever you like," said Greff, without enthusiasm. He rubbed his hands together.

Rothmann asked his prepared list of questions. How tall was the angel, was it male or female, did Greff hear it speak, and so on. Greff's answers were predictable, even boring. He did not strike Rothmann as a man who had been brushed by the divine. Although you might, if you wanted to believe him, put his woodenness down to his having already told the story too many times.

"How did it move?" asked Rothmann. "Did it walk along the ground, or seem to glide above it?"

"It glided above it," said Greff firmly.

"Its wings were folded?"

"Yes."

"You never saw them unfurl? To carry you back to Münster?"

"No. I don't remember anything about that part." He began suddenly to massage his knuckles and then to rub his hands together as if they were cold. It was quite warm in the room.

"Did you notice anything on its breast?" asked Rothmann.

Greff frowned. "What sort of thing?"

"They are said to bear the name of God in fiery letters on the breast."

Greff seemed alarmed. "No, I didn't see anything like that." He thought for a moment. "It was so bright I could hardly look at it at all."

"Thank you for your patience," said Rothmann. "You must be tired of answering questions. Your imprisonment must have been a terrible ordeal."

"It was. But I never lost hope."

"Were you tortured?"

There was a tiny hesitation before Greff answered, "No."

"You should let a doctor look at those hands," said Rothmann.

Greff shot him a look of naked terror.

Rothmann stood up and took his leave. Walking the short distance back to his house, he thought it was perfectly clear what had happened. The only mystery was what purpose it served.

No more had been heard of the army that was marching from Groningen. Jan calculated over and over how long it would take them to reach Münster. He had revised his plans for their arrival. He would not go out to meet them, since he had so much to occupy him in the city, but he would welcome them in through the gates with banners and the thunder of cannon, and together they would all await the Day of the Lord. Then, at last, he did receive news. It came in the form of a letter, hastily penned, sweat-stained and muddy, that was fired one morning into the wood of what the people still called Jews' Gate. The archer had taken a terrible risk, shooting from a knoll behind the Bishop's camp.

The letter said that the men from Groningen had fought fiercely but in the end had been wiped out by the Duke of Gelderland's troops. Only a handful had survived. The letter was signed with a code name which guaranteed its authenticity.

Jan scrutinised it for telltale signs. He knew it was a trick.

He was at dinner with his wives when he noticed that there was something wrong with the wine. A metallic edge. He tried eating a bit of spiced pork and then sipping the wine again, but he could still detect it, that flat, menacing bottom to the taste.

It was poisoned.

He put the goblet to one side and called his youngest servant over.

"Go to the cellar and get me a jug of wine," he said. "Draw it from the cask yourself. Bring it straight back to me. Speak to no-one on the way."

Devera, sitting beside him, picked up the glass.

"Leave it alone," said Jan. "There's something in it."

Devera sniffed the wine. She was about to raise it to her lips. He grabbed her wrist and forced it down. "Don't disobey me," he muttered.

The other wives were watching this. He looked round at them, forcing them to lower their eyes, and gestured to the musicians to play something lively.

The boy came back with the wine and set it before him. Jan tasted it. It tasted exactly the same as the other.

He would have to behave as if nothing were happening.

The music was still wretched. Scrape, scrape. Pitter-patter. His irritability had increased to an almost unbearable pitch already, and the evening still stretched ahead without hope of respite. He would have to get through this poisoned meal, and then he would have to dance with his wives, and then he would have to choose one of them to bed (he had devised a means of indicating his choice: it had been amusing at first, and was now hopelessly tedious), and then he would have to bed the one he had chosen, and then he would try, and fail, to sleep. The drowsiness that enveloped him as he lay pillowed on top of the woman would lift as if a cloth had been whisked away the moment he rolled off to lie on his back.

Wide awake, he would lie there while the night passed, hearing the watchman's calls and the sounds of slumber from the creature beside him, whom, as the hours went by, he would start to hate. Hate not only for her ability to sleep but for her simplicity.

He pushed the plates away and rose from the table. The wives, too, rose to their feet, abandoning the unfinished meal.

The adjoining room was well lit with candles but otherwise empty. The wives formed a ring and stood waiting. As the musicians began a dance tune, he took the hand of one of the women and began to dance her in and out of the ring. The other wives clapped in time to the music, and tossed their heads and smiled, for all the world as if they were enjoying themselves. Perhaps they were.

He was dancing with Anna. Black hair and blue eyes, a pretty mouth, small white teeth. She came of a large family—dyers from Brabant—but did not look like any of them. He was sure she was a love-child, and that was what had kindled his interest. It hadn't lasted long: she had a shrill voice and was always asking him for new shoes.

He left her with a bow, and took the hand of the next in the ring, Clara. He had married her after Devera, and had hopes that she was carrying his child. That was good. That made him feel better. They had to have more children. That was why he had to sleep with a different one of his wives every night, whether he felt like it or not.

Time for a new partner again. This was Lisabeta, Dolling's daughter. A pretty child: he had married her in order to be sure of Dolling. Devera had taken her under her wing. He never knew what went on among women. It didn't matter as long as they obeyed him.

The musicians played, and the wives clapped in time.

After he thought he had danced enough, he held up his hand for the music to stop and walked to the wooden board which hung on the wall at the end of the room. The wives, seeing him standing there, all turned their backs with a swish of skirts. He took the peg from its rest and stood with it in his hand. The name of each wife was inscribed on the board, and next to each name was a circular hole. The name at the top, in a central position, was Devera's. The rest came below, in two columns.

Anna? No. Magda? No. She chattered, and he did not feel like listening to it. Eva? This was the Frisian girl. He hesitated between Eva and the one he had most recently married, but hadn't he slept with her the previous night? He inserted the peg into the hole next to Eva's name. Then he turned away and walked to his quarters.

Reaching his bedroom, on an impulse he sent to ask Devera to come to him straight away. She was still the first and best and the one he trusted, although sometimes her very constancy made him angry because he suspected that it was not constancy to him (and, earlier, had not been to Matthys) but constancy in some way to herself. This evening he had a mind to overlook it.

Devera sat on the side of the bed and ran a searching eye over him. "What is it?"

"I'm ill. Or someone is trying to poison me. Or both."

"There was nothing wrong with the wine, Jan. I tasted it afterwards."

"I told you not to."

"If someone is trying to kill you, I want to share the danger."

He was touched. He bent to kiss her, and found himself wanting her.

As he prolonged the kiss his desire increased. Perhaps that was what had been in the wine? An aphrodisiac! And perhaps Devera herself had dropped it in. He wouldn't put it past her. He wouldn't put anything past this clever, loyal, beautiful woman whom he had now completely repaid for her marriage to Matthys and could love with simple affection.

He sat down beside her and began to talk, and meanwhile he was running his hand up and down the back of her dress. After a while he lifted the dress and slid his hand under it, and teased her by stroking the top of her thigh with a finger. Then he unlaced his clothes. He pushed her down on the bed, flinging up her skirt, and went in, covering her mouth at the same moment with his own and dwelling on it as if he would suck out her essence. She cried out; he lunged and lunged, and when at last, with a shudder, he finished, he knew that Eva was standing behind them in the doorway and he felt, for the first time in days, a measure of relief.

With February came renewed hope.

"Three ships have left Amsterdam, their decks crowded with our brothers in the faith, all praising God and talking of Jerusalem."

Jan held in reverent fingers the letter which Dolling had brought him. He had trusted, and his faith had been rewarded. Three ships had left Amsterdam, their decks crowded…

He summoned the court. Ministers, preachers, deacons and all his wives. He wanted them all to hear.

"I know you have doubted," he said. "You are only human. Even the disciples doubted. Our Lord forgave them, and I forgive you. The news we have waited for has come! Three ships have left Amsterdam, their decks crowded with our brothers, all praising God and talking of Jerusalem."

He held up the letter for them to see. His face was alight with joy. He seemed taller: the news had brought him life. A great cheer went up in the room, followed by fervent cries of "Praise God!"

"Praise God," said Jan, "for by Easter He will truly redeem His people."

He went round the room embracing them all one by one, and they embraced each other. Then he said, "Let us give thanks," and led them in prayer.

Within the next week, astonishing proof was received that God was working His will and that the time would not be long. A youth managed to get through the enemy lines and reach the city. When he was brought before the King he revealed that he had come from Minden, where the townsfolk had risen and were setting up a model of the New Jerusalem following the description in Rothmann's book.

The third piece of news, which seemed final confirmation that the tide of events had turned, was that in West Frisia nearly a thousand Anabaptists had seized control of a fortified monastery and were holding it against the authorities.

Jan was ecstatic. "What did I tell you?" he declared. "From west and east they gather. Flocking to the banner of the Lord."

That Sabbath he preached to a huge crowd. He told them that the seaborne army from Holland and the new city of God to the north-east were just the beginning. Soon, the righteous the whole world over would be on the march, driving back the forces of darkness, breaking the chain that bound the New Jerusalem, flooding through the open gates to worship alongside the people of Münster.

The congregation's response was puzzlingly muted. He wondered if they had understood.

"The siege will be over by Easter!" he cried, making it as plain as he could.

"Give us bread!" called out a man in the crowd.

Jan stopped in surprise. He decided he had not heard properly. "What did he say?" he asked of Rothmann, at his side.

Rothmann coughed, which was getting to be a habit of his. "Give us bread."

Jan stared around for the man who had said it, and fixed on a rough fellow, rather wild-looking. Not right in the head.

All the same, he must reply.

The cobblestones gleamed in the winter sunlight, their smooth roundness washed by early rain. It seemed to him no more a miracle that these should be turned into loaves than that Greff had been released from prison. Perhaps that would satisfy them.

"Your Father will turn these stones into bread for you, when you need it," he said. "Be patient."

Jan's newest wife was the woman he had taken out of prison. He had meant to execute her, but at a certain stage in the conversation had realised that he was intended to marry her instead.

Her name was Lisa. She was eighteen and already a widow. Her husband had been killed in one of the first salvos fired from the Bishop's camp. She said frankly that his death had been a relief because he had beaten her so violently that she had been afraid that one day he would kill her.

"Why did he beat you?" Jan asked sternly.

"For anything. Because the fire was smoking. Because his belt buckle was broken."

After his death she had returned to live with her parents and said she did not want to marry again. Then the law was passed making it compulsory for women to have a husband.

Suitors began arriving at her door. She refused them. Her father told her she would have to marry one of them sooner or later. She told him she would rather die. The preacher told her she had six weeks to make up her mind, after which she probably would die if she continued obstinate.

She prayed. In answer to the prayer, she felt an inner certainty that it was wicked to throw her life away. She thereupon resolved to marry the next man who asked her, since "they were all the same."

"And did you?" asked Jan. He found this woman astonishing.

"Yes. A man came to the house the next morning. I said yes, and we were married the same day."

"You felt... no particular liking for him?"

"No. Nor any dislike, either."

"But then you refused to enter his bed."

"I had obeyed the law. I thought that was enough."

"But what do you think marriage is for?" he laughed.

"I think it is a way for men to govern women," she said.

He could at any moment have her impertinent tongue cut out of her head. However, he decided to continue the conversation. He was quite enjoying it.

"There is a natural love between the sexes," he said. "You won't deny that, I suppose?"

"Everyone talks about it, but I have not felt it myself."

"You didn't love your first husband, either?"

"I was ready to. He could not love me."

"Women must respect their husbands."

"Then husbands should respect their wives," she said, looking him straight in the eye.

It was the Devil that made women speak like this. He felt a little thrill of pleasure.

"If all women behaved like you, there would be no order in the world and no children either."

"I can't help that," she said simply, and pushed the hair out of her eyes with a child's gesture which showed him how young and how defenceless she was. "I can only do what's in my heart."

He saw with a sudden sweet clarity that there was nothing of the Devil in her after all, that she was just misguided and had been in the hands of stupid men. There was no reason why she should not make a good wife, if she was married to a man who was wise and patient. He understood that he was that man, and that he had been guided to the prison that night to save her.

He smiled at her. She was so surprised by the smile that at first she did not know how to respond. But as he went on smiling and looking gently at her, an uncertainty crept into her eyes and for the first time in their interview she looked away from him. He saw her bite her lip. It was a shapely lip. Then she glanced at him again, and it was a glance that spelt disaster for her composure, because he was still smiling, a warm and already affectionate smile of which her mouth could not resist quirking into a tremulous reflection.

He said, "Do you still consider it a sin to throw your life away?"

"Yes, I do."

"I have come to help you save it," he said.

He had her bathed and decently dressed, and brought to the palace the following day. He talked to her again. He promised he would never beat her. Then he summoned the husband and asked him privately if he agreed to a divorce. The man fell over himself to say yes. The two ceremonies, divorce and remarriage, were performed on the same day.

He did not regret his decision. The beauty he had glimpsed under her prison dirt and pallor emerged swanlike when clothed in silk and linen. He lavished jewels on her. (The treasury was full of these pretty toys. They might as well have a use.) He wanted her to feel his kindness in the weight of gold on her fingers.

She was obedient to him, and she seemed grateful. She thanked him for taking her out of that wretched place and giving her a chance to live. She admitted her pride. A sort of melancholy, which he thought came from the prison, still sometimes hung over her, and on those occasions he took pleasure in diverting her and making her laugh.

He explained that she must not go out without his permission. None of the queens did. The streets were dangerous, he said, and there was plenty to do in the palace. She seemed surprised, but accepted it.

It was not long after the man had shouted "Give us bread!" that there was a further unpleasant incident.

Jan was talking to all the preachers in the palace one morning, suggesting, as he often did, texts they might use in their exhortations. He was focusing these days almost entirely on the Book of Revelation. The preachers stood in a respectful row, waiting for the next utterance. One of them seemed restless, however. He shifted his feet and looked out of the window, when he should have been looking at the King.

"What is the matter with you?" demanded Jan.

"Nothing, Your Majesty. I beg your pardon."

But he had lost the thread. He dismissed them, except for the one who had fidgeted. A youth who'd always been reliable before. Came from Brabant.

"What is it?" asked Jan. He knew there was something.

"Your Majesty... May I speak freely?"

"Of course you may."

"The people are hungry."

"Hungry?"

"The food stocks are nearly exhausted."

"You're mistaken. There is plenty of food."

"Your Majesty, there is growing hunger."

"You're lying," shouted Jan. "Didn't you eat breakfast?"

"No, I couldn't bring myself to."

Jan summoned the guard. He knew the enemy when he saw it. "Put him in one of the towers," he said. "Alone."

This kind of thing had to be sealed off from the healthy body of the people. It was an infection. The Devil sent it. Its purpose was to undo God's work.

One day, Jan realised that he was making a stupid mistake by keeping Greff in the city. It was like not playing an ace.

He decided that Greff should be sent out at once to add fuel to the revolutionary fires which were burning all over the region. He discussed the best strategy with Dolling and others, and then with Greff himself, who came up with his own suggestion. He wanted to be sent to Deventer, in the Netherlands. It had a strong and radical brotherhood, and was in the geographical centre of all the revolts.

"Deventer," murmured Jan. He knew it: he had passed through it on his journey to Münster. Yes, Deventer was a good choice and fertile ground. From it, Greff could make contact with all the important brotherhoods.

In a state of high excitement, he spent the day discussing plans with Greff, Dolling, Krechting and—at the last minute—

Rothmann, who had to be included in things these days because of his fame as the author of "Restoration." Rothmann obligingly made several useful suggestions. A list of names and places was drawn up (by Dolling, naturally).

Jan's eye rested on the list. In his mind's eye he saw them gathered, glittering hosts. Their banners flew. A holy singing tide, they converged on the New Jerusalem.

"So," he said, "it's settled. Greff will leave tonight. Are you ready to go, brother?"

Greff said he was.

"Which road will you take?"

"I shall travel west until I reach the border, and then follow the river."

"Better to go through Gronau," said Rothmann. "We have friends there."

Greff did not want to go to Gronau.

"Greff knows what he wants to do," said Jan. "He consorts with angels: I think we can trust him to reach Deventer."

Greff was avoiding Rothmann's eye.

"You must take a companion," said Jan. "Choose the man you would like to go with you."

"I'll go alone."

There was a surprised silence.

"The Spirit is telling me to go alone," said Greff. "It tells me that to travel with a companion courts danger."

Dolling raised his head from the lists and gave him a penetrating look. Bernard doesn't trust him, either, thought Rothmann: but why does he say nothing?

"Your companion will be the Holy Spirit, then," said Jan. "In that case you hardly need my blessing. Nevertheless, you have it." He took a ring from his finger and put it on Greff's. "This is my personal seal. It is the guarantee that I myself have sent you."

Strange that Jan should think that a man who consorted with angels and travelled with the Spirit should need his authentication,

Rothmann thought; but then saw that the King was in such awe of Greff that he would seize any means of associating himself with the apostle.

"Would you like my armour?" Jan asked suddenly. He leapt up. "Yes, he must have it! Bernard…"

"No, Your Majesty, thank you, it's a most generous offer but the armour would not fit me, and it would be too conspicuous…" Greff could not decline fast enough. Quite understandably. Whatever he was up to, the armour of the King of Münster would not help him one little bit. Rothmann, despite his tension, his guilt and a horror at what was happening, was hard put to it to suppress a smile.

"Do you have anything to add, Rothmann?" asked Jan. "I have the feeling there's something you haven't said."

Greff turned his eyes, reluctantly, to Rothmann, and he and Rothmann looked at each other.

"No, Your Majesty," said Rothmann. "I'm in agreement with everything that's being done. I think the sooner our brother leaves, the better."

Greff slipped out of Our Lady's Gate in the west wall during the first night watch. The King himself, with Dolling and a few others, came with him to the outer gate. They watched him step into the shadows, and within a few moments the darkness had swallowed him up. Listening for his footsteps, they heard only the distant sounds of the camp, a sentry's cough, a horse neighing, and nearer, a swish of water in the moat and the sighing, sucking sound of the marsh.

The heavy wooden gate was pulled almost silently back into place, and the little party retraced its steps without speaking through the empty streets.

There was nothing to do now but wait. Deliverance would undoubtedly come, but its means was uncertain. Since its means was uncertain, not to mention the time of its arrival, it was not possible to prepare for it beyond maintaining the state of alertness that was now normal for them. Jan barely restrained himself from telling Dolling to abolish the routines of the watch and the inspections because two weeks would see the end of the siege and the Bishop's army and all the rest of their troubles... but he did not tell Dolling to abolish them, because there was a voice in his head, of prudence, which was not yet stilled.

Daily he mounted the steps of the watchtower and scanned the flat, fertile landscape, from which the snow had retreated and into which the green of new leaves had come. He did not see the glint of steel he longed for.

Holy Week came, and there was nothing.

Good Friday came, and still there was nothing.

Easter Sunday came and went, and there had been no deliverance.

12 The Last Days

The failure of the relieving armies to arrive at Easter plunged the King into despair. He locked his doors and forbade anyone to speak to him even through the wood. Then, hating to hear the sound of other voices anywhere, he left a written order that no-one should speak, laugh or make any other noise within earshot of his room. A dire hush descended on the palace and the streets outside.

But after a couple of days of this the reason why the armies had not arrived occurred to him. He had mistaken the nature of the promised deliverance. It was a spiritual deliverance: the rescue from the hands of their enemies would come later.

He rushed through the corridors of his palace, shouting "Praise God!"

The women in the cell had been taken away by ones and twos during the past month, until only Sister Agnes and the woman who had cut off her husband's ear were left.

This woman was called Emilia. She was a short, wide, heavily built woman with features which did not seem to have enough room, so that when she looked worried or angry they got in each other's way. Sister Agnes imagined them doing this at the moment when Emilia cut off her husband's ear.

"I didn't mean to do it," said Emilia. "It just happened. The blade was sharp. I didn't know it was so easy to cut off someone's ear."

"I suppose it is," said Sister Agnes, thankful that she had not done it. She and Emilia were sitting together on the straw in a little patch of sunlight that came through the high barred window at a certain time every day. It was summer now, or nearly: you could hear the birds.

"He might have bled to death," speculated Sister Agnes.

"Not on your life," said Emilia. "I didn't cut it all off, although the way they went on about it you'd think I did. There was quite a lot left."

"But it must still have bled."

"I expect it did. I didn't stay to look. I ran out of the house before he killed me."

"Did you still have the sword?"

"I can't remember. No, I think I dropped it."

"It would have been sensible to hold on to it for a bit," said Sister Agnes thoughtfully.

"Yes, that's what a man would have done."

"Did he divorce you?"

Emilia gave a cackling laugh. "I'm sure he has by now. I'm probably the only woman in Münster under fifty who hasn't got a husband." She clutched Sister Agnes in a sudden access of mirth. "And you've got two!"

They were sitting laughing when the jailer came in. "What are you laughing about?" he said, and was quite angry when they wouldn't tell him. Not that he was a bad man, Sister Agnes thought: he had one eye and a limp, and liked to put his hand on her breast although she didn't want him to, but she forgave him the last thing and the others he couldn't help.

He had brought their food. He set it down just inside the door, as usual. This time he stood looking at it. There wasn't much to look at: a hunk of bread and a bowl of greasy liquid in which a green leaf or a sliver of carrot might be floating. He said, "D'you know how lucky you are to get this?"

They thought it was a joke, so they gave him a smile, because a jailer who makes jokes is better than a jailer who doesn't, and a jailer must in any case be humoured.

"No," he said, "you don't. You've been in here half a year. You don't know what it's like outside."

"What is it like outside?" asked Sister Agnes, struck with anxiety for her husbands, but he didn't answer.

"The King's own kitchens, this food comes from," he went on. (Surely that was a joke!) "So you and me, we've got to stick together. Because as long as you're here, I'm here. See?"

He fixed them with his one eye. He was obviously trying to say something to them, but they had not the faintest idea what it was.

"So don't you go falling sick, or escaping," he said, "or it's the end of me as well." Then he grinned at them with his toothless mouth, and they realised that it had been a joke, and laughed to oblige him.

There was something wrong, and no-one would tell him what it was. A miasma, a deadly exhalation, lay over the city. Sound was muted as if there had been a snowfall, but it was spring and there was no snow. The streets, when Jan rode through them, were empty. Where were all the people? Sometimes he saw a shadow-like figure at some bizarre occupation, like picking at the ground with its fingers, but often he saw no-one. Perhaps they were all so afraid of him that they had run back into the houses. He was sorry if that was so: it was good and natural for them to be afraid of him, of course, because of the majesty that clothed him and the mystery that invested his being, but he wanted them to love him, too. He didn't want them to run away, to be unable to look at him, or to look at him, if they did, with those strangely darkened eyes.

One day when the smell was rather worse than usual some visitors arrived. They entered his presence with great politeness, holding handkerchiefs to their noses. They said they were ambassadors, and from a neutral party. They were the

Burgomasters of Nuremberg and somewhere else, and hoped to negotiate a peace settlement before any more lives were lost.

"There will be many more lives lost," observed Jan. He could barely understand what they said, it was such strange German. It had been translated for him by Dolling. The Burgomasters looked like plump black partridges. Their hats were ridiculous, and if they thought they could conceal them by holding them under their arms they were mistaken. "It is written," he told them, "that hundreds of thousands will die. The earth will groan with the weight of dead."

He thought that the less portly one said, "It's starting to do that already," but since he didn't understand what this might mean and since Dolling did not translate it, he ignored it.

"It doesn't matter to me who you are, where you come from, or what you say," he said. "The only thing that matters to me is that I carry out the will of the God whose instrument I am."

"Do you imagine that you are carrying out the will of God by allowing your people to starve to death?"

Dolling translated this with great unhappiness, as well he might.

"What does he mean?" Jan demanded.

"I am only translating, Your Majesty…"

"Tell him that no-one is starving to death. No doubt he heard that lie from the Bishop."

"We can use our eyes," said the plumper one. "As we came through the streets we saw people who were walking skeletons, trying to eat the whitewash from the walls and the grass between the cobbles."

"Some of them were even trying to eat the cobblestones," said the other.

Jan understood all this perfectly, although Dolling mangled it beyond recognition. These ambassadors were both mad, he concluded. He had better humour them. They would leave soon enough.

They were asking now if he knew that a conference of the German states had just met at Worms. No, he did not. Or perhaps he did, he had forgotten. The states had each pledged to contribute five thousand gulden a month to prosecute the siege until it was concluded, they told him.

Did they hope to impress him by talking about sums of money? He laughed at them. "This city will endure for a thousand years. Don't talk to me about gulden."

They were silenced by this. He followed up his advantage. "Our allies will arrive any day. Three ships have left Amsterdam, their decks crowded..."

"They were sunk on the Ijssel," said the fat one. "I'm surprised you haven't heard." He was taken aback for a moment, then brushed it aside. "In Minden..."

"That uprising was completely crushed by the Town Council," said the second. "Though I believe there was quite a fight. Cannon had to be used." He would ignore this, too. It was a pathetic lie. He played his best card. "A thousand of our brothers are marching from Groningen to help us. Many more will join their ranks on the way."

"They were marching," said the fat one. "They were routed by the Duke of Gelderland, weeks ago. I don't think any of them survived."

"Lies, lies, lies! Everywhere our brothers are in arms. In Frisia they have captured a monastery..."

"They are dead, sir. You must believe us. They are all dead."

He shut his ears to these taunts of the Devil. Dolling was quaking in his shoes. He had been worse than a girl since he came out of prison. Jan rose with dignity from his throne.

"Have them conducted to the gate," he said.

"May God have mercy on you," said the fat Burgomaster.

There was still Greff. Greff in Deventer. And in any case it was all lies. Lies and plots. There were plots everywhere.

A letter was brought to him. It had been fired over the battlements. It was addressed to the common people of Münster, was signed in the Bishop's effeminate and wavering scrawl, and offered them a free pardon for their rebellion if they would rise against the man who ruled them.

Jan redoubled the guard on the royal apartments. All his food and drink was now tasted before he touched it. He stopped riding through the city. He had already ceased his solitary visits to the prison.

Then Dolling astonished him by saying they should slaughter the horses. He said they were an incitement to revolt. A trooper riding alone had been mobbed and nearly killed by the populace the previous day because they wanted the horse, he said. They wanted it to eat.

"To eat?" Jan tried to stare him down, but Bernard for once stood his ground. "They're a military necessity," Jan said. "Keep them in barracks, if you think they shouldn't be seen."

"They have to be exercised."

"Then exercise them at night. Good heavens, I don't know. It's a ridiculous problem."

But perhaps it was not such a ridiculous problem if the horses were really an incitement to revolt. He began to brood over it, not over the horses, on which he would not give way (he could not; in the last resort, a mounted bodyguard was his only defence), but over the threat his own people might pose him, simply by virtue of their numbers and their ignorance and fear. If they were told they were starving, and that the armies which had been coming to their rescue were all defeated, would they not believe it? These things were much easier to believe than the things he told them, about spiritual deliverance and the thousand-year reign of the Elect, in which they showed no interest at all. He began to feel very angry with them.

So that when Rothmann turned up for the tenth time with a humble request that those people who wanted to leave the city should be allowed to do so — "to ease the pressure on resources, Your Majesty" — he agreed. Rothmann recovered from his surprise and was about to rush off on another precipitate errand when Jan stopped him, assailed by a vague memory of Matthys.

"They mustn't be allowed to take anything with them," he said.

Rothmann looked at him oddly. "Your Majesty, they don't have anything."

"Oh, don't they? Very well, then."

And it was swiftly arranged, or so it seemed to him. Very swiftly. They must have just been sitting there waiting for the word. Otherwise how could they have lined up the very next morning, hundreds of them, holding their vacant-eyed children by the hand, waiting for the gate to open?

When it did open, they shuffled and shambled out in a manner that enraged him to see. He felt like cursing them. They were traitors. For them there would be no shining hereafter, no reign of a thousand years. However, that being so there was no point in cursing them, because they had their punishment.

In fact, leaving did them no good. He watched them often during the following weeks, from one of the siege towers or from St Lambert's, as they wandered about the strip of land between the walls and the camp. They could not get beyond the ring of blockhouses that had recently been built. The commander would not let them through. Equally, it was impossible to let them back into the city, since they had elected to leave it. They would just have to stay where they were. They had no food and there was only grass to eat, so they ate it and it made them ill. Well, he had not forced them to leave. They cried pitifully. They went from begging the soldiers for food to begging the soldiers to kill them, but the soldiers did not grant either request. When they began to die the stench was very bad, and in the end the commander was obliged to do something for those that remained alive. By then, more than a month had passed and the stench inside the city was also horrible, but he, the King, was not responsible. He had not forced them to leave.

And where was Greff?

The leaflets urging the citizens to revolt continued to be fired into the city. There was no point in sending men out to pick them up before they were read, because everybody knew about them and in fact nobody now bothered to read them, and they blew about the streets when there was a squall of wind.

Jan realised that only the strongest measures would save him. The city had become a hostile place, an enemy town which had to be garrisoned. He turned to his compatriots to help him control it.

For the last time, he took Dolling's map, now so fingered and overwritten as to be in many places quite illegible, and divided the city into twelve sectors of equal size, ignoring the old districts. He drew the lines between the sectors in a red ink that looked to him like blood, with a hand that shook from sleeplessness. He would put honest Dutchmen in charge of these sectors. Men whose will would be his will and who would count it glory to lose their lives in his defence. He would call them...what? This was a kingdom: they would be dukes. When the Kingdom came (or rather when it was re-established, because of course it had come but it could not yet be seen by mortal eye), they would rule over real dukedoms, not these miserable streets.

He looked at the unbroken red lines, each islanding its sector. This told him that the dukes must not confer. Each must speak only to him. Each must know only what happened in his own territory: he, the King, would alone have the eagle's-eye view of the whole. Good.

And the people —wretched, deceitful, thieving—they must not confer! Why had it taken him so long to think of this? It was bad enough that they lurked in their houses, where husband talked to wife and Heaven knew what treason was mulled over. That he could not prevent. But he could and must prevent their meeting outside their homes. No more than two would be permitted to meet for any purpose. Then conspiracy could not grow.

The dukes would need an efficient police force. Well, that had never been difficult to provide in Münster. What else? As he looked at the map with its clear divisions and its uncompromising perimeter, it became obvious. He had made a mistake in allowing those people to leave. No-one had thanked him for it, and half of them had died anyway. The thing had looked bad. In future, no-one would be allowed to leave in any circumstances.

The starkness of this pleased him. To abandon the city was betrayal. After all, he remained at his post.

Since it was treason to leave, they would be executed if they tried it.

Then he saw the final step he must make, and did not shrink from it. He must carry out the executions himself.

Even at this late hour, Jan expended himself in efforts to stop the New Jerusalem from turning into the graveyard it seemed bent on becoming.

He had written a play. It was in loosely rhyming verse and was based on Greff's escape from prison. This was an ideal subject because it allowed him to present, on one side, the holy city and its King, and on the other the villainous Bishop, whom the audience would enjoy hissing and jeering. There was also scope for a fine dramatic effect with the appearance of the angel.

The play ended with Greff's rapturous vision of the armies which would relieve the city. His final speech, delivered from the battlements with the King at his side, Jan considered to be the finest thing he had ever written. He could not read it without the tears forming in his eyes. It was a pity that the play could only be performed in Münster, because he would have liked the whole world to see it. But even amongst this sullen and shadowy population it could not fail to have an effect.

It would be performed in the Cathedral. The bare stone and dark recesses, the pillars and steps and long perspectives, gave him, not the best stage, but one that challenged his ingenuity. He had to accept that some of the audience would be unable to see some of the action. He had tried to get over that by making the actors move about a lot and by making the speeches explain to a great degree what was happening. The Cathedral would be full. Everyone would want to see the play. Just in case, out of spite or indolence, they decided to stay away, he would make it a test of loyalty.

The play would be performed by the preachers. He rehearsed them daily, but was dismayed by their ineptitude. He had to show them how to speak a line, cross the stage, address the audience and perform the simplest action. At one point he called them a troupe of jackasses. They all sulked at that. He had to talk them round. He, the King!

He had wanted Rothmann to play Greff. Rothmann had refused. Respectfully and humbly, but without giving an inch. Jan was very surprised. Rothmann had never refused to do anything. Why on earth should he refuse to do this? He could hardly plead that he was frightened of an audience! Rothmann said, however, that he greatly looked forward to the play and was sure it would be the most remarkable thing that had ever been seen in Münster. Mollified, Jan decided not to punish him.

It happened that on the day of the performance he was not feeling well. The old suspicion that his food was poisoned had resurfaced. For days he ate only food which he took from the warehouse shelf with his own hand and had cooked under his own eyes. Strangely enough, that, too, had a tainted and threatening taste. Despairing, he ate nothing, but then the thought occurred to him that perhaps the plot was not to poison but to starve him, so at breakfast he crammed himself with bread, cheese, salt bacon and pickles. That was the day of the play's performance. His stomach was leaden. His head ached.

When he took his seat in the front row of the audience, the nave and both aisles were full. What struck him unpleasantly was the smell; Heaven knows, the streets had long been full of it, but here in the confined space it had doubled its potency. They had brought it with them, in their rags and on their breath and their scabbed skin. He felt nauseous, and clutched Devera's arm for support.

The wives settled themselves. Devera was on his right hand, Lisa on his left. There was something wrong with Lisa: she was tense and trembling. He asked her irritably what was the matter, thinking that this was her first outing since their marriage and he had confidently expected her to enjoy it. She didn't reply, but took out a handkerchief and buried her face in it.

Displeased, he turned to Dolling in the row behind him and asked if everything seemed ready. Dolling was looking rather ashen, too, or perhaps it was just the thin, clerical light filtering through the leaded windows. Dolling said that everything was ready and the audience had settled down. Jan gave the signal for the performance to begin.

The prologue was spoken by the actor who also played the King. Jan had with conscious modesty written only a small part for the King. The play was, after all, about Greff, and also Jan did not want to write a part that would frighten the performer. (It was enough, he thought wryly, that it frightened him.) He thought it was sufficient to convey the King's majesty by his costume, and the burden that rested on him by a few well-turned speeches. Well then, you would think that the idiot preacher, having no more than eighty lines to memorise for the King's part, would be able to get the Prologue off by heart as well without too much difficulty — it was no more than twenty lines and he had the rhyme to help him. But no, he stumbled over it, had to be prompted, kept staring at the audience as if it might rise and bite him, and managed to mangle the cadence of the speech as well, so that by the end of it Jan was barely able to restrain himself from shouting at the man and had no hope at all that he would make anything but a disaster of the main role.

The rows behind him, filled with members of the court, applauded. He was disturbingly aware of the lack of applause from the great mass of the audience to right and left and further back. Perhaps they hadn't understood the speech. Well, they would surely understand what followed. The subject of the play had been kept a secret, so that surprise would make it more enjoyable. He tried to relax, preparing himself to experience the play through the eyes of those who had never seen it before. But beside him Lisa was snivelling into her handkerchief. In exasperation he told her to be quiet.

The first scene was unfolding. Greff and his companion were making their way through dangerous countryside to Warendorf. They discussed their mission, and made jokes about the things they had seen while creeping through the Bishop's lines (there was no laughter, except the odd nervous titter from the front rows). They fell in with a peasant travelling to market, who told them about the hardships of the local people and how the city of Münster was a beacon of hope to the land around.

The scene was played reasonably well, in view of Jan's gloomy expectations, but the audience remained still and silent. He had expected some excitement when they realised what the play was about, but he had overestimated them. It would take the angel to wake them out of their lethargy. He should have started the play with Greff already in prison. It would have been shorter, but with an audience as half-asleep as this one, that might not have been a bad thing.

The next scene took place in Münster. It showed the King and his advisers conferring on how best to defend the city from the enemies who surrounded it. Jan had considered having Dolling, Krechting and other prominent members of the court play themselves, but decided against it since he did not intend to play the King, which he thought might make everything confusing. But now he wondered, listening to the silence where he had expected murmurs of recognition, whether most of the audience understood what was going on in any case. He turned his head to stare behind him into the comparative obscurity—how dark in fact it was, this church: if he lifted his eyes to the clerestory windows and then looked down again to where the people sat in their rows, he could barely make them out—and then, on turning to look at the play again, he found his view occupied by the snivelling Lisa.

"What is the matter with you?" he hissed.

"These poor people."

Despite the tremulousness, it came out quite clearly. He had no idea what she meant.

"Where?"

"Here."

He shrugged. Something had distressd her, but he could not be bothered with it now.

"Be quiet," he said. "Watch the play."

The one who played the King was even worse than Jan had feared. Wooden. Trampling the lines. Jan grew angry. The man had performed better than this in rehearsal. He seemed to be mocking the play. Much more of this, and Jan would go up there and speak the lines himself.

Devera put a hand on his arm. It was her way of telling him to be patient. Very well, he would be patient, he would once again be patient, the exercise of patience was almost his sole occupation these days. He tried to erase the frown from his face, and bent his attention again on the stage, where the pretend-king and his pretend-courtiers were shambling off to make way for the Bishop.

This would make them laugh! He had spared no pains in his portrayal of the Bishop: fat, lascivious, wine-bibbing, money-grubbing, incapable of organising his own household let alone a siege. He had looked forward to the roar of laughter that would greet the Bishop, strutting on stage preceded by his enormous stomach (a feather cushion) and followed by his enormous sword. And indeed all his own row and the two rows behind him laughed quite loudly, but the laughter sounded forced to Jan, he could hear no enjoyment in it, and below and behind it he heard again the silence.

It would not get any better until the angel appeared. And perhaps even the angel would not lift this play out of the pit into which it was descending.

Scene succeeded scene, each more leaden than the last. But perhaps, in fact, it was nothing like this at all and he was ill, perhaps there was something interfering with his sight and hearing, perhaps the play was really a great success and he was the only person in the Cathedral who did not know it. He looked around him to see if this might be true, and then he saw something which almost caused him to give up belief in his senses on the spot.

In the obscurity of the rows behind him, people had got up from their seats and were apparently trying to leave. But for some reason they had become disoriented, and now they were wandering the aisles like ghosts who cannot find their way back to the graveyard. They were as thin and insubstantial as ghosts, and the unnatural largeness of their eyes horrified him. And although they resembled ghosts, they did not flit or glide like ghosts but dragged themselves along and staggered, as if they were drunk, and fell down, yes, some of them fell down.

He took a grip on himself. He was King of the New Jerusalem. He could speak the word and everything would stop.

"Bernard," he whispered hoarsely, and Dolling craned forward. "Stop them. They are trying to leave."

Bernard sat motionless. What was the matter with him? What was the matter with all of them? Now Lisa was saying something to him. Well, that was an improvement at any rate. Unfortunately he couldn't make head or tail of what she'd said.

He turned back to the stage. He had no idea what was happening around him: perhaps he would understand what was happening in the play, since he'd written it. And no doubt he would have been able to, if the man who played the King had spoken his lines in an intelligible manner, if the one who played Greff had not mumbled and fumbled and started a speech which belonged in a different scene entirely, so that the other players didn't know where they were or what to do, and if Lisa, beside him, hadn't suddenly launched into a dialogue of her own, unscripted and incoherent but nevertheless making terrible lunges at meaning.

"Jan, stop the play, please."

"What?"

"It's horrible. These people…" (a bit he missed) "… and you're making them watch a play."

"I wrote it for them. Why shouldn't they watch it?"

She said, in a voice which must have carried to every corner of the Cathedral, "They are dying."

"Will you hold your tongue?" he screamed. And then, as Devera and others intervened and he thrust them away, "There's a contagion in the city, the ambassadors brought it. Watch the play."

She shrilled, "There are corpses piled in the street!"

The performance had stopped. The players stood with stupid expressions on their faces, eyeing each other wildly.

Devera said, "Jan, perhaps you should stop the play. Perhaps this is not the right time for it."

"I will not stop it. It will go on until it is finished. And no-one will leave before it is finished. And no-one will speak again before it is finished."

And so a hush descended that was only broken, once or twice, by the soft falling of something behind him, and they were all able to give their full attention to the glorious appearance of the angel, at which the entire court applauded hysterically. As a result his expectations revived somewhat, only to be dashed again by the abysmal way in which the king-player handled the last scene, by which time Jan's patience, so sorely stretched, found itself completely exhausted and he strode on to the set, booting the player into the transept, and spoke the lines as they should be spoken, with dignity and hope.

The words he had written, so moving and so noble, rekindled his faith. As he heard Greff speak of his miraculous release and prophesy the glory that was to come, his mind cleared of its mists and his heart leapt like a young man's.

Jan counted the morning on which he had to execute his own wife as the most wretched of his entire existence.

He had given her a last chance. There were no lengths to which he wouldn't go for this woman, who had touched him so in prison and who was now again dressed in prison garb, looking like a wan little bird. Inside, however, she was still unregenerate.

He asked her if she repented of criticising him in public. She asked why that was a crime.

"Don't you understand who I am?" He marvelled at his own restraint.

She looked strangely at him. "Perhaps not."

"I am the Second Messiah."

She lowered her head and looked at the floor.

"You must believe it," he said gently. "If you don't, you're damned."

"I don't believe it."

"Don't you believe that this is the New Jerusalem?"

"It is Münster, in Westphalia."

"God is trying to save your soul, Lisa."

"It is Münster, or it is Hell."

There was nothing he could do. Her obstinacy was Satanic. In the corner of the room, he half-glimpsed the swishing of a tail.

The entire court was gathered for the execution. Also a number of the common people, winkled out of their holes.

Lisa was led in and blindfolded. Her hair, normally pale and loose on her slender shoulders, was tied up on top of her head. She knelt. He was profoundly moved by the sight of the soles of her feet, grimed from the roadway, sticking out under the edge of her penitent's gown.

He grasped the two-handed sword that was held out to him. He thought, soon all this will be over.

He swung the sword.

Afterwards, standing with his feet in the blood that was spurting everywhere, he remembered that he had meant to say, "May God have mercy on you."

Rothmann had taken to visiting the walls in the evening. He observed the camp and talked to the men on watch. The physical condition of some of them was now so bad that he was not sure they would be able to fight when the assault came.

He stood one evening beside a young watchman who was almost as thin as the lance he grasped, although he grasped it firmly.

"They've finished that blockhouse," Rothmann observed, nodding towards one of the most recent outworks.

"Yes. I reckon it won't be long now before they have another go."

"The armies from Holland may get here first."

"Yes, of course," said the boy in a tired way.

Both of them scanned the landscape behind the camp. There was nothing to be seen in it beyond a few peasants sowing their fields.

"No chance of a breakout with this lot all round us."

"No," agreed Rothmann.

"And he can mass his troops very nicely behind those earth walls."

"But all the same," said Rothmann, resting his hand, and his gaze, on the massive stonework of the ramparts, "these defences are impregnable."

"No, they aren't," said the young man.

Rothmann turned to look at him.

"There's a weak spot where the river flows in."

"But that's heavily fortified!" said Rothmann, visualising the place.

"Yes, because it isn't defensible. You can't bring the guns to bear where you want to because of the shape of the walls, and you can't get enough men up there in a hurry because there's only one stairway. If they can get across the river at that spot, they're as good as inside."

Rothmann was silent.

"Everybody thinks they're impregnable, though," said the young man.

Rothmann was suddenly overcome with a fierce tenderness for him, for all of them. "What's your name?" he asked.

"Martin."

"Do you have any children, Martin?"

"Yes." A smile lit up the hollow face. "A baby boy."

"Good."

The smile faded. "Mind you, Susi's having trouble feeding him."

Somewhere to the north, a cannon discharged itself against the walls. Let it come soon, thought Rothmann. Dear God, let it come soon.

He felt in his pocket and brought out a square of cloth in which he had wrapped some cheese. This was one of the reasons why he visited the walls.

Give her this," he said.

The young man looked at the cheese, and then at him, incredulously.

Rothmann walked away before he could be thanked. He went home, and then almost at once went out again.

13 Deliverance

To Dolling, surveying the camp in the bright light of early morning, a change was apparent.

It was hard, in fact impossible, to pinpoint, it was as subtle as the difference between the look of a blunt knife and a sharp one. Turn your eyes away for a moment, and you couldn't see it any more.

He set off to walk a complete circuit of the walls. Once, he had done this every day; recently he had rarely taken the trouble, infected by the fatalism which now governed the entire city, from the thoughts of the king downward. The enemy had seemed gripped by the same fatalism, sunk in the same lethargy: the siege would go on, it could not be brought to a conclusion.

But today, yes, there was something different.

He stepped briskly along the stonework. He felt more cheerful than he had for months.

It was as he approached Our Lady's Gate that the arrow was fired. It landed twenty paces ahead of him, falling on the walkway of the rampart. As he went towards it he saw there was something wrapped around the shaft.

He picked it up and ducked back below the shelter of the wall.

A letter. He unpeeled it from the shaft with clumsy fingers and held it open.

It was from Greff.

The King sat on his throne like a marionette whose strings have been cut.

"Betrayed," he said.

Greff had betrayed everything there was to betray. Names, places, what was planned and how. He said so in the letter.

"I believed in him," said Jan.

"We all did." It wasn't true, but what did it matter? What the King believed was of a different order from what anyone else believed.

"How could he do it, Bernard?"

Greff had gone straight to the Bishop. But it was worse than that: he had been sent by the Bishop. The story about the angel, that story which had been told over and over to give heart to the people: a fabrication. It was the Bishop who had released him from prison, and the Bishop's soldiers who had escorted him under cover of darkness to the gates of Münster.

In a sense, none of this surprised Dolling, although it horrified him. He was only surprised that Greff had been able to keep up a lie for so long, and with no assurance that the trick would ever work. He wished now that he had voiced his suspicions, but it was only for the sake of his conscience that he wished this. Jan would not have listened: he had fallen in love with the miracle.

"God knows how many of our people he has killed," said the king. "Hundreds. Thousands. They were on their way to rescue us."

Dolling said nothing. He did not believe the information Greff had given away had much military importance. Small groups of Anabaptists, many of them having no interest at all in revolution, would have been rounded up and killed in distant towns; perhaps some weapons had been seized. But in any case he did not think any armies would have come to rescue them. They were on their own and always had been. No, it was not on that level that Greff's betrayal really operated. It operated in the mind. Greff had mocked the thing their community was founded on: faith.

There was something else he had to tell the king. Dared he? Yes, because it was nearly over and he was not afraid of Jan any longer.

"A rope was found hanging over the walls this morning."

"A rope?"

"A bell-rope. We checked all the belltowers, and it came from St Lambert's."

"Rothmann."

"No-one has seen him since yesterday evening."

"So he has gone to the Bishop as well. I always knew Rothmann would betray me."

"He doesn't know anything of importance."

"It doesn't matter if he does."

Jan had drawn himself into a normal posture on the huge carved chair.

"They sent that letter from Greff to make me despair," he said.

"Yes. They will send more of them, for the people to read."

"It doesn't matter," said Jan. "The end is coming." He looked out of the window. It was a bright summer day. "Are you going to leave me, too?"

"No," said Dolling.

Sister Agnes heard the rumbling in her dreams. It was a cliff falling. The cliff separated into a mountain of boulders and the boulders began to topple towards her. She couldn't move; she just stood there paralysed, waiting to be engulfed by the mountain of stone.

She woke up. The floor was shaking. The cell was filled with white dust, which hung like a gauze curtain in the early morning light from the grilled window. Sister Agnes began to cough. Emilia was awake, and looking in terror at the ceiling as if expecting it to fall.

"It's the guns," said Emilia. "It must be an attack."

A boom! close at hand made Sister Agnes almost jump out of her skin, and left her ears muzzy and tingling. But then came another and another, rocking the ground and even the air, and the little window filled with smoke. As the terrible noise and the trembling of the ground continued, and the walls of the prison seemed to shiver, Sister Agnes remembered her dream and wondered if they were all to be buried alive. She tried to tell Emilia that God would protect them, but Emilia wasn't listening.

In the occasional lulls between the firing of the cannon, you could hear shouts and running feet. Once, Sister Agnes heard the king's voice. He was quite close to the window. He was shouting, "Where did they get in?" and then there came another rush of feet, followed by horrible cries.

After this, nothing seemed to happen for quite a time. Sister Agnes began to wander around the cell. She felt strange. In fact it was not an unfamiliar feeling. It was just strange that she should get it in such circumstances. Usually...

Lie on your stomach, said the Lamb clearly. Cover your head. NOW!

Sister Agnes lay down and put her hands over her head.

The world filled with roaring and light. The air rushed out of the cell as if sucked by a giant lung, and when it rushed back it brought things falling out of the sky which fell around her and cut her skin. Under her elbows, for some reason, the straw continued to exist.

Get up, said the Lamb.

Sister Agnes stood up a little shakily. She saw dust and light, all mixed together. Then she saw a ghostly figure covered in white struggling to sit up a short distance away.

She was just stepping towards Emilia, over the hill of rubble the floor had become, when she saw something else. In front of her a shape was forming. A very odd shape which had no meaning. She looked hard at it, and then she had the idea of looking at it inside-out, as it were, and as soon as she did that the shape became a gaping hole in the prison wall.

Walk out, said the Lamb.

Sister Agnes reached Emilia and got her to her feet. Emilia was dazed and her ear was bleeding. Pulling Emilia behind her by the wrist, Sister Agnes made her way to the hole in the wall and looked about her. Fire-flashes, swirling dust. Shouting. Screams.

Go on, said the Lamb. Sister Agnes and Emilia went through the gap in the wall. They were on an apron of stone on which stood a cannon with a headless man draped over it. Sister Agnes felt faint. Go on, said the Lamb.

Ahead of them was a narrow bridge, with no-one on it. It went across the moat. Sister Agnes moved towards it, grasping Emilia's wrist, then stopped, assailed by an urgent thought. Her husbands! She must go and look for them.

No! said the Lamb, and she had never before heard him angry. Walk away.

So Sister Agnes and Emilia walked. They walked over the bridge and across the grass that was wet with dew. They walked on and on, and no-one stopped them.

Spinsters Ink Books

Spinsters Ink Books is one of the oldest feminist publishing houses in the world. It was founded in upstate New York in 1978, and today is located in Denver, Colorado.

The noun "spinster" means a woman who spins. The definition of the verb "spin" is to whirl and twirl, to revert, to spin on one's heels, to turn everything upside down. Spinsters Ink books do just that—take women's "yarns" (stories, tales) and enable readers to see the world through the other end of the telescope. Spinsters Ink authors move readers off their comfort zones just a bit, pushing the camel through the eye of the needle. These are thinking books for thinking readers.

Spinsters Ink fiction and non-fiction titles deal with significant issues in women's lives from a feminist perspective. They not only name these crucial issues but—more importantly—encourage change and growth. We are committed to publishing works by women writing from the periphery: fat women, Jewish women, lesbians, old women, immigrant women, poor women, rural women, women examining classism, women of color, women with disabilities, women involved in social justice issues, women who are writing books that help make the best in our lives more possible.

To Order Books

Spinsters Ink titles are available at your local booksellers or through Spinsters Ink Books. Call 1-800-301-6860 to place an order. A free catalog is available upon request or visit www.spinsters-ink.com. You may order directly online, or mail your order to: Spinsters Ink Books, P.O. Box 22005, Denver CO 80222. Please include $3.00 shipping and handling for the first title ordered, 50¢ for every title thereafter. All major credit cards accepted.

Other Titles Available from Spinsters Ink Books

The Activist's Daughter, Ellyn Bache	$10.95
Amazon Story Bones, Ellen Frye	$10.95
Angel, Anita Mason	$14.00
As You Desire, Madeline Moore	$ 9.95
Booked for Murder, V. L. McDermid	$12.00
Cancer in Two Voices, 2nd Ed., Butler & Rosenblum	$12.95
Clean Break, V. L. McDermid	$12.95
Closed in Silence, Joan M. Drury	$10.95
Common Murder, V. L. McDermid	$10.95
Conferences Are Murder, V. L. McDermid	$12.00
Considering Parenthood, Cheri Pies	$12.95
Crack Down, V. L. McDermid	$12.95
Dead Beat, V. L. McDermid	$12.95
Deadline for Murder, V. L. McDermid	$10.95
Deadly Embrace, Trudy Labovitz	$12.00
Desert Years, Cynthia Rich	$ 7.95
Dreaming Under a Ton of Lizards, Marian Michener	$12.00
Fat Girl Dances with Rocks, Susan Stinson	$10.95
Finding Grace, Mary Saracino	$12.00
A Gift of the Emperor, Therese Park	$10.95
Give Me Your Good Ear, 2nd Ed., Maureen Brady	$ 9.95
Goodness, Martha Roth	$10.95
The Hangdog Hustle, Elizabeth Pincus	$ 9.95
I Followed Close Behind Her, Darleen O'Dell	$14.00
The Kanshou, Sally Miller Gearhart	$14.00
Kick Back, V. L. McDermid	$12.95
The Lesbian Erotic Dance, JoAnn Loulan	$12.95
Lesbian Passion, JoAnn Loulan	$12.95
Lesbian Sex, JoAnn Loulan	$12.95
Lesbians at Midlife, edited by Sang, Warshow & Smith	$12.95
The Lessons, Melanie McAllester	$ 9.95
Living at Night, Mariana Romo-Carmona	$10.95
Look Me in the Eye, Macdonald & Rich	$14.00

The Magister, Sally Miller Gearhart............................	$14.00
Martha Moody, Susan Stinson............................	$10.95
Moon Creek Road, Elana Dykewomon................	$14.00
Mother Journeys: Feminists Write About Mothering, Sheldon, Reddy, Roth...	$15.95
Night Diving, Michelene Esposito.........................	$14.00
Nin, Cass Dalglish..	$12.00
No Matter What, Mary Saracino........................	$ 9.95
Ordinary Justice, Trudy Labovitz............................	$12.00
The Other Side of Silence, Joan M. Drury.............	$ 9.95
The Racket, Anita Mason..................................	$12.95
Ransacking the Closet, Yvonne Zipter......................	$ 9.95
Report for Murder, V. L. McDermid......................	$10.95
Roberts' Rules of Lesbian Break-ups, Shelly Roberts.......	$ 5.95
Roberts' Rules of Lesbian Dating, Shelly Roberts.............	$ 5.95
Roberts' Rules of Lesbian Living, Shelly Roberts..........	$ 5.95
Silent Words, Joan M. Drury............................	$10.95
The Solitary Twist, Elizabeth Pincus......................	$ 9.95
Sugar Land, Joni Rogers..................................	$12.00
They Wrote the Book: Thirteen Women Mystery Writers Tell All, edited by Helen Windrath.........................	$12.00
Those Jordan Girls, Joan M. Drury......................	$12.00
Trees Call for What They Need, Melissa Kwasny..........	$ 9.95
Turnip Blues, Helen Campbell............................	$10.95
The Two-Bit Tango, Elizabeth Pincus......................	$ 9.95
Vital Ties, Karen Kringle.................................	$10.95
Voices of the Soft-bellied Warrior, Mary Saracino.......	$14.00
Wanderground, Sally Miller Gearhart....................	$12.95
The Well-Heeled Murders, Cherry Hartman................	$10.95
Why Can't Sharon Kowalski Come Home? Thompson & Andrzejewski...............................	$12.95
A Woman Determined, Jean Swallow........................	$10.95
The Yellow Cathedral, Anita Mason......................	$14.00

Anita Mason

Mason's life and works have been shaped by growing up in the port city of Bristol in post-World War II England. She is the only child of her mother, a housewife, and her father, who work at a Spitfire airplane engine manufacturing plant. All of these have combined to produce Mason's forceful inner drive to be a writer of serious novels.

Mason has taught writing at Bath Spa University College in Bath, England. She lives in Bristol, and writes fiction.

A writer with a fine eye for detail, a mind focused on the usual as it is twisted about by the unusual, a penchant for unearthing curious history, and a thorough command of the craft, Mason continues to do quality research, find conundrums, draw excellent characterizations, and write interesting stories.

Mason read English at Oxford, lived in London and worked in the publishing field for five years. She then settled in the deep English countryside of Cornwall and tried to be, among other things, an organic farmer at a time when no one knew what that was. During that time she began writing fiction, building upon her base of non-fiction, magazine writing, and newspaper reporting. Her second novel, *The Illusionist*, was shortlisted for England's prestigious Booker Prize.

Mason has spent a good deal of time in Mexico, researching her interest in the Chiapas Indians, which has resulted in her work, *The Yellow Cathedral* (2002). She is currently working on another book about the European conquest of Mexico.

For an in-depth interview and more background on Anita Mason, visit www.spinsters-ink.com.